FALLING DARK

THE WATCHERS, BOOK 1

CHRISTINE POPE

Dark Valentine Press

This is a work of fiction. Names, characters, places, and incidents are either the product of the author's imagination or are used fictitiously. Any resemblance to actual events, places, organizations, or persons, whether living or dead, is entirely coincidental.

FALLING DARK

ISBN: 978-1-946435-01-9
Copyright © 2017 by Christine Pope
Published by Dark Valentine Press

Cover design by Christian Bentulan
Book layout by Indie Author Services

To learn more about this author, go to
www.christinepope.com.

FALLING DARK

CHAPTER ONE

YOU KNOW THAT FEELING WHEN YOU'RE POSITIVE YOU'RE being followed?

Well, I couldn't shake the feeling that someone was following me right then. Creepy-crawly sensation on the back of my neck, cold trickle down my spine that didn't have anything to do with the gray clouds looming overhead.

Problem was, as I stood on the sidewalk just outside Trader Joe's and let my gaze sweep the store's parking lot, I didn't see anything out of the ordinary. The usual mothers with kids too young for school in tow, hipster-looking couples who might have been students at Art Center…or Caltech, since these days being a science type was no excuse for not also being vaguely hip, too. A couple of oddballs like me, people

who should have been at work but, for whatever reason, weren't.

The lot was a little more than half full. I tried to
time these trips at hours when the place wouldn't be
too crowded, hence the availability of all those precious parking spaces. Since I set my own schedule,
there was no reason to cram myself in with all the
other people trying to grab a couple of bottles of
cheap wine on their way home from work.

A cool breeze ruffled my hair. Overhead, the sky
looked more and more threatening, even though the
rain had held off so far—and I hoped it would wait
until I got back to my condo. Then it could come
pouring down. Lord knows we needed the rain here
in Southern California, needed every drop to help
prevent the parched land from blowing away altogether the next time we got a round of Santa Ana
winds.

Once again I scanned the parking lot, then
glanced down at my phone. The little dot on my
Uber app crawled along, clearly caught in some kind
of heavy traffic as it made its way from Old Pasadena
down Arroyo Boulevard. I let out an exasperated
breath and looked up from the phone. As far as I
could tell, no one was paying any attention to me.
I'd been the target of unwanted advances here in the
past…nothing like some random guy trying to hit on
you in the frozen food section…but today I'd been

left alone. Even though I'd escaped this shopping trip unscathed, for some reason, I was still having a massive case of the heebie-jeebies. Then again, what was new about that? After the past few years, I should have been used to my brain messing with me.

Anyway, the distance to my condo from where I stood was less than a mile. Even carrying a couple of shopping bags, it shouldn't take me more than fifteen minutes at the most. And I doubted the Uber driver would care if I canceled the trip—he could stay safely in the old town area instead of having to venture down here, where his fares would be more widely spaced.

That seemed to settle it. I tapped the screen, canceling my ride request, then shoved the phone into my purse and picked up the two shopping bags I'd set down on the sidewalk. After glancing around one last time—and telling myself I was being totally paranoid—I headed out across the parking lot.

I decided to go up Marengo since it was a nicer walk, one that would take me through a quieter, more residential area. Besides, a lot of large old trees overhung the sidewalks there, promising some shelter in case the rain did arrive.

No one paid any attention to me as I crossed the street and headed north. I didn't even know why I thought they might, except for that nagging sensation, the one that wouldn't quite go away, of unfriendly eyes somehow fixed on me.

Once upon a time, I hadn't been nearly so paranoid. But now that I was a...actually, I still didn't quite know what to call myself. "Psychic" sounded so pretentious. And it wasn't as if I could read minds, or hold a set of keys and know who they belonged to, or speak to the dead and deliver messages from beyond the grave. No, the only thing that made me out of the ordinary was my dreams. Visions. Premonitions. Whatever you wanted to call them.

Most days, I didn't call them anything at all. My family didn't like me to talk about that sort of thing, so with them, I pretended that the visions didn't exist. They still desperately clung to the hope that one day I might get better...whatever that meant. So I didn't tell them anymore. I wrote everything down in a little book I kept by my bedside, since sometimes the visions came in the form of dreams, and sometimes they visited me when I was wide awake. As far as I'd been able to figure out, there didn't seem to be much rhyme or reason as to why or when they would descend. Usually, those visions would be proven true within a day or a week—or much more rarely—in a month or two. Every once in a great while, they didn't seem to come true at all. But even with an overall decent batting average, I did my best not to talk about them.

Who would believe me?

All right, I had a couple of people who actually did believe me…but neither of them were my family members.

The wind picked up, tugging at my loose hair, and I thought I felt a drop of rain hit my cheek. Damn it. Yes, the forecasters had been saying that the storm would come in this afternoon, but I'd thought I'd be able to beat it.

So you'll get a little wet, I told myself grimly as I trudged along, wishing I hadn't bought that third bottle of wine. At the moment, it felt as if it weighed a ton. *It's not the end of the world. You can change your clothes, take a hot bath.*

Ignore the world. That was something I'd gotten pretty good at over the past couple of years.

Another drop of rain followed the first one, and then more. No, it wasn't coming down too hard yet, but I knew how these things went. In a few minutes, I was probably going to get hammered. Yes, I had on a jean jacket over my tank top and long skirt, but denim wasn't exactly waterproof.

My sunglasses shielded my eyes somewhat, although I still kept my gaze fixed downward, watching the pavement, trying to keep the increasingly heavy rain from hitting directly me in the face. Probably not the smartest thing to do. After getting that rampaging case of the creepy-crawlies back at Trader Joe's, I should have been paying better attention.

The property I was passing had a low wall that separated it from the sidewalk, and on the other side of the wall grew some thick bushes and several stubby, spreading trees of a variety I didn't recognize. The bushes rustled, and then out of them burst— well, I suppose you'd have to say he was a man, maybe a few years older than I, with a shock of pale hair and equally pale eyes, and a pasty complexion.

That was all the time I had to take in his appearance, because in the next instant he had lunged for me, wrapping thin but surprisingly strong fingers around my bicep. I let out a startled cry, but I wasn't so shocked that I completely forgot to fight back. Out of instinct, I swung one of my shopping bags at him, the one that had two of the three bottles of wine I'd bought inside.

The bag connected with his shoulder with a sharp *crack*, but the blow wasn't enough to stop him. As the bag fell to the sidewalk with a crunch of glass, he didn't even blink, instead maneuvering past so he stood in front of me, blocking the sidewalk. He grabbed my other arm with his free hand, squeezing so tightly that I dropped the second bag of groceries.

Adrenaline zinged through my bloodstream, pushing past the initial shock, telling me what I should do next.

"Help!" I called out. Surely there had to be someone around, even though it was a little before eleven in the morning, a time when probably most of the people who lived in the neighborhood had to be at work or school. *"Help!"*

In response, my assailant let go of my left arm and clapped his hand over my mouth. His fingers were cold and hard, and my lip stung as it was ground into my teeth. The metallic taste of blood ran over my tongue. "Shut up," he growled into my ear. "No one is going to help you."

The rain fell faster, harder, soaking my hair, stinging my cheeks like little chips of ice. Right then, I wondered if he was right, if he'd chosen this spot on purpose because he knew no one was close enough to come to my aid.

Maybe that was true. In which case, I'd have to help myself.

Without even stopping to think, I drove my right knee into his groin, using all the strength of my yoga-trained muscles. Surely the force of the blow would be enough to make him let go of me, if only for a few seconds. Then I would run like hell, or at least as fast as I could. The old injury in my leg had begun to ache, and it might have slowed me down.

But I never got the chance to find out, as my attacker didn't let go. A harsh breath escaped his lips, but his grip on my arm only intensified. Tears of pain and fear stung my eyes. Right then, it seemed all too likely that he'd be able to drag me off that sidewalk—maybe to the shabby Volvo parked a few yards away—and take me wherever he wanted.

And why the hell hadn't he doubled over in agony the second I kneed him in the balls? Was he hopped up on something, like bath salts or PCP?

So maybe I should be more worried about him eating my face off, or—

A dark blur. I didn't really see where it had come from, because I had been struggling in my attacker's grip, still trying to wrench my arm out of his hand, even though he might as well have been holding me in a set of shackles for all the good that did. But in the next instant I saw a fist come out of nowhere and hit the man who held me, striking him in the jaw with such force that he did finally let go, right before he reeled back a pace or two and bumped into the wall behind us. I pulled in a breath, wondering if I should scream again, but then I stopped, staring. A man I knew I'd never seen before, tall, with shaggy dark hair, advanced on my assailant, left fist coming up to connect with the other side of his face. Improbably, my attacker began to laugh, even as blood trickled down from his pale mouth.

"You think that's going to stop me?" He swung, but the man who had hit him moved so fast my eyes could barely track the motion. All I really saw was his left hand coming up to catch that fist before it ever connected.

A sickening crunch, one that could only have come from all the bones in his hand being crushed at once. At last my attacker flinched, the remaining blood draining from his face so he barely even looked human, seemed more like a wax figure before any color had been painted on its features.

"No," said the man who had stepped in to save me. "But this will."

He grabbed my assailant's other hand, crushing it just as he had the first one. The pale man sank to his knees. An odd keening noise escaped his lips, a sound that didn't even seem as if it could have come from a human throat.

And then—maybe it was pain, or maybe it was shock. I didn't know, because I couldn't come up with a rational explanation for what I witnessed next. The man who'd come to my assistance reached in his pocket and pulled out a small vial filled with a strange silvery liquid. He took out the stopper and splashed the liquid on my attacker's face.

It dissolved. Or rather, *he* dissolved. All of him, melting down into a pool of a pale oily substance that quivered briefly, as if it still possessed some kind of hideous life. And in the next second it was gone as if it had never been.

"What—?" I managed. "Who—?"

"Later," said my savior, his tone curt. He bent to pick up my dropped bags of groceries, one of them clinking with the sound of broken glass. Even though the bags were the heavy plastic reusable kind, red wine still began to drip from the bottom. "Let me drive you home."

My mind was still reeling, attempting to process what I had just seen, but I knew I sure as hell wasn't going to let this stranger drive me to my condo. I'd had enough encounters with crazy men for one day. Letting this one get me alone in his car? Not going to happen.

"No, that's fine," I said. Somehow, I even managed to smile. No doubt my mother, who'd made it her goal to ensure that both her daughters could handle every social situation with grace and ease, would be very proud of me.

Not that I would ever tell her what had just happened. That would be the final piece of evidence she needed to be convinced that I was completely crazy.

"It is not fine," the man said. For the first time since he'd come to my rescue, I was able to take in some more of his appearance, to note that he also looked to be a few years older than I—maybe around thirty—and had dark brown, longish hair that brushed against the collar of his black T-shirt. His eyes were also dark, piercing as he stared down into my face. Tall. Definitely over six feet.

"No, really," I returned. I pulled in a breath and added, "Unless you'd like to stay here with me while I call the police."

"To report what?" he asked. His gaze flicked to the spot on the sidewalk where my attacker had melted into nothingness. "Police require evidence."

"I—"

"I mean you no harm, Serena Quinn."

My protests died there. "How do you know my name?"

"That isn't important. Let me get you off this street."

Mind churning, I said, "Give me my groceries."

"No. You're in no condition to carry them. I'll give them to you after you're safely home."

"Fine," I told him. "Keep them."

And I turned away and began walking up the street. Yes, my knees wobbled, and I honestly didn't know if I had the strength to make it the extra half mile to my place, but the one thing I did know was that I sure as hell wasn't going to get into a car with him.

From behind me came a muffled curse, followed by the sound of footsteps. A second later, he had caught up with me, thanks to his much longer legs. "You are a very stubborn woman."

"So I've been told." I didn't dare let myself look up at him. For some reason, I had the feeling that if

I looked too deeply into his eyes, I'd discover things I didn't want to see, would begin to find some answers to the craziness I'd just experienced.

Right then, I wasn't sure I wanted answers. I wanted to go home and pretend this morning had never happened.

The rain arrived in earnest then, pouring down in that shocking way it did sometimes in California, as if giving the finger to the endless commentary about the seemingly never-ending drought. The stranger's hair plastered itself against his cheeks and his neck, glistened in the dark stubble on his chin, but he barely seemed to notice, only kept walking along at my side.

Because I'd stubbornly refused the offer of a ride, I was getting soaked as well, raindrops beating through my jacket as if it was made of thin silk rather than heavy denim. My cotton skirt was equally soaked, beginning to cling to my thighs.

Had he noticed? I couldn't tell, because I was trying so very hard not to look at him.

Eventually, the silence grew too terrible. I said, desperation clear in my voice, "Really, I'm fine. I'd appreciate it if you could leave me alone."

He only shook his head. "No, I don't think you're fine. And I cannot leave you alone."

Oh, that was just wonderful. So apparently I'd traded a crazy would-be rapist for a stalker. Or something. True, the man who walked calmly along beside me was an order of magnitude better-looking than the one who'd attacked me, but I wasn't about to let his looks lull me into a false sense of security. After all, Ted Bundy had been attractive.

Don't forget about Jeffrey Dahmer, my mind whispered at me, even though I was forced to admit that I wouldn't exactly have been Mr. Dahmer's type.

Since I didn't know how to respond to the stranger's words, I lapsed into silence again, walking as quickly as I could. At least I'd had the sense to put on low-heeled boots, faux leather ones that did a pretty good job of keeping out the rain. My feet would be dry, even if the rest of me was a lost cause.

Not for the first time, I wished that my powers— or whatever they were—might be of a little more use in situations like this. A vision might come to me of a bus crash or a kidnapped child, but I never seemed to see anything that affected my own life, whether present or future. Every once in a great while I'd get an odd tingle like the one I'd experienced at the Trader Joe's parking lot. Even that hadn't done me any good, though. The danger hadn't been there at the store at all, but waiting for me up the street.

Damn it, I should never have canceled that Uber.

At last we reached Cordova—my street. I turned right and trudged down the sidewalk, and couldn't quite repress the sensation of relief that went over me as I spotted the awning that led into the lobby of my condo complex. No way would I go in through there, though. Not looking like a drowned rat and with a tall, grim-faced stranger in tow...especially a stranger who carried a trashed Trader Joe's shopping bag with wine dripping out the bottom.

Instead, I went down a side path that led to the dumpsters. "Toss it in there," I instructed the strange man. "I don't want red wine dripping all over my floor."

His eyebrows lifted. "You don't have other items in there that you'd like to salvage?"

"No," I replied wearily. I could live without the bag of dried apricots and the box of gorgonzola crackers. Well, maybe not the crackers....

With a shrug, he raised the cover of the dumpster and dropped the bag inside. Since I somehow knew that trying to take the other bag of groceries from him so I could go up to my place alone wouldn't do any good, I headed back up the path, then zigged off toward the building where my condo was located.

As I'd feared, he followed, staying only a pace or two behind me. Clearly, he didn't intend to let me out of his sight. Why, I really didn't know. Did he think another pasty-faced man was going to leap out of the bushes and assault me? I was shaky and feeling shell-shocked, and all I wanted was to get inside my house and lock the door against the world...including the man who had just saved me. Right then, I needed time to think.

When I reached the door to my condo, I came to a dead stop and turned to face him. "If you think I'm going to let you in—"

"I would not expect that," he said calmly. "Here are your groceries."

I stared at him for a second, then took the bag from his hand. "So...that's it? You're not going to stop me from going inside?"

"Of course not. It is safe for you there."

Usually, I would have found such a statement reassuring. But after what had happened over on Marengo Street.... "How do you know it's safe?"

"Because I do," he replied, which of course didn't help at all. If I hadn't been freezing and soaked through, I probably would have gone hot with anger at his apparent nonchalance. "That doesn't mean they won't still try to get at you in the future. But your home is safe...as long as you don't let them in."

"'Let them in'?" I repeated. Assuming an ironic tone that I was sure he didn't believe for one second, I added, "What, they need an invitation? Are they vampires or something?"

"Or something," he agreed. "Take care, Serena Quinn."

And with that parting shot he was gone, walking swiftly down the path that led to the community pool. A second or two later, he had turned a corner and disappeared.

Vampires. Or something.

Hands shaking, I pulled my house keys out of my purse and went inside.

CHAPTER TWO

AFTER GETTING SOAKED THROUGH LIKE THAT, NORMALLY I would have taken a long, hot bath. But I was far too shaken up after my encounter with the strange pale man—the one who had apparently been melted into a puddle of goo—to allow myself to feel so exposed. Soaking in a tub for a half hour or more, just lying there, naked? No, thanks.

Instead, I turned on the shower as hot as I dared and stood there until I'd banished the worst of the chill. Then I got out and dried myself off and got dressed in record time. Once I was done, I went to the window as I towel-dried my hair. With my free hand, I cautiously pushed the drapes to one side. Of course I didn't see anyone, since the rain was coming down in earnest, and anyone with any sense would have retreated inside.

Even so, I couldn't shake the feeling of still being watched.

I fought back a shiver as I let go of the drapes. The condo had a gas fireplace in the living room, so I paused and flicked the switch to turn it on before heading into the kitchen. That one unbroken bottle of wine beckoned, but I knew better than to indulge myself when I was still so shaken up. Besides, it was barely noon, a little early to start on a bender. Mouth set, I got out a mug and nuked some water in it, then dropped in a bag of my favorite Darjeeling tea.

The warm mug felt good in my trembling fingers, which were still far too cold despite that hot shower. I sat down in my favorite chair, the big overstuffed one placed to the left of the sofa. A flat-screen TV hung over the fireplace, but I didn't turn it on. No, I cradled the mug of tea in my hands and stared at the wall, and wondered if I'd finally gone crazy.

What I really wanted to believe was that the incident had only been another of my visions, or whatever you wanted to call them. Problem was, even when I was still coming to terms with what they were, I'd always been able to differentiate my waking visions from reality. Reality was bright and sharp-edged. The visions—even the ones I had when I was asleep—always had a hazy sort of quality to them, as if being seen through a camera with a thin layer of gauze over the lens.

The encounter with the crazed man...or whatever he was...felt far too real. I could still see way too many details about him, from the spiky, oily texture of his white hair to the faint line of a scar that had etched its way down one cheek. I rarely got that level of detail from a vision, only enough to know what was going on, and not much more than that. Anyway, my arm still ached where he'd grabbed me. Not once had I ever experienced any physical after-effects from one of my visions, except a brief disorientation. But disorientation rarely left bruises behind.

And then there was my nameless rescuer. He was far too real as well. Handsome, with those level dark brows and that firm mouth. His shaggy hair and the three days of scruff on his cheeks seemed to indicate he didn't care too much about his appearance...or that he was the kind of guy who actually cared a lot but tried to affect that he didn't.

I had a feeling he was the former, just because the metrosexual types I'd known would have put a hell of a lot more effort into their clothes, not to mention a lot more product in their hair. And the way the stranger had dispatched my attacker.... Sure, I'd seen that kind of fighting before, in movies or on TV. Not right in front of my eyes.

What I'd never witnessed before, even in make-believe, was a man dissolving into nothing like that, just like the Wicked Witch of the West or something. It wasn't possible. It *couldn't* be possible. And yet I'd stood there and watched the whole thing.

Which meant it had to be possible. If that was true, then pretty much everything I thought I knew about the world had suddenly turned upside down.

My hands wouldn't stop shaking. Right then, I really wished I had wine in my mug, not tea.

I made myself take a sip, though, telling myself that I needed to stay sharp right now. Anyway, the tea felt good going down, warm and strong.

Even though I wanted to go to the window and look out again, I stayed where I was. The last thing I needed was to turn into the crazy neighbor who was always peering out through the drapes, trying to catch make-believe intruders creeping around in the bushes.

Although in my case, the intruder wasn't exactly make-believe.

The stranger had said I would be safe here in my condo, though. Whether I could take his words at face value was up for grabs at the moment, but I chose to believe him. After all, I was the next thing to a recluse anyway. No one would think it terribly strange if I didn't venture outside for a day or two. Most of the time, that was my standard behavior. My work—such as it was—kept me at home. I only went out for groceries or to catch the odd movie when I was sick of streaming them from my solitary living room. Even more rarely, I'd meet for lunch or dinner with the one friend who had stuck by me through everything: Candace Neely, my college roommate. Everyone else had slipped away, not sure how to handle the change in my circumstances.

At any rate, it wasn't as if I had the kind of active social life where people would even notice or miss me if I stayed inside for days at a time.

I set my mug down on a coaster and frowned. Although Candace had believed me, had never tried to deny my visions, I wondered what in the world she would think if I called her now and told her what had happened to me. Would she think this was the final straw, that I'd really lost it at last?

Not that I would blame her. I was beginning to think the same thing.

If I hadn't seen my attacker melt away into nothingness, I would have thought he was just some whacko who was trying to get at my brother through me. Yes, I kept a low profile, but Jackson was still the junior senator from California, the one being groomed for a run at the White House. He hadn't announced his candidacy yet, but we all knew it was a foregone conclusion. My parents and my sister were thrilled. I, on the other hand, could only think of the increased scrutiny and shudder. How long would it take before the tabloids started screaming about Senator Quinn's crazy little sister?

But politically motivated whack jobs didn't melt into pale puddles of slime. What had just happened to me an hour earlier couldn't be explained away. Not by any rational means, that is.

Vampires. Sort of.

How could a person be "sort of" a vampire? That was like being "sort of" pregnant.

Anyway, vampires weren't real. That silvery stuff my protector had thrown at the guy…it had to be some kind of weird experimental chemical, something capable of making a human body melt away and disappear. I was far more ready to believe that kind of cloak-and-dagger CIA stuff than confront the reality that my assailant was some kind of strange supernatural being. After all, the conspiracy websites were full of that kind of thing, always talking about the sort of tech the government kept hidden. My brother laughed at those rumors, but…wouldn't he be compelled to do so, because of his position in the government? Being a member of the Senate's Select Committee on Intelligence, Jackson had to keep pretty close-mouthed about a good number of subjects.

However, I had to admit that my savior—whoever he was—didn't exactly fit the profile of a Secret Service agent. Families of senators didn't rate that level of protection, but I'd seen enough Secret Service men and women when my family traveled to D.C. for Jackson's swearing-in that I knew the man who'd stepped in to protect me wasn't exactly sporting regulation hair or clothing. Ditto for the scruff of beard on his chin and cheeks.

Undercover agent? Maybe, but someone like that wouldn't have been assigned to protect me unless some sort of serious threat had been leveled at the family, and I hadn't heard of anything along those lines. Oh, sure, I wasn't naïve enough to think that Jackson didn't get his share of hate mail—that was just part of the job—but I knew he would have contacted me if something of sufficient gravity had occurred. Or rather, he would have called my mother, and she would have called me, no doubt begging me to come home and live with them.

That was a constant refrain of hers. The condo had been a compromise, close enough to the family home in San Marino that she could come flying to the rescue if necessary, but also far enough away that I could pretend I had a modicum of independence.

There was a joke. They'd bought this condo for me, bought the Mercedes GLA SUV that was sitting, barely driven, in the condo's one-car garage. The freelance editing and script-reading jobs I used as a way to fill up my empty days brought in some pocket cash, nothing more. I hated the feeling that I lived on my parents' sufferance, but there wasn't much I could do about it. With the way the visions could come over me at any time, I couldn't hold down a real office job. My dream of being a teacher—and the master's degree I'd been pursuing when the accident occurred—were both long gone, shattered forever the second that Ford Explorer slammed into me and knocked my limp body across the street, breaking multiple bones and sending me into a coma that lasted for days.

I had to stop myself there. Brooding over what might have been wasn't going to help me one bit. Anyway, I'd had three years to get used to my change in circumstances. Better to focus on what had just happened this afternoon and try to come up with a reasonable explanation for what I'd seen.

Problem was…I didn't think there was a reasonable explanation.

Three days later I did finally leave the condo. My friend Candace called and wanted to have lunch, and by then I was going stir-crazy enough that I agreed. True, I'd had a hefty editing job to keep me occupied, but a person could only fix comma placement and misplaced modifiers for so long before she started to get restless. Besides, I was going to be driven straight to the restaurant and retrieved there once I was done. It wasn't as if I would be wandering the streets of Pasadena by myself.

I told myself that would be enough.

The storm that had descended the day of my attack was long gone. Now the skies were blue, the air mild, just about what you'd expect of Southern California in late February. An Uber came and picked me up, and transported me to Lucky Baldwin's in Old Pasadena, a place Candace and I both loved, mostly because it was unpretentious and kind of a hole in the wall, and had the best fish and chips I'd ever tasted.

Why the Uber, when I had approximately forty thousand dollars' worth of Mercedes sitting in my garage? Because I'd had a vision come over me once when I was driving and ended up parked on the curb. Thank God I didn't hit anyone—or anything—and the tires and alignment survived the incident well enough, but ever since then I'd been terrified of the same thing occurring with a far less favorable outcome. Once a week I backed out the car and drove it around the block, just to make sure everything was in good working order, but I didn't dare do much more than that.

Candace was waiting for me in the restaurant, which occupied an old brick building and had all sorts of nooks and crannies, one small room opening on the next. It was the kind of place that worked well when you wanted to have a private conversation, especially on a weekday when it wasn't all that crowded.

As I approached, Candace waved and smiled. When I sat down, though, she took one look at me and said, "Out with it."

Maybe I neglected to mention that she was a lawyer. Her firm's office was just a few blocks over from the restaurant, on DeLacey Street. Anyway, part of the reason she was so good at her job was because she could take one look at a person and know whether something was going on.

In my case, something was definitely going on.

I sat down in the booth, not bothering to pick up a menu, since I knew exactly what I planned to order. "Out with what?"

She lifted an eyebrow. "Are you really going to try that with me?"

"No, I guess not." I noticed she had an iced tea sitting on the table in front of her, which meant she had to be back in court later that afternoon. On non-trial days, she generally would relax enough to have a beer with me. But clearly this wasn't one of those days.

The waiter came by, and I asked for an iced tea as well, and ordered some fish and chips, since I figured I might as well get the whole thing out of the way. Candace got fish and chips, too, and then, once we were alone again, she settled against the wooden back of the booth and shot me an expectant glance.

I'd already resolved to tell her as much as I could, but now that the moment had come, I wasn't sure of the best way to approach the topic. Hedging, I said, "Well…something strange happened on Monday."

"Strange? Like…?" She trailed off there, but I knew what she was hinting at. She wanted to know if I'd had another vision.

If only it was something that prosaic.

I shook my head. "No. I was at Trader Joe's, and…." I had to stop there, because the waiter had returned with my iced tea. Once he was gone, though, I continued with the story, telling Candace everything that had happened that rainy Monday morning. Well, almost everything. I did leave out that little tidbit about my rescuer's comment concerning "sort of" vampires, but I didn't hold back when it came to describing how my attacker somehow got reduced to a pool of viscous-looking liquid. That was one detail I would have liked to leave out, except that it was the only real way to explain why there wasn't any evidence of the assault.

During the narrative, Candace's brows kept pulling together until she had a serious crease happening in the middle of her forehead. "Why didn't you call the police?"

"And tell them what? They would have thought I was crazy." It certainly wasn't out of bounds for me to think that most of the local cops would have

probably decided I was off my rocker, and would
have sent over a mental health worker rather than
an officer. However, I did have a good relationship
with Raoul Ortiz, a detective with the Pasadena P.D.
Several years earlier, when a little girl had gone missing from her home up on Oakland Avenue, I'd gotten a vision of who had taken her—the boyfriend of
a former babysitter. And Detective Ortiz had listened
to me, and caught the guy responsible before anything too terrible could happen. But just because he
didn't think I was a fraud, or crazy, didn't mean the
rest of the department shared that opinion.

"You said the guy grabbed you pretty hard.
Didn't you get any bruises from that?"

"Yes, on both arms." I paused then, thinking
of the mottled bruises on my biceps, the ones that
the elbow-sleeve T-shirt I wore covered pretty effec-
tively. "But that still doesn't prove much of anything.
It wasn't as if there was DNA evidence or anything
like that."

"And the man who stepped in to help. He didn't
give you a name?"

"No...but he knew mine."

"So you have a stalker?"

The thought had crossed my mind more than
once during the past few days. I'd also begun to
wonder if the whole thing had been a setup, a fake
attack so the man who appeared to be my rescuer

could show up and look like the hero. To what end, I had no idea, and my theory still didn't explain the way he'd made the other man melt away to nothing, but....

"I don't know," I admitted. "I haven't seen him since, though."

"Because you haven't left the house," Candace pointed out.

"Well, true, but I've tried to keep an eye out on my surroundings, and I haven't seen him anywhere near the condo. So if he is a stalker, he's not a very consistent one."

After taking a sip of her iced tea, my friend said, "Or he's a really good one. Maybe he's trying to lull you into a false sense of security."

Great. And here I'd hoped I would feel better after unburdening myself to Candace, rather than the exact opposite. "I suppose that's possible. Jesus, at this point I can only say that *anything* is possible. I'm still trying to wrap my head around what I saw, trying to come up with some sort of rational explanation, but there just wasn't anything rational about what happened."

"What about the goo? Some kind of acid?"

"I don't know. Maybe." I'd played the scene over and over in my head, and I still couldn't quite figure out what had happened. "I can't think of any other explanation that fits."

She nodded, as if agreeing that there really couldn't be any other reason for a body to melt away to noting like that. "And you're sure it wasn't connected to Jackson."

"I'm not sure of anything," I replied. "But no, I don't think so. He's probably going to make his announcement in the next few weeks or so, at which point I'm sure the crazies will start to come out of the woodwork, but right now, things have been pretty quiet."

"So he's really going to do it."

I drank some of my own iced tea before answering. "It's pretty much a foregone conclusion at this point. He's just working out the timing with his team."

Candace's coral-glossed lips pursed. As usual, she looked impeccable, from her sandy blonde shoulder-length bob down to her three-inch heels. How she could stand in those things for hours in court, I had no idea. "And he really doesn't care about what all this might do to you?"

The same thought had crossed my mind a number of times. Right then, though, I found myself defending my brother's decision. The last thing I wanted to do was sound selfish, as if my privacy was more important than someone who might be the next person to occupy the White House. "It's not going to do anything to me," I said. "I'm a big girl. If someone tries to go up my ass with a microscope, I'll tell them to shove it."

Candace let out a reluctant laugh. "Yeah, I suppose you probably would."

"Anyway," I continued, "I can't let my own problems get in the way of this. We're talking about being the President of the United States. That's far more important than my own neuroses."

Candace's nose wrinkled slightly at the "neuroses" comment, but clearly she intended to let it slide, since she asked, "You think he'll do a good job?"

"I know he will," I said. "Don't you?"

"Yes. Probably. I mean, I voted for him for Senate, and I've been watching what he's done for the last three years. His record is pretty impressive. But…."

All I could do was shrug. I knew why she was concerned. She was my friend, had stuck with me through a serious amount of crap. Her job was defending people, and she had always defended me, too. It was just part of her makeup. But I'd already told myself that being made uncomfortable by reporters and paparazzi wasn't quite enough of a reason to tell someone he shouldn't run for President. At least, not when the person in question was so eminently suited for the office.

Jackson and I had never been that close, mostly because he was eleven years older than I, and so our lives had followed completely different orbits. He

and my older sister Vanessa were much more intimate, since only two years separated them. I was the
caboose baby, the one I was pretty sure my parents
hadn't really planned on, although of course neither
one of them had ever come out and admitted such
a thing. Even so, it wasn't too hard to read between
the lines.

But even though Jackson had never been the big
brother who played catch with me, or helped me
with my homework, or done any of the sorts of
things my idealized version of a big brother might,
I'd always been proud of him. Yes, one could argue
that, coming from our family, he'd been given a massive head start in life. However, he'd always been
an overachiever—class president and valedictorian
in high school, fast-tracked through law school,
mayor of the town where he'd settled after college
before he even hit thirty. His Senate term came after
he was mayor of Claremont, and almost as soon as
he'd landed in Washington, the murmurs about a
possible presidential run had started. People wanted
to rally around someone young and energetic and
handsome, someone with a unique combination of
hard-headedness and idealism. And really, who could
blame them?

Maybe the would-be candidate's slightly odd little sister, but no one had asked me for my opinion.

"But nothing," I said, trying to sound more confident than I actually felt. "It'll be fine. I'll be fine."

Candace didn't reply, only gave me a speculative glance. If she'd intended to say something, it was interrupted by the arrival of the waiter with our food. And I was glad of that, glad of having a reasonable excuse to dig into my plate of fish and chips, and remain quiet for a few minutes.

I should have known she wouldn't let it go.

Yes, she ate as well, and washed down her own fish and chips with some iced tea, but then she said, "So what are you going to do about your stalker?"

"I don't know for sure that he's a stalker."

"And you don't know that he isn't, either." She tapped her French-manicured fingertips on the tabletop. "Would any of your neighbors help, if it came right down to it?"

I really didn't like the question, although I could see why she had asked it. "The people on my left moved in a couple of months ago. I don't know them very well, although we've waved and said hi a few times. But you know Brian and Lewis keep an eye out for me."

Which they did. Brian and Lewis were already there in the condo complex when I moved in, and they'd become sort of my surrogate big brothers, inviting me over for dinner, occasionally trying to set me up with their straight friends. I'd always declined those offers, because the last thing I'd felt like doing after my breakup with Travis was to try to explain to a new guy why I might suddenly bug out in the middle of a conversation, going all glassy-eyed and completely unconnected to the world around me. Or at least, that was how Candace said I looked when I was having one of my visions. I'd had one several years earlier, during another time when we'd met for lunch. Since we'd been seated in a booth in a corner, no one else had noticed, but I'd been mortified by the incident, even though such things were completely out of my control.

She'd offered to record one of my episodes on her phone, just so I could see for myself, but the idea hadn't appealed at all. It felt odd enough as it was happening; I didn't want to actually witness one of those spells as an outsider.

Luckily, neither Brian nor Lewis had ever seen me suffer a vision. I'd told them I did have "spells" every once in a while, although medication kept things mostly under control. A harmless lie, I supposed, although I hated telling it. But making them think I suffered from a mild form of epilepsy was better than trying to explain the truth to them. In fact, I even wore a MedicAlert bracelet when I went out, just to be safe. That way, if I did have a vision, any strangers who came to my aid would think I was having a seizure…rather than just going crazy.

"Thank God for Brian and Lewis," Candace said. She twirled the straw around in her half-drunk glass of tea. "If it weren't for them, I'd probably worry about you a lot more than I do."

"You don't need to worry."

That comment got me a raised eyebrow, followed by a shake of the head. "It's what I do. And this latest incident? What the hell am I supposed to think about that?"

"Nothing," I said, unable to keep the weariness out of my voice. "That is, I know you're going to think about it...and worry. It's what you do. And believe me, I thought about going to the police. But there just isn't anything to go on. Not a single shred of evidence. Even Detective Ortiz might have a tough time believing this one."

Candace was silent for a moment. I could almost see her ticking over possible responses in her head, attempting to decide if anything she might say would make a difference. Problem was, I didn't see any real answers to my situation. I was about as safe as could be—Brian was a graphic artist who worked from home, and so he was around most of the day. My condo had an alarm system. Really, short of hiring a bodyguard to follow me everywhere I went... not that I went a whole lot of places...I didn't see what else I could do, except be vigilant and make sure I didn't walk anywhere alone.

I knew my friend was worried about my "stalker," but for some reason, I wasn't. Not really. He could have dragged me off to his car if he'd wanted to. Hell, he could have forced open the door to my condo and dragged me inside. But he didn't. He'd seen me safely home and then left.

Yes, he'd rattled my nerves with that "sort of" vampires comment, but I knew better than to mention that to Candace. She'd start asking delicate but pointed questions as to whether maybe it was a good idea for me to go back on my meds.

Never again. None of those prescriptions had done a damn thing except make me foggy and not myself. The visions…they weren't a sign of mental illness, whatever else they might be.

"You're probably right," she said at last. "Just… be careful, okay?"

"Aren't I always?"

She couldn't argue with that. Problem was, I didn't know if being careful would be enough.

CHAPTER THREE

CANDACE HAD TO LEAVE A LITTLE AFTER ONE, SINCE SHE was due in court at one-thirty. After reassuring her for the umpteenth time that an Uber was on its way and I would be going straight home, she finally headed off to the parking garage where she'd left her car…but not before giving me one last backward glance over her shoulder, as if she thought someone was going to pop out and grab me the second her back was turned.

That sort of maneuver would be a lot tougher to do here. At the tail end of the lunch hour, Raymond Avenue was jammed with cars trying to turn onto Colorado Boulevard or people looking for nonexistent parking spaces on Raymond itself. The sidewalks were equally crowded. I waited at the red zone just in front of the entrance to the garage, simply because there wasn't any place else an Uber would be able to pull up.

I glanced down at the app. Still three minutes to go. From what I saw on the map, it looked like the guy was stuck at the light at Fair Oaks and Colorado. Good luck with that.

When I looked up from my phone, I caught a glimpse of a shaggy dark head across the street. Deep-set eyes locked on mine for a second before he turned away and began walking south, toward Green Street.

Goddamn it. I hadn't seen hide nor hair of him for the past three days, but clearly my stalker hadn't given up.

For the longest moment, I stood there, unsure as to what I should do in response. Just that one glimpse of him had been enough to send a tremor through me, as if seeing his face again was enough to awaken my memories of the assault, memories I'd tried damn hard to keep locked down the past few days.

The logical—and intelligent—thing to do would be to stay right where I was. Just sit tight and wait for the Uber driver to show up. Since the stranger was walking away from me, it seemed obvious enough that he didn't have any plans to engage. No, he'd only been watching, and as soon as I'd noticed him, began to beat a retreat.

But....

I wanted to know just what the hell he thought he was doing. What possible harm could he think might come to me here, in the heart of Pasadena, surrounded by people?

Unless the Uber driver isn't really an Uber driver? my mind suggested, and I went cold all over, even though the day was mild, a nearly perfect seventy-four degrees.

That settled it. I pushed the "cancel" button on the app, then took advantage of the stopped traffic to weave in between cars as I crossed Raymond Avenue before turning down the sidewalk in pursuit of my stalker. Since he was tall, I didn't have too difficult a time keeping an eye on him as I threaded my way through the people who were window shopping or heading out for a late lunch.

There he was, paused in front of Stat's Floral Supply. I had to wait for the light so I could cross Green Street safely, but the delay didn't allow him to get away. In fact, it seemed that he waited for me, an incongruous figure in his dark T-shirt and jeans and boots, standing there in front of a display window filled with obnoxiously pastel Easter-themed floral arrangements.

"You were following me," I said as I approached him.

To my surprise—and irritation—he merely smiled. I noticed that his teeth were white and even, and for some reason that silly detail made me that much more annoyed. "Some might say you were following me."

I huffed out a breath. "Actually, I was following you because I noticed you following me."

"Semantics. But," he added, as I opened my mouth to argue, "I will go ahead and concede you that point. Yes, I was following you. I needed to make sure you were safe."

"Because otherwise I would be attacked by 'sort of' vampires while eating fish and chips at Lucky Baldwin's?"

His smile faded. I couldn't miss the way his gaze slid up the street, in the direction I'd just come from, and then past us, to the much less crowded sidewalks in front of Stat's and the historic Castle Green apartment building across the street. "Not in the restaurant," he said quietly. "But coming to and from it. Possibly. How much can you trust the people who drive these hired cars you ride in?"

"Ubers," I corrected him automatically, while at the same time a trickle of cold moved its way down my spine. How could he have known I'd just experienced those same misgivings? "They have very detailed background checks—"

"Which would not turn up anything useful," he cut in. "Or at least, useful in the sense of keeping out those who might wish you harm."

"And you don't?" I asked, my tone sharp with disbelief. "Wish me harm, that is."

"Of course not," he replied. A spark of anger came and went in his dark eyes, to be replaced with something that might have been weariness. I didn't know him, so I couldn't be sure. "Very much the opposite. It's my duty to keep you safe."

"So you're Secret Service after all?" Even as the words left my mouth, I realized how ridiculous they sounded. Whatever else he might be, this guy was definitely not Secret Service.

But he looked serious enough as he said, "No, I am not. But I suppose you could say that our duties aren't that dissimilar." He paused, then sent another one of those searching glances up and down the street. Without any change in expression, he continued, "Let me take you home."

This had to be part of an extended ploy to get me alone in a car with him. But he'd planted a seed of doubt in my mind about using an Uber, and I realized a taxi wouldn't be any safer. Walking wouldn't be all that wise, either, even though I was only about a half mile from home. Yes, the streets in between here and my condo were busier than the stretch of Marengo where I'd been attacked, but....

"It will be safe," he said quietly. "I promise this to you."

Maybe I was going crazy after all. Because I stood there and looked up at him, and didn't see anything except gentle concern in his eyes. But there was no reason for me to trust him. No reason at all. And yet....

"What's your name?" I asked.

"Silas," he replied.

An odd, old-fashioned name. But it suited him somehow. "Silas what?"

"Just Silas."

I raised an eyebrow at him. "Are you a musician or something?" Only a musician could try getting away with the "single name" thing these days.

"Hardly." He shifted away from me, and pointed toward a dusty black pickup truck parked at one of the meters on Green Street. "That's mine. Shall we?"

I hesitated. Now was the time to back out. I could tell him thanks but no thanks, then head up to Colorado Boulevard and call a taxi from there. Surely not every single one of the taxi and Uber drivers in the city could have been compromised....

No. The voice sounded clearly inside my mind, although it hadn't come from a vision. I could still see Silas clearly enough. The world hadn't taken on that strange glow which always accompanied my visions. But I'd still heard that single syllable, wherever it had come from.

Oh, well. Most of the world already thought I was crazy. Even so, I knew I'd take a quick snap of his license plate and mail it to myself as I walked to the passenger-side door, just to be safe.

"Sure," I said.

We didn't talk on the way back to the condo. It wasn't as if I had to give him directions; he knew where I lived. By some miracle, one of the guest parking spaces near the entrance was available, and he pulled the truck into the spot, then turned off the ignition.

"Thanks for the ride," I said quickly, my fingers already pushing down on the door handle.

"I will walk you to your door."

"That's not necessary—"

"But it could be." His dark eyes met mine, and I swallowed. Yes, I'd felt safe enough on the grounds of the condo complex, but was I?

"All right," I conceded, and pushed open the door.

He got out of the truck's cab as well, then locked the vehicle with the remote. Despite the dust, it was a nice truck, a newer Dodge half-ton model. Expensive, actually.

For some reason, that reassured me, which I knew was just silly. Owning an expensive truck didn't make a person any more trustworthy. But I'd been raised with money, and grown up around people with money, and as much as I'd tried to erase that part of me, hidden somewhere inside would always be the snobby little girl who didn't understand what it was like to live paycheck to paycheck, who couldn't figure out why people would drive cars with dents instead of just fixing them. I knew better now, of course, but that didn't change where I'd come from.

Silas trailed a few steps behind me as I followed the walkways and then headed up the stairs to my condo. The complex was three stories high—the bottom level held everyone's individual garages, and then the units themselves had two stories, with the bedrooms and a loft sitting area on the top floor. Townhouses, really, but it was just easier to call them condos.

I stopped at the door to my place so I could pull my keys out of the inner pocket of my purse where I kept them. Again, Silas stood a few paces away, as if he understood that I didn't want to be crowded… that I would be able to escape quickly inside if I needed to.

Then I shocked myself by saying, "Do you want to come in?"

Surprise flickered over his features. "Are you sure?"

"Of course I'm not sure," I retorted. "But…I guess just promise me you aren't a vampire."

"I am definitely not a vampire," he replied. The faintest of smiles touched his lips, as if he knew all too well that I'd invited him in because my desire to know more about this whole crazy situation had overridden my innate caution. "And thank you."

I shrugged, trying to appear nonchalant. Already I was beginning to question my hasty invitation, but there wasn't much I could do about that. Yes, I supposed I could take it back, but an entire lifetime of being schooled in what was polite and what wasn't somehow prevented me from telling him I'd changed my mind.

We stepped inside, and I quickly entered the code for the alarm system to disarm it. Then I closed and locked the door behind me. "Do you want something to drink?" I asked. "I don't have much, but there's water, and I think I have a bottle of Perrier shoved in the back of the fridge somewhere—"

"Regular water is fine," he said.

Relieved, I poured us both a glass, then handed one of the tumblers to Silas. He was careful as he took it from me, making sure that our fingers didn't touch.

I was glad of his caution. Or at least, I thought I was. This whole situation was too weird on a multitude of levels, and yet I couldn't help thinking, as I stole a glance up at him, that he really was good-looking enough to be an actor, or a model.

Either possibility seemed plausible enough, considering that we were in Southern California.

Although I didn't know too many male models who could fight like something out a Bourne movie.

"Do you want to sit down?" I asked.

"Thank you," Silas said again, and went to the couch and seated himself on the left side, close to the wing chair that was my favorite.

It seemed clear enough that he expected me to take the chair, and so I did. I set my glass down on a coaster and gave him an expectant look. "All right... we're someplace private. And safe, according to you. So can you please tell me what this is all about?"

For a long moment, he didn't reply. His gaze moved around the room, taking in the gas fireplace and the flat-screen TV above it, the neutral flat-weave rug that covered the floor in the living room, the hardwood beyond that. The furniture was simple, spare, but I liked it that way. My parents' house felt fussy to me, with the expensive antiques everywhere and the original oils that crowded the walls. I knew it was partly that way because the house had originally belonged to my paternal grandfather, and the only updating had been to the kitchen and the bathrooms, but I'd still made sure that my own home would be a polar opposite of the house where I'd grown up.

"Telling you what it is all about would take a great deal of time," Silas said. "Let's just say, for lack of a better term, that I've been assigned to you."

"'Assigned'?" I repeated. "By whom?"

"That's not important. What's important is that you have a very important gift, Serena Quinn. That gift can't be allowed to fall into the wrong hands."

"Let me guess," I said, not bothering to keep the sarcasm from my tone. "The 'sort of' vampires."

"Not exactly," he replied, and I raised an eyebrow.

"Then who?"

"The real vampires."

I wasn't sure how in the world I was supposed to respond to that little piece of information. To cover my uncertainty and unease, I retrieved my glass of water and took several swallows before I returned it to its coaster. "So there are 'sort of' vampires and real vampires?"

"Exactly. That person—that creature—who attacked you on Monday was controlled by the true vampires. Of course, one of them could not attack you in broad daylight."

"Because vampires burn up in sunlight." I made the comment as if it was the most natural thing in the world, but something inside me wanted to scream at the utter insanity of the conversation we were having.

"Precisely. I know there are many books and films these days that make it seem as if vampires can walk in the daytime, but that's simply not the case. They must have agents to carry out their dirty work."

"So who are these 'sort of' vampires?"

Silas' expression sobered, a frown turning down the corners of his mouth.

Damn it. I probably shouldn't have been looking at his mouth. It was a lot more distracting than it should be. Actually, all of him was. For the first time I noticed how his biceps strained against the faded black T-shirt he wore, the width of his shoulders. I tried to tell myself that I was only paying attention to these things because it had been a hell of a long time since I'd had a man who wasn't my neighbors Lewis or Brian here in the condo—and even longer since I'd actually *been* with a man—but that line of thought was even less productive. I shouldn't be thinking about Silas as a man at all.

He was…what? My protector? My bodyguard against all things supernatural?

God, that sounded so crazy.

If Silas noticed my distraction…or the way I'd been looking at his shoulders and biceps…he didn't give any sign of it. Voice grim, he said, "The 'sort of' vampires are those we refer to as the 'semivives.'"

"The what?" The word sounded Latin to me, or maybe French. I'd taken Spanish in high school and college, though, and so couldn't make sense of the term.

"The half dead. Half living. They were once ordinary people, those who were taken by the vampires to be their servants." He lifted one finger to his neck and touched it to the tanned skin there. "They bite their victims, as you would expect, but they don't actually share their blood, not in the way that they would to turn someone into a full vampire. Instead, they inject enough of the vampire antibodies from their blood into their victims, making them their slaves."

I tried not to shiver. "So the man who attacked me—was he that strange-looking because of the vampire virus, for lack of a better word—in his bloodstream?"

"No," Silas said. He reached for his glass and sipped, then put the tumbler back on its coaster. "The 'virus' does not change a person's appearance. The whole point is to have servants...slaves...who look the same as everyone else. In fact, it often takes weeks or even months for loved ones to begin to notice something strange about a semivive. Which means your attacker must always have been a rather odd-looking fellow."

"Wow," I said, trying to absorb what Silas had just told me. "That is...so not reassuring."

"I didn't intend it to be reassuring. But also know that we track the semivives as carefully as we can. Your family is safe, as are your friends."

All three of them, I thought. *There aren't too many "friends" to keep track of.* Of course I didn't voice those words aloud. They sounded self-pitying enough within the echo chamber of my mind. Instead, I drank some more water, then said, "Okay. But…why now? I've been dealing with these visions for more than three years. If they're valuable to the vampires, why did they wait so long to come after me?"

His jaw clenched, and I noticed the way his brows drew together, as if he was wrestling with how to respond. Eventually, though, his shoulders lifted in a helpless sort of shrug. "We really don't know. Something has changed, but we can't determine exactly what. But we've watched over you for some time, ever since you began working with Detective Ortiz."

That remark sparked so many more questions, I wasn't sure which one I wanted to ask first. But I supposed I should start with the fundamentals and work from there. "And who is 'we'?"

"I can't tell you that."

Of course he couldn't. Anger began to boil within me, although I tried to force it back as best I could. Losing my temper wouldn't do me any good. I couldn't say that I knew Silas at all, but even in our brief interactions, I'd gotten the distinct impression that he wasn't the sort of person who would respond well to being provoked. Better to be as calm and in control as I could, and see if he might let something important slip. "So what can you tell me?"

"That your gift is a singular one. While we can't always predict what the vampires will do next, we do know that they always try to press their advantage whenever possible. Which means that someone like you could be very valuable to them. That would shift the balance of power to their side, which could be very damaging to your world."

"'To my world'?" I echoed. "Isn't it your world, too?"

"Yes, of course," he replied—a little too quickly. "All I meant was that many people would suffer if the vampires ever got the sort of power they desire."

Vampires. I still was having a really tough time wrapping my head around that concept. Because it felt beyond weird to sit there and discuss vampires so calmly, as if we were talking about the weather, or the latest Star Wars movie.

My mind in turmoil, I got up from my chair and went to the window. Because it was a sunny day, I'd left the curtains drawn back so my houseplants could get enough light. Right then, however, I felt too exposed, even though I tried to tell myself that no one could actually see inside my condo. At eye level were only the units directly across from my building, after all, and I knew the people who lived there by sight if not by name. And anyone standing on ground level wouldn't really be able to see anything at all, thanks to the angle. Maybe at night, if the lights were on and someone was standing in exactly the right spot....

I found I didn't like that line of thought much at all.

The sofa creaked slightly. I turned from the window to see Silas getting up from his seat so he could approach me. Not too close, though; he stopped a little more than a foot away, as if he was all too aware of how much distance needed to be maintained between us.

"I know this must be unsettling," he said. "It can be difficult to absorb this kind of information, to realize that another world has existed alongside the one you thought you knew."

"So how do you know about the vampires? Are you part of an ancient order of vampire hunters or something?"

"Not exactly." His gaze moved to the bright, sunny day outside the window and back to me. Those dark eyes were calm, assessing, and I hoped to hell my cheeks hadn't chosen that moment to flush bright red. At least, because I knew I was meeting Candace for lunch, I'd put on some makeup and used a waver on my hair, and wore a long skirt and boots and a nicely fitted wrap top. Not like those times when I hung around the condo in yoga pants and an oversized T-shirt and no makeup, since I wasn't planning to go anywhere.

Then I tried to tell myself it was really stupid to be thinking about my appearance. I hadn't caught the slightest hint of interest from Silas…not that I'd ever been terribly great when it came to picking up those sorts of subtle signals. Men practically had to inform me beforehand that they were flirting before I got the hint—unless they skipped the flirting altogether and went straight for asking me out, as had happened at the grocery store more times than I would have liked.

Some psychic I was. But no, I wasn't actually a psychic at all. I still didn't know what I was, except brain-damaged in a particularly spectacular way.

"It's not our place to engage, unless we're given no choice," Silas went on, still in that calm, unruffled manner. "We observe, and only step in when we must. The vampires have their constraints, which help to keep them in check. But in the past they've tried to gain an advantage by binding psychics to them, so they might use those powers for their own gain."

"What is it they want?"

This time he smiled slightly, but it was a grim smile, one that didn't reach his eyes. "Power, of course. The power to influence the world, to make it their plaything. By necessity, they've kept to the shadows. But they're always looking for that one tipping point, the one thing that will give them the upper hand."

I shivered, even though the temperature in the house was comfortable enough. "I assume they haven't found it."

"No," he replied. "Not yet, anyway. But because we know psychics can be vulnerable—*true* psychics, not those who use simple tricks to dupe their customers—we do our best to keep an eye on them. Which is why you came to our attention."

"I don't see how," I protested. "Detective Ortiz has never outed me. No one else in the department knows that he works with a psychic. He hasn't even told his partner about me."

"Yes, Raoul Ortiz has kept his promise to you that your involvement in his investigations would remain hidden. But that doesn't mean we weren't able to find out on our own."

"What, you have spies in the Pasadena P.D.?"

"'Spies' is an ugly word. Those who watch, yes. Because vigilance is everything."

All right, so Detective Ortiz hadn't betrayed me. The knowledge reassured me somewhat, because I liked the man, knew him to be honest and possessed of a sort of understated courage. However, that didn't mean I wasn't still upset that my secret wasn't quite as secret as I'd hoped. I'd been loath to approach Raoul Ortiz at all that first time, not just because I didn't want to get laughed out of his office, but also because I'd promised my parents that I wouldn't tell anyone about my visions. They'd been kind about it, had couched their request that I keep quiet on the subject based on what they claimed was a concern for my welfare, but I knew better. What they really wanted was for me not to embarrass them any more than I already had, no matter how much I needed them to accept what had happened to me, to let me know that they still loved me despite everything.

But all that was uncomfortable family history… and we weren't the sort of family that aired its dirty laundry in public. No, on the surface, we were all pretty much perfect—Jackson, the golden boy senator, Vanessa, the successful clothing designer, and Serena…well, poor little Serena really didn't do all that much, to be fair, although my mother often spoke in arch tones about my editing work, trying to make it sound as if I was on the masthead at the *New Yorker*, instead of a freelancer who scraped a pittance out of editing for people who were trying to self-publish their novels or who needed their websites proofread. I knew that some people did really well at that sort of work, but since I didn't use any kind of advertising and had the most basic of web presences, most of my jobs came to me through word of mouth.

I didn't sigh…mostly because I didn't want Silas to think I was being overly dramatic. At the same time, though, I couldn't help thinking that life had dumped more than its fair share of crap on me. As if getting hit by a car and going into a coma and waking up three days later with a new and entirely unwelcome talent for having visions wasn't bad enough. Now I suddenly had vampires to deal with.

He seemed to understand, though, because he said, "I know it's a great deal to take in. But you must remind yourself that you're not alone. I'll make sure that nothing happens to you."

As he'd already proven on Monday. Once again I saw my attacker dissolving into a pool of pale, slimy ooze. I had a feeling that particular memory would play out in my mind far more often than I would like. But, thinking of the events of that morning and of everything Silas had just told me, I couldn't help experiencing a tremor of unease. "That semivive…."

"Yes?"

"You said that the semivives are people the vampires have enslaved. Wasn't there any way to, I don't know, turn that guy back into a regular human instead of…?" I trailed off then, since I didn't want to put into spoken words the horrible scene I'd witnessed. It already felt far too real.

At once Silas shook his head. "In that case, no. I could tell by his strength that he had been enslaved for a long time. Occasionally, we have been able to intervene when someone is newly infected, reverse the vampire virus, but when it has lived within the bloodstream of a semivive for years and years, it's impossible to remove." He stopped there and watched me carefully. "I had no choice, Serena. You must not feel guilty about what happened. In fact, dispatching those creatures is the best way to do right by them. At least in death their souls are free."

Souls. Vampires. Half-human creatures who couldn't call their minds their own. Right then I wished that I might open my eyes, roll over in bed, and realize this had all been a terrible dream. But unfortunately, it was far too real. I couldn't wish it away.

"What did you use on him?"

Silas didn't pretend to misunderstand the question. "A solution of silver...and other things."

"I thought silver was for fighting werewolves."

"It works against vampires and their semivives. We don't know exactly why."

Fair enough. After all, modern medical science still didn't understand the precise mechanics of why aspirin worked. "What am I supposed to do now?" I asked, and wished my voice didn't sound so weak.

So afraid.

"Only what you can," he said. This time Silas' tone was gentle. Probably too gentle, the voice of a man who was trying to keep someone from bursting into tears. "Just as you have been. The way you have set up your life, you are safer than someone whose work requires them to be in the world all the time. But...." He paused there and pulled a white business card out of his pocket, then handed it to me.

The card was plain white with black print. On it was a phone number with a 213 area code and nothing else.

"Your number?" I asked.

"Yes. If you need to go out, call me, and I will drive you. As long as we're not sure whether the methods of transportation you use have been compromised, it's better to be safe."

I stared down at the card, feeling slightly flummoxed. What, so I was supposed to have Silas ferry me to the grocery store...to the movies... the hair salon? To my dentist and...shudder...my gynecologist?

"I really couldn't impose on you like that—" I began, but he shook his head.

"It is my duty to make sure you're safe. It is not an imposition. It is an imperative. Do you understand?"

Did I? All that stuff about vampires and world domination hadn't completely sunk in yet. However, it wasn't too hard to understand that some bad people had apparently taken an unhealthy interest in me. Not after Monday's attack.

Unless that had been an isolated incident, and Silas had stepped in to take advantage of someone who was vulnerable, who would believe his story because it was just plausible enough that it couldn't be easily denied.

And the magical melting man? I asked myself then. *That was a pretty good parlor trick. How do you explain that one away?*

Well, I couldn't. Yes, I lived in Southern California, the land of make-believe, where, not twenty miles from where we stood, the studios made movie magic every day. I supposed it wasn't outside the bounds of possibility that the whole thing could have been some kind of elaborate special effects setup.

But…why? It seemed like a lot of work simply to go after one not particularly interesting female.

Silas stood and waited silently as I wrestled with myself. He had a quality of stillness that I hadn't encountered in many people, the ability to be quiet and watch. But then, it sounded as if that was what he and the rest of the people in his organization did. Some kind of weird supernatural surveillance. Or was it? He still hadn't said anything about who he was, where he'd come from. Something about the way he spoke sounded almost too formal, but he didn't have any kind of an accent, nothing to indicate that he wasn't a native of California, same as I was.

Nothing about his looks was out of the ordinary. Well, all right, he was far more attractive than the usual guy you'd see walking down the street, but still, he looked like a normal man. Surely I'd be able to pick up some kind of a hint if he wasn't.

"I understand," I said after a long hesitation. "I don't think it's necessary, but…."

"But you'll do as I've asked."

"Yes." I gave an entirely unconvincing chuckle and added, "I don't think you'll be on call too much. As you might have noticed, I don't get out a lot." There was an understatement. But it was so much easier to hide inside, rather than go out where I might have a vision—a seizure, to someone who didn't know better—in front of complete strangers.

"This is true. But when you do have to leave—"

"I know." I waved the business card at him. "I promise. I'll call."

"Good. Then I'll leave you now."

Why did I feel a pang right then? Was it just that suddenly being alone didn't sound quite as appealing as it once had? Or maybe it was simply the thought of being by myself after spending this time with him.

No. I didn't dare let my thoughts stray in that direction. Silas had a professional obligation to make sure I was safe, and that was all. I seriously needed a reality check.

"Thank you, Silas," I said.

He nodded, and headed toward the door. Once there, he turned back toward me. "Take care, Serena."

Then he let himself out, pulling the door closed with a solid *thump*. Obviously, he was making sure that the lock had engaged.

Not that I was taking any chances. I went to the door as well and turned the deadbolt.

After that, I leaned my head against the smooth wooden surface and closed my eyes, wishing more than ever that I could somehow undo the events of the past few days.

Silas had just pulled me deeper into the rabbit hole, and I had no idea what to do about it.

CHAPTER FOUR

LESS THAN A MINUTE LATER, MY DOORBELL RANG. I jumped, my heartbeat speeding up more than I wanted to admit. Had Silas forgotten something?

When I opened the door, however, I saw my neighbor Brian standing outside, one sandy eyebrow lifted at a quizzical angle, shirt untucked as usual in an attempt to hide the small paunch he'd begun to develop. "Who in the world was that?"

"Who was what?" I asked, even though of course I knew exactly who he was talking about.

"That piece of man-candy who just left. Have you been holding out on us?"

I shook my head, even as I opened the door all the way so Brian could come in. Once inside, he headed to the fridge, opened it, and pulled out a bottle of pinot grigio, the half-drunk one I'd put in there the night before. After setting the wine on the countertop, he went to the cupboard and got out two wine glasses, then poured some pinot grigio for both of us. He handed one of the glasses to me and said, "Spill it."

"There's nothing to spill."

Another lifted eyebrow. Brian always had been someone who could use his eyebrows to ferocious effect. "You expect me to believe that? I haven't seen anyone over here except your friend Candace or one of your family members for longer than I can recall. Now suddenly you've got someone who looks like he's straight out of *True Blood* or something coming and going from your apartment? Details. Now."

The *True Blood* comment shook me, although I knew Silas wasn't a vampire. Or at least, I didn't see how he could be, since he'd said that vampires couldn't walk in the daylight. But then, maybe he was a different kind of vampire. Or a semivive. Maybe there were factions in the vampire world fighting with one another, and that's what this was all about.

I pushed those frenzied thoughts away and took a sip of my pinot grigio. "There aren't any details, Brian. Sorry. His name is—" I broke off there, because I had a feeling that Silas wouldn't be too thrilled to have me bandying his name around, even if I didn't know anything except his given name. "His name is Sam Willis. He's a friend of Candace's. We met him after lunch today as we were coming out of Lucky Baldwin's, and he offered me a ride home. That's all."

There. That sounded plausible enough. After all, Candace knew people all over town because of her work. It wasn't so strange that she'd have a friend whom Brian had never heard of.

"Oh, really?" Brian drank some of his wine, his skeptical expression telling me exactly what he thought of that story. "And came up to your place afterward? And stayed for half an hour?"

"Well...." Time to pile more lies on top of lies, since of course I couldn't tell him the truth. "Turns out he works for the *L.A. Times*. It wasn't exactly a chance encounter. He'd heard rumors about Jackson getting ready to announce his candidacy, and he wanted to get a statement from me."

Brian's sharp features shifted from skeptical to concerned. "I hope you told him to get lost."

"I did. Mostly."

"Mostly?"

I lifted my shoulders. After all, I knew I couldn't entirely close the door on this "Sam Willis" person, if only because of the very real possibility that Silas might be returning at some point for Driving Miss Daisy duties.

"I get it. He's a hottie, and you've been going through a hell of a dry spell."

Right then I pondered the drawbacks of having a neighbor who knew a little too much about your personal life. I loved Brian, but sometimes a girl needed her space. "No, really—"

Brian raised a hand. "Serena, you don't have to make excuses. It's worried both Lewis and me. There's something not right about a girl like you living like a nun."

"I'm not a nun," I protested.

"Well, I'll admit your cell is a little nicer." His gaze flicked from me to the living room and back. "And your wardrobe is better...marginally...but otherwise?" It was his turn to shrug. "If it walks like a duck, it's a nun."

"Not funny."

"I wasn't trying to be funny. But I'd watch out for this Sam Willis guy. I'd hate to think he's acting interested just so he can try to pry information out of you."

"He can try. But he won't get very far."

"Good girl."

We both fell silent for a moment as we drank some more of our wine. Actually, although some people might have been annoyed at the high-handed way Brian had come in and commandeered the pinot grigio like that, I was actually relieved. I needed a drink more than I'd realized, and somehow he'd understood. He was like that.

Actually, in a lot of ways, he was much more of a big brother than Jackson had ever been.

"How's work?" I asked, and Brian raised another eyebrow at me.

"Talk about your obvious changes of subject."

It was my turn to lift an eyebrow at him. "All right, yeah. But I don't have much more to contribute on the subject of Sam Willis, so I thought I might as well be polite."

He chuckled then. "Work is…fine. Busy. You?"

"The same." Actually, it wasn't the same at all. Just another polite lie. Brian always seemed to be taking on new work, whereas I wouldn't be getting my next project until the middle of the following week. But that was fine. I usually took advantage of breaks like that to binge-watch a show I hadn't seen before. Up next was *Westworld*.

By the way his mouth curled at my reply, I could tell Brian didn't believe me. We'd known each other long enough that he had a fairly good idea of my workload…or lack thereof. But it was something we really didn't discuss, because talking about my work in any great detail would bring up the sad fact that my parents were really the ones who made sure I had a nice roof over my head and health insurance and everything else I needed to get by. What I earned from my editing jobs was barely enough to keep me in groceries and cable.

"Well, then," Brian said, and put his now-empty glass down on the counter. "Speaking of work, I'd better get back to it. I need to deliver some comps to my client by noon tomorrow. But if you do end up on a hot date with this Sam Willis person, I want to hear all about it."

"You'll be the first to know," I promised. A promise I'd never be able to fulfill, because of course Silas and I were never going to be connected intimately. Or in any other fashion, except in a decidedly odd bodyguard kind of way. But I couldn't tell Brian that.

"I'd better." Those were his parting words, because he shot me a final grin as he let himself out and closed the door behind him.

Once again, I found myself turning the deadbolt, followed by activating the alarm system. This time I didn't stay over by the door, but went to the kitchen so I could pick up my glass and finish the last of the wine it held. As I set it down, I found myself thinking about Silas, trying to figure out where he had gone after he'd left me. The area code of his phone number indicated that he must live in the heart of Los Angeles somewhere, or possibly Hollywood. Then again, these days, area codes didn't matter that much, since people held on to numbers for their cell phones long after they'd moved out of a particular city. He could be anywhere.

Well, maybe not anywhere. His comments about coming up to Pasadena to drive me around made it sound as if he wouldn't have that far to go. The distance from downtown to where I lived didn't look that far on paper, but traffic could be hideous on the 110 Freeway, depending on the time of day.

I should have asked him where he lived.

Right, like he would have told you that, I mocked myself. *The guy wouldn't even give you his last name.*

True enough. I finished the last mouthful of wine, then rinsed out both glasses and put them in the dishwasher. As I did so, I wondered if Silas drank wine...or anything at all. He didn't seem much like the type.

I had a feeling I wouldn't find out anytime soon.

That night, I had a vision. It had been a while since the last one...almost a month. Problem was, they never came on any kind of schedule. It wasn't as if I could look at my calendar and think, *Oh, it's the second Wednesday of the month— time for a vision!*

No, it was definitely not that easy. I never knew when one would strike, hence the nun-like lifestyle that Brian had been giving me grief over earlier. It was just easier to stay home whenever possible, rather than risk losing contact with reality in such a visible fashion. A near car accident and an incident at the local Ralphs where the manager was about to call the cops because he thought I was drunk or high or both was enough to convince me that it was better to limit my exposure to the outside world.

At least this time I was sitting down. I'd just finished my dinner—salad and a few strips of cold chicken breast, penance for the fish and chips I'd had with Candace at lunch—when the familiar, and hated, hazy pearlescent glow descended on my field of vision. At once my living room disappeared, and instead I saw a house.

Well, a mansion, actually, if you wanted to get technical about it. The place was huge, the sort of faux chateau-style that you might find out in the upscale San Rafael section of Pasadena. Or in my hometown of San Marino, but if that were the case, then I should have recognized the building. But I was sure that I didn't know this house.

It stood on the edge of a cliff, overlooking an arroyo. Actually, it was *the* arroyo, the one that sliced through the western edge of Pasadena. Although even a decent-sized lot in that location had to be worth over a million, this house sat alone, with a large wall surrounding it and trees crowding on every side. In fact, a normal observer would never have been able to see the house itself because of the heavily wooded lot, but of course I wasn't a normal observer. It was almost as if I hovered, drone-like, over the property, looking down at it from a height of fifty or sixty feet.

But I wasn't a drone, and so I didn't see anything in exact detail, instead getting a hazy impression of gray stone and multiple chimneys...a flash of color that might have been stained glass. I couldn't tell for sure, because the light shifted and warped, harsh and dark gold in my eyes, as if I was staring directly into the sun as it set.

The wind rose, cold, pulling at my loose hair. For the first time, I realized I was present in the vision, which had never happened to me before. Always I'd been a sort of bodiless observer, but this time I drifted on the wind, floating over the treetops. All around me there came a cacophony of harsh caws, crows rising up from the trees to surround me, their heavy wings churning at the air, chilling it further. So cold, the kind of ice that went straight to your bones. I'd never felt that kind of cold before. How could I, when "cold" in Southern California usually meant temperatures in the low fifties at most?

And then I saw those eyes. Cold as the chill that penetrated me, glinting silver-gray, like chips of ice. I had thought I was cold before, but now my entire body was wracked by shivers. Frantic, I paddled at the air, as if I could swim through it like water. But of course that maneuver didn't work. The wind's current carried me closer to the house, closer to a dark doorway. Standing in it was a shadowy figure shaped like a tall man, but I couldn't see his face. I couldn't see anything except those eyes.

I put up my hands to shield myself. What exactly that gesture would accomplish, I didn't know, but I had to do something. I had to defend myself.

It felt as if I was drowning, as if his eyes were growing larger and larger, not eyes at all, but a swirling vortex of freezing water moving up to swallow me, to pull me into its depths. Once when I was a little girl and was swimming at the beach, I'd gotten sucked into a fierce undertow and dragged along the bottom, heart pounding and lungs aching as I held my breath, knowing that if I opened my mouth to scream, the water would rush in and choke me.

That was what it felt like now as I struggled against that inexorable force. I pushed and pushed, trying to break free, and the cawing of the crows in my ears changed to mocking laughter.

The sound of that laughter made me want to scream. It tore across my eardrums like nails on a chalkboard. At the same time, however, a burst of rage shot through me, bringing an impossible heat with it. I was not going to drown. I was not going to fall into the darkness. I'd survived three days in a coma. I could survive this.

A cry escaped my lips, one that contained no words, was only a long, drawn-out wail of negation.

And then suddenly I was back to myself, back to the couch and the television blathering away in the background.

I gripped the sofa cushion and drew in deep panting breaths, as winded as though I had fought against that undertow in real life, rather than in the most horrifying vision I'd experienced to date. My heartbeat didn't have much time to calm down, though, because in the next instant someone was knocking on the door.

"Serena? Are you all right?"

Brian. So had that scream been real, rather than something uttered only in my vision? I didn't know. But I did know that Brian wouldn't go away, not until I went and reassured him that everything was fine.

Not that it was fine, of course. But I'd gotten pretty good at pretending.

My legs shook as I got up from the couch and walked over to the foyer. I gulped in some air, told myself that I needed to get it together, and then opened the door. Arranging an expression of innocent surprise on my face, I said, "What's the matter?"

"'What's the matter'?" he repeated, eyebrows working overtime. "You were screaming bloody murder!"

"I was?" Then I gave a silly little giggle and said, with a lift of my shoulders, "Oh, there was a spider."

"A spider."

"Yes. A huge one. It was in the bathroom when I went in and turned on the light. So I guess I might have screamed."

"'Might have screamed'? It sounded like you were getting axe-murdered."

That's probably exactly what it sounded like, because I knew from my teenage experiences at local amusement parks that I was a damn good screamer. One of my high school boyfriends had told me that I should scream professionally, like for horror movies or whatever. Unfortunately, it wasn't a very good talent to have when you were attempting to keep a low profile.

"Well, I hate spiders," I said. "I'd show you the evidence, but I hit that sucker with my shoe and then flushed him down the toilet. So really, everything is fine."

"You're sure."

"Of course I'm sure. And aren't you glad I can handle that sort of thing on my own instead of running next door and asking you to do it?"

Brian shuddered slightly. "Ugh. You'd have to ask Lewis, because I can't stand bugs. So I forgive you your scream. Just maybe try to tone it down next time. Lewis was about to call 911."

"I will," I said. "It's the first time I've seen a spider that big around here, so hopefully it'll be the last, too."

"One can only hope." He peered past me into my condo, as if to reassure himself that no axe murderers were lurking behind the half-wall that separated the living room from the dining room. "All right, gotta get back. My manicotti is getting cold."

"Sorry." And I was. Just because I'd sentenced myself to an extremely unappealing dinner didn't mean I'd intended to deprive Brian of his vastly superior meal.

"No problem."

He left after that, and I locked the door and returned to my neglected salad. Actually, I realized that I'd lost my appetite, so I took my plate to the kitchen and scraped everything into a Pyrex storage bowl with a rubber lid. Experience had taught me that salad wasn't exactly the sort of thing that traveled very well, but it felt wasteful to just throw it out. The food needed to season in the refrigerator for a few days before I could justify getting rid of it.

I was out of wine, too. Maybe that was all for the better, but right then I wanted to blot out the memory of that vision, and the only way I could think of to do it was to have a couple of glasses of wine, then go to bed and pray I'd be able to fall asleep.

All right, it was barely seven-thirty. Sleep probably wasn't an option, as much as I would have liked it to be.

So I poured myself a glass of water and went back to the living room. Because I didn't like to watch anything terribly meaningful while I ate, I had *House Hunters* on. Usually I found it soothing to watch all the made-up drama, the earnest conversations about granite versus marble or hardwood versus laminate. Right then, though, I just wanted to throw the remote at my TV.

Something crinkled in my jeans pocket. I set down my water and reached into the pocket to locate the source of the noise. My fingers closed around Silas' business card, and I pulled it out and stared at it for a long moment.

213-555-5929.

He'd said to call when I needed a ride, but surely he'd want to know about this latest vision. Had I just seen a vampire? I had no idea what a vampire was supposed to look like—resolutely, I pushed away the image of Bela Lugosi and his silky cape—but shouldn't I let Silas know what I'd just experienced?

All right, maybe that was only an excuse. Maybe the vision hadn't shown me a vampire at all. However, the background noise of the television notwithstanding, I felt terribly alone right then. Just hearing the sound of his voice would help.

Quickly, so I wouldn't lose my nerve, I went over to the dining room table where I'd left my purse, and got out my phone. Then I returned to the sofa, sat down, and tapped out Silas' number.

It rang once. Twice. Three times, and I felt my heart begin to sink. One more ring, and I knew it was going to roll over into voicemail. Would I have the courage to leave a message?

But then I heard him say, "Serena?"

For the barest second, I wondered at this evidence of psychic powers, then realized he must have looked at the caller ID on his phone. "Yes. Um…hi, Silas. Sorry to bother you, but I've just had a vision."

I couldn't see him, but it was almost as if I could feel the way he stiffened with shock at that revelation. "Just now?"

"Yes. I—"

"Don't say anything about it. Not over the phone."

A protest rose to my lips, one that died away quickly as I considered his words. I certainly wasn't naïve enough to think that phones couldn't be surveilled. One might have said there wasn't much point in listening to my sparse conversations…except for that little detail about my brother possibly running for President.

Silas spoke into the silence. "May I come over?"

Of course he could. Until he asked the question, I hadn't realized how much I dreaded being alone. "No—I mean, yes, it's fine. Have you eaten?"

"Not yet."

I wasn't going to count those few mouthfuls of salad as dinner, especially not when I now had the prospect of being able to sit down to eat with him. In fact, just thinking about it was enough to bring my appetite roaring back. "I can call for some pizza," I said, trying to sound casual. "Or there's an Indian place that's good."

"Whichever you prefer," he replied. "I have no dietary restrictions."

Well, there was a relief. Crazy visions notwithstanding, before I'd basically given up on men, going on dinner dates had begun to feel like negotiating a mine field—you never knew when someone would be vegan, or vegetarian, or avoiding gluten, or lactose-intolerant. I was none of those things, thank God, but I couldn't say the same for some of my former dates.

"I'll get pizza," I said. "It's probably easier."

"That sounds fine." A pause, and then he added, "I should be there in about twenty minutes."

"Okay. Thank you, Silas."

"It's why I am here."

He hung up then, and I speed-dialed Z Pizza and got one of their gourmet pizzas in the works—gorgonzola and prosciutto and pear. Then I rushed around like a madwoman, turning off the TV, getting some quiet background music going, setting the table. Maybe it was silly of me to go to all that effort, but some habits were too deeply ingrained. No matter how impromptu this dinner might be, I still needed to make sure the table looked right and that dead silence didn't reign in the house when my guest came over. I'd say that my mother would be proud, but I knew better.

As I headed back downstairs, I remembered the complete dearth of wine in the house. Quite possibly that was all right, since I had no idea whether Silas even drank…but what if it wasn't?

Out of desperation, I headed over to Lewis and Brian's place, and knocked. Brian opened the door a moment later and stared down at me in some mystification. "Another spider?"

"No," I replied. "It's just—Sam is coming over… kind of a last-minute thing…and you and I drank the last bit of wine in the house. Could I borrow a bottle? I'll get you a replacement the next time I go shopping."

"The reporter wearing you down already?"

"No, it's not that…it's…."

Apparently taking pity on me, Brian cut in, "Sweetheart, if you're actually having a man come over to your place for dinner, then consider the wine a gift."

"No, I couldn't—"

Of course Brian ignored my nervous spluttering. "I insist. What are you having?"

"The gorgonzola from Z Pizza."

"I've got a nice unoaked chardonnay that would be perfect. Hang on."

He disappeared into his condo. I could hear a low, murmured exchange, probably him explaining the situation to Lewis, and then a minute or two later he came back with an already chilled bottle of white wine. He handed it to me with a grin and said, "I want to hear all the gory details."

"I'm pretty sure there aren't going to be any gory details," I replied. "But if there are, you'll be the first to know."

"That's my girl."

I returned his grin with one of my own. "Thanks, Brian."

He waved a hand, and I went back inside my condo and put the wine in the refrigerator. Then I had just barely enough time to go to my bathroom upstairs and brush my hair and refresh my lip gloss. Yes, even as I primped, I knew I was being foolish. This wasn't a date. This was only a meeting to exchange information. I wouldn't lie to myself and say that I didn't find Silas attractive. But that had nothing to do with any of this.

No, I had a feeling that the real reason I was distracting myself with my hair and makeup was because that way I wouldn't have to stop and think about that vision, recall how terrifying it had been.

Unfortunately, I'd have to do that very thing just as soon as Silas got here.

CHAPTER FIVE

IF HE WAS SURPRISED BY THE BACKGROUND MUSIC AND THE wine glasses waiting for us on the dining room table, Silas didn't show it. I told him the pizza should be here any moment, and then I added, rather diffidently, "I didn't know if you drank or not. That vision rattled me, and I'd like some wine, but if you have a problem with it—"

"No," he said at once. "That is, I will only have one glass, since I have to drive home after this, but it's fine."

Thank God, I thought, but I only offered him a smile as I went into the kitchen to fetch the chardonnay and a bottle opener. When I returned, Silas said, "I can do that for you," and reached out for the items I held.

Right then the doorbell rang, so I didn't have to indulge in a battle of wills over who would open the wine. That was actually a relief, since my hands still felt a little shaky from the aftermath of my vision, and I wasn't sure whether or not I would have botched the job.

But dealing with the wine kept Silas distracted while I got the pizza from the delivery guy and handed over a twenty and a ten, telling him to keep the change. I had offered dinner, and so it was my responsibility to pay for it, but I wasn't sure whether Silas would see things in the same light. He did seem a little old-fashioned in some ways.

However, he didn't say anything as I came back to the dining room table with the pizza and set it down. He'd filled each glass halfway, so there wasn't really anything left for us to do except sit down and get started.

Silas lifted a piece of pizza onto my plate, then served one to himself. His gaze flicked to his wine glass, but he didn't touch it. Instead he asked, "This vision?"

Well, if he wanted to get right into things, then I was going to need some fortification. I curled my fingers around the stem of my wine glass and took a large swallow of chardonnay before saying, "Mind if I eat something before we launch into that topic?"

"Of course," he replied immediately. "I'm sorry. It was bad?"

"Yes," I said, but didn't offer anything more than that. I picked up my pizza and ate a few mouthfuls.

Once again my appetite seemed to have deserted me, but I knew I needed to eat. Besides, the warmth of the food and the mellow combination of flavors did help to steady me a little, giving me the strength I'd need to relive that vision.

Taking the cue, Silas ate as well, then allowed himself a very small sip of wine. As I watched him from beneath my lashes, I realized that he'd switched out the black T-shirt he'd worn earlier for a long-sleeved black button-up. His hair brushed against the collar, heavy and silky and dark.

You're staring, I scolded myself. *Stop it.*

So I set down my pizza and drank some more wine, then said, "This one was different."

He rested his hands on the tabletop and watched me carefully. "Different in what way?"

"Because I was in it. Usually my visions are sort of like watching a movie, although hazier, not as distinct. But still, I always have a very clear sense that I'm an observer, that I'm not involved in the action at all. This time, though…." I let the words trail off, and fought the shiver that wanted to run an icy finger down my spine.

"You were there?"

"Yes." After allowing myself another fortifying swallow of wine, I did the best I could to describe the house, the malevolent presence I felt there, even though I hadn't seen him, hadn't seen his face. At the moment, even though I knew his appearance must be a vital piece of information, I was glad I hadn't seen anything of that person except the dark outline of his body.

Silas listened as I related what I had seen. His mouth tightened, and his dark brows drew together. When I was finished, he gave a grim nod, then said, "You must have seen their lair."

"Lair?"

"Of the vampires."

"They live here?" I asked, aghast. I wasn't even sure why Silas' revelation should have startled me so much, except I supposed I had the dim notion that those blood-sucking ancients must be holed up in an abandoned country house or something, living someplace where they couldn't be easily detected. That they might be right here in prosy suburban Pasadena had never occurred to me.

"Some of them do." He lifted his wine glass and drank—a much larger swallow this time. "Or at least, we suspected they did. We observe the comings and goings of the semivives, but we have never been able to track them to their destination when they go to give their reports to their master. His magic is very strong, and he keeps his home shrouded in darkness." Silas stared across the table at me then, eyes narrowed. "It's impressive that your own powers

were able to pierce that darkness, to see his house…
and him."

"I didn't really see him," I protested. *And thank
God for that….* "Just something that seemed to be a
man."

"He is no man. Or rather, he hasn't been one for
centuries."

I wanted to shiver. But I also didn't want to
seem like a coward in front of Silas. Maybe one day
I could be as casual as he when it came to discuss-
ing an inhuman being who'd walked this earth for
many human lifetimes. Now, though…. I picked up
my rapidly cooling piece of pizza and forced myself
to take a bite, and another. That was a little better.
Pizza was such a wonderfully prosaic thing. It was
hard to imagine that vampires and pizza could exist
in the same world.

But—according to Silas, at least—they did.
Which meant I'd have to find some way to come to
terms with all this. "How old is he?"

"Old enough that he saw the beginnings of this
nation, and the death of many others. It is difficult to
say for sure, because he has borne many names over
the years. But at least three centuries, and probably
more." At last Silas picked up his own slice of pizza
and took a bite, followed by another.

Three hundred years old. And that was a minimum estimate. I tried to think of all the events this

vampire must have witnessed, all the changes in the
world he must have experienced, but my brain had
to back off after a moment. It was all too much.

"So what does he call himself now?"

"Lucius Montfort." A wry glint entered Silas'
dark eyes, and he added, "Don't bother to Google
it. You won't find any record of him anywhere. Any
property he owns would have been purchased by
a trust, using layers of semivives and unknowing
agents to manage the deal."

"If he's so secretive, how do you know his name?"

"Because we have been watching him for a very
long time."

Something about that reply spurred me to ask,
"And how old are you?"

Far from appearing offended by my question,
Silas only smiled. "I'm thirty-one. Does that surprise
you?"

It actually did, sort of. From the way he'd been
talking, I'd begun to form the impression that he
must be part of some secret order of vampire-chas-
ers, equally old and equally powerful. Apparently,
that wasn't the case. "Sort of. So you yourself hav-
en't been tracking this Lucius character across the
centuries?"

"No. It was only in the last few decades that he
resurfaced in Southern California. Before that, he
lived in a mansion on Long Island. Before that, in

London. And before that"—Silas didn't quite shrug, but I saw his shoulders move slightly—"we really don't know."

"That's quite a change. I'm surprised that a vampire who'd lived in London and the Northeast would end up someplace so…sunny."

A lift of the eyebrow, and Silas shook his head. "The intensity of the sunlight is not a factor. No vampire can tolerate any kind of daylight, whether it's the hot sun beating down on the Mojave Desert, or a rainy afternoon in New York. He must stay hidden during the daylight hours, no matter what."

"But he can come out at night." It seemed like a logical conclusion, but I had to admit that I didn't like it very much. This vampire master didn't seem quite as frightening if I could think of him as being confined to his lair, unable to move around in the real world.

"Yes. And before you ask, taking up residence someplace like Alaska or Norway, where during the winter there are many hours of darkness, isn't something that would work. For one thing, they would have to move during the summer, when it is light just as long, and vampires like to find a place of refuge and stay with it for as long as possible. Constantly disrupting their routine in such a way is not optimal. And second, they would be far more conspicuous in a place with such a low population. It is easier to hide their activities in large cities, or suburban areas with many people to choose from."

"To hunt, you mean." Damn it, my voice had shaken slightly as I made the remark, despite my best efforts to steady it.

"Sometimes. But vampires do not need living blood as often as one might think. A fresh kill—so to speak—can keep them sustained for many months. It's a survival trait, because even in as populated a place as Southern California, too many missing persons will invite far too much scrutiny."

Well, that was something. I'd always wondered how vampires managed it in books and movies, killing people right and left, without every local police and sheriff's department, and probably the FBI to boot, descending to figure out who the culprit was. But if this Lucius and any other vampires around him were able to space out their kills, then the whole thing didn't seem quite as logistically difficult.

"How many vampires does he have with him?"

"We don't know for sure. At least three or four. But probably not many more than that, because too high a concentration of their kind in a given area will lead to far too many killings, even if they are attempting to go the maximum length of time between victims."

"Three or four doesn't sound too bad."

Silas' mouth pursed slightly, as if he was attempting to decide how much of the truth I could handle. I had to repress a flicker of irritation. What, did he think I was too fragile to handle what he had to tell me? Without answering right away, he reached for his glass of wine and drank some, then took a bite of pizza. At last he said, "I assure you, even a single vampire can do a great deal of damage. They are inhumanly fast and strong, and able to draw on powers of illusion, of darkness, to give themselves even more of an upper hand. No human can go up against them and hope to prevail."

"But you're hunting them."

An uneasy silence fell, and Silas' gaze shifted away from mine. What his lack of response meant, I wasn't quite sure. That he wasn't human, either? He certainly looked like a normal enough man. That is, an extremely strong and attractive man, but even so, I hadn't been able to detect anything about him that would signal there was something strange going on.

"Observing," he said. "Not engaging."

"It sure looks like you engaged with that semivive."

"That was different. A semivive has some peculiar traits, true, but fighting one is very different from going up against a full-blooded—so to speak—vampire."

I had to take his word for it, because of course I'd never seen a vampire fight. I hadn't seen one at all, unless you could count the hazy, malevolent figure I'd spotted in my vision. Those icy gray eyes would haunt me forever. I didn't want to see the whole person in the flesh. A vision was bad enough.

"And what happens when a vampire realizes you've taken out one of his minions?"

"Acceptable losses. A semivive can be replaced. In fact, that is their whole reason for being—to be the eyes and ears of the vampires, their foot soldiers. Cannon fodder when necessary." Silas paused there and ran a finger over the glass tabletop, tracing a pattern I couldn't quite make out. "That's not to say that a vampire is exactly happy when he loses one of his servants, but they can be replaced."

"So a vampire can't be replaced?"

"No more than you or I could be replaced." He looked up then and gave me an unreadable look. Our eyes met, and a small shiver passed over me. Not an unpleasant one, but…not the kind of shivers I should be getting from someone I barely knew, no matter how attractive I might find him. "Far fewer survive the transition from mortal to vampire than do those who survive being made a semivive. The master vampire—in the case of the local coven, Lucius Montfort—must be very sure of his disciple before he attempts to take them on that journey."

"Journey? So it's not just a matter of being bitten by a vampire?"

"No. The disciple must drink the blood of the master, and he must hold that person as their body turns from mortal flesh to undying matter. It is a journey into death...and back from it. So the disciple must be entirely sure of his or her purpose, and must possess unwavering devotion and belief in the master vampire."

Lovely. I supposed in a way it was good that the process was so difficult, or else we'd probably be knee-deep in vampires, despite their need to remain as low-profile as possible.

"So you see," Silas continued, "why the loss of a vampire he created is a true blow to a master vampire."

"How would you know for sure if you aren't hunting them?"

He reached for his wine glass and lifted it by the stem, then gave the contents a slight swirl so the liquid glinted pale gold under the light of the brushed-steel chandelier hanging above us. "Just because we don't actively hunt them doesn't mean we don't do our best to kill them when we come across them. They are...an abomination."

Strong word, but I wasn't inclined to argue with it. One could say that all creatures under the sun had their place in the world, no matter how vicious, but vampires weren't exactly the same thing as polar bears or mountain lions. They certainly were outside the natural order…or at least the natural order as I understood it. .

"Where did they come from?" I asked softly.

"No one knows for sure. They have existed alongside humanity for most of recorded history. Always in the shadows, always hunting in stealth. Some say they are merely a mutation of humankind, while others believe they carry some kind of rare infection. The fact that vampirism is transmitted by blood, and that an extract of their blood creates the semivives, seems to indicate the latter theory is the more accurate one."

"I'm surprised you don't try to study their blood when you do manage to kill one."

"I wish that were possible. But since vampires turn to dust as soon as they are dispatched, it's a little difficult to get a sample from them."

"What about the semivives?" I asked. "Do you always kill them the way you did that man last Monday? Couldn't you isolate the disease in their blood?"

Silas broke off a piece of pizza crust but didn't eat it. Instead, he set it back down on his plate, as if he'd lost something of his appetite. "We don't think of it as killing. More…releasing the soul that the vampire has suborned. The serum we use is a lethal mixture of quicksilver and holy water, the easiest way to eliminate a semivive. However, even in the times we've dispatched semivives in a more conventional way, it's still been of no use to study them. Once they're dead, whatever catalyst existed in the bloodstream dies with them."

So much for that. I didn't know why it mattered to me what precisely created a vampire, except that I supposed my modern brain would find the whole situation much easier to accept if it turned out that the vampires' condition was caused by some sort of exotic virus. Admitting that they were purely supernatural creatures took a huge leap of faith.

But then, I knew my visions were real, even though most people would probably do their best to explain them away, since they didn't fit into one's neat little ideas of how modern life should work. So, if I accepted the visions as part of my world, then I had to accept vampires, too.

"This house," Silas went on, in a very different tone of voice. "Could you try to describe it in more detail to me?"

"I can do better than that," I replied, glad that he'd changed the subject. "I can draw it for you."

An almost startled expression passed over his face. "I wasn't aware that you were an artist."

"I'm not, really," I said. "But once I realized it was easier to keep track of my visions if I put down

a representation of what I saw, I started taking drawing classes at Pasadena City College. And the more
I practiced, the better I got. I didn't have time to
sketch out what I saw in today's vision, because Brian
came over, and then I called you, and—" I broke off
there, realizing that those excuses really didn't matter. "Anyway, let me run up to my office and get my
sketchpad."

"That would be excellent."

So I pushed back my chair and headed upstairs to
the little loft area that had been turned into my home
office. Just a desk and a table for when I needed a flat
workspace, and a chair I could roll between them,
but it was still nice to have a separate area for that
sort of thing.

My sketchbook lay on the table. I scooped it up,
along with a couple of pencils and a gum eraser,
then headed back downstairs. Silas had finished the
rest of his piece of pizza and started in on another,
for which I was relieved. At the rate we were going,
talking much more than eating, I was going to end
up with a lot of leftovers.

Instead of going back to the spot where I'd been
sitting across from him, I took the chair to his right so
he could watch as I drew. "The house was definitely
located on the edge of the arroyo," I said, sketching
quickly, filling in the sharp edges of the cliff that led
down into the ravine. "Unfortunately, I didn't see any

other landmarks, like the Colorado Street Bridge, so I can't tell you where it was located in relation to the actual town. But it was a large plot of land, maybe as much as an acre."

"That makes sense," Silas murmured. "Vampires do like their privacy."

"There was a wall," I continued, pencil moving even more swiftly across the paper as more details began to return to me. That seemed to be how it worked—once I got going, it was as if my pencil had a will of its own and was able to pick up subtle features that I wasn't sure I would have otherwise recalled with my conscious mind. "Low…gray stone at the bottom, black iron with fleur-de-lis spikes along the top. A lot of trees. Some were bare, so I couldn't tell exactly what kind they were. But also some pine and fir, I think. There was some grass, but nothing like an actual lawn because of all the trees."

"Again, so they can have their privacy."

"I suppose so." After roughing in the trees, I moved on to the house itself. "The place was massive. A mansion. Lots of chimneys." The scratching of the pencil on the paper seemed to create a counterpoint to my description, as if my voice and my pencil were working together to tell the story. "I think I saw at least one stained-glass window, but I didn't get any details as to the design. There was a wide series of steps leading up to the front door.

The stone around it was carved, I think…it's hard to remember, because that's where *he* was standing."

"Was it daylight in your vision?"

"I…." My words trailed off as I attempted to recall the exact specifics of the vision. Yes, I'd seen everything clearly, but, now that I thought about it, I didn't remember seeing the sun. It was more as if everything had been clearly illuminated, but for all I knew, the light that had revealed all those details had come from the moon. "I don't think so. I think it's more that I was able to see, despite the lack of any kind of obvious light source. Because how could he have been standing in the doorway if the sun was out?"

"True." Silas rubbed a hand over his chin as he stared down at the sketch. "I only asked because you've provided a great deal of detail here."

"Thanks." Now that I'd stopped sketching, I realized how close we sat. Maybe not bumping-knees close, but still. I'd done a fairly good job of keeping a safe distance between us when we were together, and I wasn't quite sure how to handle the way my heart rate seemed to speed up slightly at his proximity, at how I now could notice subtle details about him, like the dark stubble on his cheeks, the faint line between his brows…the scar that stood out nearly white against the tanned skin of his right hand. How had he gotten that scar?

I didn't dare ask.

He had to have noticed the sudden increase in tension in the room. Sitting up a little straighter—and thereby widening the space between us, although only slightly—he said, "Do you mind if I take this sketch? I'd like to show it to my—that is, there are some people I know who would like to see it."

"Sure," I responded, glad of an excuse to look away from him. Working carefully so I wouldn't tear the paper, I eased the drawing loose from the metal spiral binding of the sketchbook and handed it to him. "Silas…."

"Yes?"

"Who are these people? Who do you work for?"

His mouth tightened. "I'm afraid I can't tell you that."

"Why not?"

"Because the less you know, the better."

I lifted an eyebrow. "Oh, is that why you just gave me a lesson in Vampire 101?"

He didn't quite roll his eyes, but from the way his jaw tensed, I could tell he wasn't exactly pleased by my question. "Because that particular knowledge won't hurt you, might in fact help you. But I can't say the same about the people I work for. There's a reason why they don't publicize who they are."

"So what makes them different from the vampires?"

"Everything," he responded, his tone so fierce that I couldn't help but recoil slightly. "They are not at all like the vampires. They are the antithesis of the vampires. Understand?"

"Um, sure." The sudden flare of anger had been unexpected, and more than a little frightening. Despite those weird twinges of attraction that I didn't quite know what to do about, I'd found myself becoming more relaxed around him. Now I couldn't help remembering the ferocity of his attack on the semivive, the casual strength of the muscles concealed beneath the black button-down shirt he wore. Acting unconcerned, I got up from my chair and headed over to my original seat across the table. "Are you going to have any more pizza? Because otherwise I'll stick the box in the refrigerator."

"No, I'm finished." He stood as well, sketch still clutched in one hand. "In fact, I think I had better be going."

"So you can take that"—I gestured toward the sketch—"to your masters?"

"They are not my masters. They—" He seemed to stop himself there, as if he knew he was on the verge of revealing too much, had possibly already let slip more than he intended to. "But yes, I need to get this to the interested parties."

"Okay." I retrieved the pizza box and closed the lid, then tried not to sigh at the amount of pizza left over. I knew what I was going to be eating for the next couple of days. As I closed the refrigerator door, I heard him say,

"Serena…are you angry with me?"

I'd never had a man ask me that question with such candor. He stood there just outside the kitchen, watching me, worry clear in his expression. And seeing him like that, the rush of irritation I'd felt disappeared as quickly as it had come. Right then, I realized it was foolish to be annoyed with him just because he couldn't tell me everything. All he'd done so far was try to keep me safe. And if withholding certain pieces of information was part of that effort, then how could I throw it back in his face?

"No, Silas," I replied. "I'm not angry. I guess I'm just tired."

He nodded. "I hope you can sleep well, then. And remember to call me if you need me to drive you somewhere…or if you have another vision. Just call if you need anything. Anything at all."

"I will."

An offering of a small smile, and then I was walking him to the door. After I'd shut it behind him, though, I felt the unexpected and unwanted sting of tears in my eyes.

And what if all I want is for you to hold me and tell me it's all going to be okay? Would you do that, too, Silas?

I had a feeling that I'd never get an answer to that question, no matter how much I might want it.

CHAPTER SIX

My phone was ringing. At the ungodly—for me, any-way—hour of eight-thirty in the morning. I briefly considered throwing the iPhone out the window, but then I realized that might be Silas calling. I sat up in bed, then climbed out and retrieved the cell phone from the top of my dresser. When I looked down at the display, I saw my sister's number there and almost put the phone back down. But I was already up, and besides, I knew if I ignored the call, she'd only keep trying until I finally gave up and answered.

"Hi, Vanessa," I said.

"Oh, thank *God,* Serena! I am in the *worst* bind!"

"Oh?" I responded, trying to sound as noncommit-tal as possible. My sister loved drama. Maybe it was holdover middle child syndrome, just an ingrained need for attention, or maybe it was simply from hanging

around so many wildly creative but not entirely sta-
ble people, but I found her theatrics exhausting.

"Two of my models are down with the *flu,* of
all things, and my show is tonight. Please say you'll
come and fill in."

My sister was a clothing designer. A very successful one, too, when you considered that she had always
stubbornly refused to leave Los Angeles and set up
shop in New York, where most of the big names in
American fashion had their studios. A number of
celebrities wore her designs, and she'd even gained
some national attention a few years past when an
Oscar nominee wore one of her evening gowns. All of
which just helped to point out what an underachiever
I was when compared to my two older siblings.

Even putting that sad fact aside, I'd always hated
it when my sister tried to recruit me for modeling
duty. Having my hair and face tormented into someone else's ideal of beauty was grueling. Besides....
"Weren't you complaining the last time I got drafted
that your clothes didn't hang right on me because I
was too short?"

"Well...." A long pause, and then Vanessa came
back with, "You *are* too short. No one five foot six
makes it as a runway model. It's nothing *personal.*"

I hated to bring up the subject of my visions, but it
seemed that was the only way I could possibly get her
to back off. "And what about that other issue?" I didn't

say the word "vision." It was sort of taboo in my family to come right out and state the matter so baldly.

A long pause. Then I heard her huff a breath into the phone, right before she replied in far too hearty a tone, "You'll be fine. You only have to be on stage for probably five minutes altogether. What are the odds?"

They were actually fairly low. While my visions didn't follow any particular pattern, I'd never had them come just a day apart. Since I'd already experienced one the evening before, the chances of one striking me while I was strutting down a catwalk tonight weren't very high. But I didn't want to tell Vanessa that. Instead, I said, "I don't know what the odds are because I can't ever predict these things. You really should get someone else."

"I can't," she said, sounding even more frantic, if possible. "It sounds as if half the models in town are down with this flu thing, and the ones that aren't are already booked. Please, Serena."

Oh, for God's sake. I pulled in a breath. Problem was, I knew I would say yes. If I turned down my big sister, I'd never hear the end of it from my mother. And while some people—namely my friend Candace—might have told me to put on my big-girl panties and grow a spine, I knew my family much better than she did. There were some hills I might be willing to die on, so to speak, but this wasn't one of them.

"All right," I said wearily. "Where and when?"

"Just come to my studio space in West Hollywood. Be there as soon as you can, because we've got to try stuff on you and do any necessary alterations."

"I'll try to be there by eleven."

"As late as that?"

"I just got out of bed," I replied with a calmness I certainly didn't feel, even as I once again repressed the urge to hurl my phone across the room. "And it's better to wait until a little later anyway. The traffic is going to be a mess until at least ten."

"Well, fine," she said, her tone ungracious in the extreme. "Just get here, okay?"

"Yes, ma'am." And then I tapped the button on my screen to end the call, because I knew if I stayed on with her any longer, I'd tell her exactly what she could do with her goddamn stupid fashion show.

I couldn't put the phone away, however. Now I'd have to call Silas and let him know that he would have to fight traffic all the way to West Hollywood to drop me off, just because I was too afraid of familial repercussions to tell my sister no.

This week was just getting better and better. What else did it have in store for me?

"Thank you so much for this," I told Silas as he maneuvered his truck through the morass that was the interchange of the 110 and 10 Freeways.

"It's fine," he replied. "It is what I told you I would do, after all."

"I know, but…."

"Serena." His voice was unruffled, even though he'd just had to tap his brakes to avoid being side-swiped by some asshole in a stake-bed truck who'd decided at the last minute that he really wanted to head west on the 10 instead of getting off at 7th Street. "Don't worry. I don't mind."

"Well, that makes one of us," I muttered. Oh, yes, part of me was glad of any excuse to spend some more time with him, but sitting in traffic had to be one of the least pleasurable ways imaginable to be spending that time.

We inched our way off the interchange and kept going west. Even though now it was well past ten o'clock, the traffic was as thick and slow-moving as slightly congealed molasses. If I'd had to drive myself, I probably would have been cursing in frustration by that point.

And that was the other thing. Vanessa knew I hated to drive and avoided doing so as much as possible, and yet she'd just assumed I'd be all right with having to pilot myself across twenty miles of some of the worst traffic in the country. Or maybe she thought I'd hire an Uber. It would have been a hell of an expensive ride, but I supposed she didn't care too much about that. Money wasn't exactly an issue in our family.

"Anyway," Silas went on, "I live downtown, so it's not that far to go back there and wait until you need me to pick you up when you're done."

Another morsel of information. I was so starved for any details about him that I had to pounce on this one, a hungry rat going after a tiny sliver of cheese. "Oh, really? Do you like it there?"

"Well enough. It's central."

A fact that not many would argue with. Unless you counted the people like my sister who liked to pretend not much existed outside the 310 area code. Yes, she'd grown up in San Marino, but she hadn't been back since she left to attend Otis Parsons when I was only eleven. Even during the summer breaks she was always traveling someplace or interning for someone, so she'd never really returned to the house where she'd grown up.

Silas glanced over at me before returning his attention to the road. "My place is just outside Little Tokyo."

Was that the faintest hint of amusement I'd heard in his voice, as if he could tell that I hadn't been exactly satisfied with the bare facts he'd offered so far about his home? "That sounds interesting. A lot more interesting than pedestrian Pasadena."

He didn't immediately reply, as he'd just stepped on the accelerator to jet us past a Prius that was slow-poking along and leaving far more following distance than was strictly necessary. Once we'd settled down in our new lane, now moving slightly faster than we had before, he said, "Pasadena is a nice town."

"Not according to my mother. She thinks I'm living in a slum. Every week she looks up the crime reports for my neighborhood and emails them to me."

A chuckle. "I would say your mother doesn't have much experience of the world if she thinks where you're living is a slum."

"And you'd be right. She's lived in San Marino her entire life."

"Then she didn't go to college."

Clearly, he knew the area well enough to realize there weren't any four-year colleges in Pasadena, except Caltech, and it was obvious enough to anyone who knew the least bit about her that my mother wasn't exactly hiding a degree in astrophysics or mathematics. "No. That is, she went to Pasadena City College after she graduated high school, but she was never ambitious about having a career. All she wanted was to marry well and be a fixture in country club society. And," I added, trying very hard not to sigh, "that's exactly what she did, so I guess you could say she was successful."

"Your family has money."

It wasn't a question. I wondered right then how much Silas actually did know about me, how much research he had done into my background. From a few hints he'd let drop, it did seem as if he possessed far more information about my family and my finances than he should. Whoever he worked for must have supplied that data, or he'd done some digging on his own.

Maybe it should have bothered me, but so much of my family's background was public knowledge that I'd stopped wasting my time worrying about that sort of thing. It came with the territory when your brother was a member of the U.S. Senate, with even loftier ambitions than that.

"What gave it away?" I asked wryly, and Silas' mouth twitched.

"A few things. Do you mind?"

"What do I mind…having money, or having people know that I have it?"

"Both, I suppose."

I shrugged and looked away from him so I could stare out the truck's window. We were just passing La Brea; a few more exits to go, and it would be time to get off the freeway. A glance at the clock on the dashboard told me it was now a quarter to eleven.

No way we would make it to Vanessa's studio by eleven as I'd promised, but there wasn't much I could do about that.

Since I could tell Silas was waiting for me to respond, I fiddled with the strap of my purse as it sat in my lap, then said, "I suppose it's more strange than anything else. That is, I grew up around other people with money, so I didn't think much about it when I was younger. When I got to high school, I started to realize that there was a difference between people who were just ordinarily well-off and my family, but it really didn't hit home until I went to college. Yes, I know that everyone refers to USC as the 'university of spoiled children,' but it isn't. Not really. There are students there from all over the world, people getting by on a patchwork of scholarships and grants, working two jobs while going to school full-time."

"So that opened your eyes?"

"It did. And that was why I decided I wanted to go into education. At first my parents were happy, because they thought I intended to get my Ph.D. in pedagogy and teach at the university level. That would have been prestigious enough for them. But it wasn't what I wanted."

"What did you want?"

For some reason, a flush heated my cheeks. Still staring out the window, I replied, "I wanted to teach high school English. I was getting my master's, just because I knew you started at a higher salary if you had one, but...." I stopped there and shook my head. The difference in salary between having just a teaching credential and a master's degree probably amounted to less than what all my father's investments earned in half a day. But the trifling numbers involved hadn't mattered to me. What had mattered was that I'd planned to set my own course, one very different from my mother's, and also very different from those of my siblings. I never wanted attention. Really, what I'd wanted more than anything was a life separate from my family's expectations.

"But then there was the accident."

I shifted in my seat and sent Silas a narrow-eyed look. His expression was imperturbable as usual, so I really couldn't tell what he thought of the whole situation. He didn't look back at me, though, as he was involved in maneuvering the truck over to the far right lane so we could get off at La Cienega. "I suppose you know all about that, too."

"Yes. As soon as it came to our attention that you were in possession of a very special talent, we found out what we could about you, about your past. Does that bother you?"

Well, of course it did. Then again, these days almost anyone could dig up an unhealthy amount of data about a person if they were sufficiently motivated. It was so very difficult to hide.

I settled for giving a shrug before I said, "I don't know if it bothers me. Maybe a little. Anyway, I thought I'd be able to go back to school and pick up my master's program once I recovered, but then the first…episode…came along, and that was the end of that."

"I'm sorry."

"It was long enough ago that I'm pretty much over it." I turned back away from him so I was looking out through the windshield, watching gleaming high-rises and careful plantings of tall palm trees go by. "Maybe this isn't the life I expected to have, but things are okay. Or at least they were okay until I learned that vampires walk among us."

I'd said that last bit with a purposely sarcastic tone to my voice, but Silas appeared to take me seriously. "Yes, it can be difficult to learn of these things, to realize there is much more to the world than is seen on the surface."

"Did you have to go through that, too?"

His brows pulled together, but only for the barest trace of a second. Then his face seemed to smooth itself, and he said, "Not exactly. I've known about the vampires my entire life."

Was he from a family of vampire hunters? But no, he'd adamantly insisted that he and his people—whoever they were—didn't actively go after the vampires, but only stepped in when necessary. I couldn't really puzzle out what was going on with him, with his own past, but I also knew that asking for more details would get me nowhere. Instead, I gave a small, bitter laugh and said, "That's kind of a heavy thing to be putting on a little kid, don't you think?"

"I suppose it depends on your point of view. There are those who would argue that it's better to possess that particular knowledge early on, so there are no surprises."

That was one way of looking at it. I wondered what it was like to grow up knowing that a supernatural race existed alongside us mere humans, to carry that secret with you everywhere you went. No wonder Silas seemed so damn serious most of the time.

I liked that about him, though. I'd been with a few guys who seemed to take everything as a colossal joke, and that sort of attitude could get very tiring very quickly.

Not that I was "with" Silas, of course. We were…I couldn't really think of a word to describe our relationship. He'd saved my life. And we seemed to be fairly comfortable in one another's company. Was that enough to say we were friends?

Possibly.

"Turn right on Melrose," I said. "Then there's a little side street called Orlando. Turn left there. My sister's studio is the gray building on the left."

Silas nodded and guided the truck along the route I'd indicated. As usual, the streets here were choked with traffic. It didn't seem to matter what the time of day, or even what day it was—you were always stuck inching along from signal to signal. I honestly didn't understand how my sister could live someplace so crowded, but she seemed to thrive on the chaos.

He had to drop me off in the driveway, since there were absolutely no spots available on the street. "I'll call you when I'm done," I told him. "The show's at seven, so…maybe around nine? I know she's going to make me stick around for the hors d'oeuvres afterward."

"Whenever you're done will be fine." His gaze seemed to rake the building, its exterior quiet and serene, even though I knew it had to be a madhouse inside. "But Serena—"

"Yes?" I had no idea what I was expecting him to say, but my heart began to beat a little faster anyway.

"Be careful. Make sure you're never alone."

I summoned a smile, forcing myself to ignore the ridiculous hope that had begun to blossom inside me. "Not much chance of that. I'm going to be surrounded by hairstylists and makeup artists and models and various hangers-on. There's no way I'd be alone even if I wanted to."

"Good."

He drove off then, leaving me to stare after his truck and wish that I was still inside, sitting only a foot away from him. We could have driven off together and....

And what? I asked myself. *Nothing is going on there. Nothing. So get in that studio and get this over with.*

I really disliked these sorts of productions, disliked having to put myself on display in such a way. Yes, people would be attending the show to look at the clothes, not me, but my inner introvert was screaming for me to dig my phone out of my purse and call Silas so he could come back and get me.

That wasn't going to happen, though. Resolutely, I ignored the urge to grab my phone and instead made myself walk down the driveway to the rear of the property, where I knew all the activity would be happening. My sister's "studio" was actually a back house built behind the main house, where she lived. I had no idea where the actual show would take place, but since I'd done this before, I knew that all the models would get ferried there in a van at the appointed time.

Models. I knew I was going to look like a plow horse next to a bunch of Arabians, but there wasn't much I could do about it at this point.

Since it was a mild day, all the windows to the studio were open, and the door stood open as well. I went inside and was greeted by the chaos

I'd expected—racks of clothes everywhere, people chattering away, the hum of a sewing machine
somewhere in the background. As soon as I entered
what used to be a living room, my sister descended.
She was a taller version of myself in some ways,
the same dark hair and hazel eyes, only hers were
half-obscured by a pair of oversized horn-rimmed
glasses, and her hair was cut severely short in a pixie
'do that I would never have been brave enough to
attempt. I liked my long hair. It helped me to hide.
That's what I felt as if I'd been doing ever since the
accident…hiding who I really was.

"Thank God you're here. What took you so
long?"

"The traffic—"

"Never mind. I know the trousers you'll be wearing in the first grouping will need to be hemmed. Go
see Marco and let him take care of it. I've got to get
on the phone with Neiman Marcus—the jewelry I
was supposed to be borrowing still hasn't shown up
yet. Off with you!"

She gave me a push toward the back of the
house, then pirouetted on her wedge-heeled boots
and took off toward what used to be the dining room
and was now a forest of bolts of fabric standing on
their ends. Since I'd done this before, I knew that
the two small bedrooms had been transformed into
alteration stations. I didn't know Marco—my sister

tended to cycle through assistants on a regular basis, driving them nuts with her insane demands—but I figured with only two bedrooms to choose between, it shouldn't take me too long to track him down.

"Marco?" I asked, sticking my head into the first bedroom.

A handsome-verging-on pretty Filipino man looked up from the sewing machine there. "That's me." He gave me a quickly assessing glance. "You must be Serena."

"That's right." I went on in and extended a hand.

He shook it, then said, "Okay, Vanessa set aside the things you'll be wearing. Let's get you out of your clothes so we can get through everything in enough time."

I wanted to quip that if he wanted me out of my clothes, he'd better buy me a drink first, but I could tell from the set of his mouth that he wasn't in the mood for any jokes. So I nodded, went behind the screen in the corner, and took off my jeans and T-shirt. There was a silk kimono draped over the screen, and I slipped into it, glad that my sister had remembered that particular detail. Last time she hadn't, and I'd been forced to wander around in my bra and panties in between trying on outfits.

Not that anyone present would have cared if I was naked. All her assistants were gay men, and none of the models would give me a second glance, even if they were into girls. Both they and I knew they could do better.

So I emerged from behind the screen, and put on the pants Vanessa wanted hemmed, along with the shoes to match—retro-styled pumps with a wedge and four-inch heels. It would be a minor miracle if I managed to make it down the catwalk and back without face-planting in front of the entire world.

Once upon a time, I might have managed it. Back in the day—high school, to be more exact—I had done some modeling, just for fun, thanks to certain contacts in my mother's circle. I'd learned how to sashay in high heels, to stop in the right places, always staring out into the middle distance, never making eye contact with anyone. That was part of the reason Vanessa knew she could call on me in a pinch. I was too short, and not exactly runway material, but at least I knew the drill. Or I did, once.

Now I stood there as Marco had me change out of one garment and into another, making sure hems were the right length, letting out a seam here and there. I was slender, but definitely not model-thin. Luckily, part of the popularity of Vanessa's clothes was that she did design for people who weren't a size double-zero, but even so, Marco did a whole lot more letting out than taking in that afternoon.

At one point, when the hunger pangs got too bad, I asked if I could order in something, and my sister looked at me as if I'd just inquired whether it was okay to axe-murder her assistant. "You can't *eat,*" she said. "You barely fit in those clothes as it is."

And then she was gone again.

So by the time seven o'clock rolled around, I was ravenously hungry and cranky as hell. The second part wasn't so bad; a vaguely hostile stare could actually work to my benefit on the runway. As for the rest of it, well, I figured I'd stuff myself at the reception after the show. I just had to hope the caterers would be providing something I liked, rather than bruised kale or some other abomination that would have me crying inside for an In-N-Out burger.

And I actually managed to get through the show without making an utter fool of myself. It took place in a warehouse over in Santa Monica—inwardly, I'd groaned when I learned where the venue was located, just because then Silas would have to drive that much farther to get me when it was all over—but it wasn't the utter fiasco I'd been fearing. I didn't trip over my heels, or get overcome by a vision at exactly the wrong moment, which was about all I could ask for. Also, I couldn't help thinking what he might make of me when he returned, because of course I was far more done up than he'd ever seen me before, with smoky shadow making my eyes look enormous, and my nearly waist-length hair worked into long, lustrous waves.

Wishful thinking, probably. I'd never seen him have the slightest reaction to my appearance, for good or ill. It made sense, if he wanted matters to stay strictly business between the two of us, but....

But nothing, I told myself as I slithered out of a hand-beaded evening gown and into the dead simple but perfectly cut short black dress Vanessa had told me I must wear at the reception. Actually, I was glad of the loan, just because if I hadn't been so rushed, I would have known that faded jeans and an army green T-shirt weren't exactly the proper attire for a cocktail reception.

After the show, everyone made their way out-side, where a large pavilion had been set up in the warehouse's parking lot. To my relief, the food provided was downright traditional—meatballs on toothpicks, little tea sandwiches, even rumaki—probably because the entire show had had a sort of retro-glam feel. Really, the dress Vanessa had loaned me would have been worthy of Audrey Hepburn. I just had to hope no one there would look at me and decide I didn't quite measure up in comparison.

I loaded up one of the small black glass plates that had been provided on the buffet table, snagged a flute of champagne, and tried to look as if I was having a wonderful time. Most of the models seemed to know one another, or the fashion critics and buyers and photographers who'd populated the audience, and my sister was off to one side having what looked like an intense discussion with a woman in late middle age, with an iron-gray bob and enormous silver hoop earrings. Probably another buyer, although I didn't know for sure. I didn't exist in this world; my orbit might cross into it every once in a while, but that didn't mean I knew who any of its players were.

So I stood off to one side and watched the crowd, who were so different from the people I bumped into at the Trader Joe's in Pasadena that they might as well have been from another planet. Vanessa had given me a tiny little black satin bag to go with the dress, and my phone was stowed inside the purse, so I couldn't tell what time it was. Pulling it out to take a look would seem rude, especially since I knew that, even though the reception felt as if it had already dragged on for hours, probably only about fifteen or twenty minutes had passed. There was no way I could call Silas to rescue me until at least eight-thirty, maybe later.

Then a chill moved down my spine, and a voice I'd never heard before, low and soft and yet somehow menacing, said, "Hello, Serena."

I turned to see who the speaker was and almost dropped the plate of food and flute of champagne I held.

Standing there before me, his gray eyes seeming to bore into my skull, was the vampire from my vision.

CHAPTER SEVEN

HOW DID I KNOW IT WAS HIM, EVEN THOUGH I'D NEVER seen his face?

No one else could have those eyes, like hard, glinting, polished silver. I felt the recognition of what he was somewhere deep within me, a wrongness that wasn't quite nausea, wasn't quite a shortness of breath or a fever, but some horrible mix of all three. The rich food I'd just eaten churned in my stomach.

I seemed to be alone in realizing that he was simply wrong, a creature that shouldn't be. All around us, people chatted and laughed and ate and drank, none of them paying the least attention to the tall man in the dark suit who had gone up to talk to one of the models.

Somehow I managed to push past my physical reaction to him to focus on the details of his appearance, the flaxen-pale hair pulled into a ponytail at the base of his neck, the aquiline nose, the dark brows, the broad shoulders beneath the black suit jacket he wore. Objectively speaking, he was quite striking, the sort of man who would make heads turn when he entered a room.

Only I knew he wasn't a man at all.

"How are you here?" I whispered fiercely. Perhaps it was the presence of the other people in the pavilion that gave me the courage to ask such a question. "You can't be here."

"Oh, I'm afraid I can," he replied, offering me a small, amused smile as he did so. His canines were slightly pointed, but not so much that they would invite comment. I'd met people who certainly weren't vampires who had the same sort of teeth. Still smiling, he reached in his pocket and pulled out a piece of cream-colored card stock. Turning it toward me, he added, "You see, I was invited."

I glared at the card, realizing as I scanned the words it contained that it was in fact an invitation to my sister's show. How he'd gotten it, I had no idea, but I supposed that didn't matter now. What mattered was that he stood in front of me, and I had no idea what to do next. Make a scene, call him out—not as a vampire, but possibly as someone who'd made an inappropriate pass at me? Anything that would get him thrown out of the pavilion.

No, that wouldn't work. For one thing, I knew I would never hear the end of it if I created that kind of a disturbance at my sister's reception. Maybe it was cowardly of me, but I knew how my family would react if I stepped one toe out of line.

But even if I could summon the courage to do such a thing, I guessed it would be in vain. This person—this thing—was a vampire, not an investor who'd gotten a little handsy. Silas had talked about how vampires could summon the darkness to help them in a confrontation. Did I really want to see what might happen if the one who confronted me now was faced with any sort of a challenge?

"Fine," I said, as calmly as I could. "What is it you want...Lucius?"

"Ah, so I see you've learned something of who I am."

"A little." A waiter went past us with a tray of champagne, and I exchanged my nearly empty flute for another. Then I summoned a mock-sweet smile and said, "Would you like one, Mr. Montfort?"

Of course I'd been hoping that he would recoil, would refuse the drink. After all, he was a vampire. Could he even consume anything except human blood?

To my disappointment, he replied, "Yes, thank you," and took the flute of champagne the waiter offered him as if it was the most natural thing in the world. After the man had gone, Lucius said, "I can drink champagne, Miss Quinn. And wine, and a number of other distracting beverages. Just as I can sit down to dinner and eat a perfectly normal meal. The only difference is that it does not provide me with the…necessary nutrition, if you will."

I added those tidbits to my admittedly scanty store of knowledge about vampires. Because I needed a little time to settle my thoughts, I sipped from the champagne I'd procured for myself, while at the same time depositing my plate of half-eaten food on the small table that stood behind me. During this operation, Lucius drank some of his own champagne, piercing silver eyes never leaving me for a second.

"So what do you want?" I asked.

His eyebrows went up, as if he was surprised—or possibly offended—by the question. "To talk," he said. "I thought that perhaps you would be more open to discussion in a neutral setting such as this one."

I highly doubted that, but I couldn't help being curious as to why he'd want to talk to me at all. As a human, wasn't I simply prey, something he couldn't possibly consider an equal? "It is neutral," I admitted. "Or rather, not the sort of place where you'd be noticed as easily. My sister's events do tend to attract an eclectic crowd."

For just a second he glanced away from me and at the crowd, all of whom were carrying on with their eating and drinking and talking, completely unaware that a dangerous, unnatural predator stood in their midst. "Are you saying that my appearance would otherwise attract attention?"

"Just making an observation, Mr. Montfort."

"Lucius, please." He smiled, but I realized then what was so off-putting about those smiles. It wasn't the sharp teeth, or the way the expression never reached those icy eyes of his. No, it was the way the muscles of his face moved, as if he had to force them to do as he wished because over the centuries they'd forgotten what a spontaneous muscle movement was supposed to look like. He went on, "You know that you are a young woman of unique gifts, Miss Quinn. I would like to see that those gifts are properly utilized."

"Oh, is that why you sent one of your lapdogs to assault me on the street?"

The smile faded. I wasn't sure which was worse—the smile, or the absence of one. Right then he looked as if he wanted to lunge for my throat, and only held back because of the crowd that surrounded us. "My apologies for the way the situation was handled. I didn't think my servant would become violent. But it turns out that you had your own protector, didn't you?"

"A Good Samaritan came to help me out, yes," I said cautiously. It was entirely possible that Lucius Montfort knew everything about Silas already. But just in case he didn't, I wanted to make sure I didn't provide any damning details.

"Oh, yes, Silas the defender." One corner of Lucius' mouth lifted, but the smirk didn't prevent him from drinking some more of his champagne. "I fear he hasn't quite told you the whole truth."

I wanted to argue with that remark, but I couldn't. Not really. I'd only be lying to myself if I didn't acknowledge how much Silas had kept to himself. Yes, he'd provided me with a good deal of information…but never quite enough, and nothing about himself. "And what is the 'whole truth'?"

"Much more than I could tell you this evening, that is for certain." He moved closer to me, and I had to steel myself to hold my ground, to not flinch away even though every muscle in my body was shrilling with a healthy burst of fight-or-flight chemicals. "But I thought I should warn you of the danger in listening to only one side. You rarely get the whole story that way."

"Maybe not," I allowed. "However, you're going to have to be a hell of a talker to persuade me that your side is the good side."

"Did I say that?" His shoulders lifted, and once again those steely eyes made a quick scan of the people closest by, as if to make sure that no one was listening to our conversation. "When you've lived as long as I have, Miss Quinn, you'll come to realize that nothing is black and white, only infinite gradations of gray."

I didn't miss the way he'd phrased that particular remark. And I really didn't like it. "Are you implying that I'll have your long life? I'll tell you now that I'm not interested."

His expression didn't change. "A slip of the tongue. My pardon. I was merely attempting to let you know that Silas is not quite the hero you think he is."

"Is that a fact."

My flat response didn't seem to faze the vampire one bit. "Oh, yes. I will not lie to you, Serena. Of course I have my own motives for reaching out to you. But Silas also has his. Perhaps you should ask him precisely why he came to your aid last week."

"Why, because seeing a woman getting attacked in the street wasn't reason enough?" Even as the words left my mouth, I knew how disingenuous they were. It was entirely possible that Silas actually would help any random stranger in that situation, but my case was different. He'd flat out told me that he'd come to my aid because of what I was, because my visions made me valuable.

"For some, it might be. In his case…." Lucius' words trailed off, but from the way one eyebrow arched slightly, I could tell that he didn't think much of Silas' motives.

Right then, I didn't know what the hell I should be thinking. I did know that Silas and I would have to have a good long talk in the very near future.

If I survived this encounter with Lucius Montfort, that is.

I lifted my champagne flute to my lips and took a sip, steeling myself for what I needed to do next. "Well, Mr. Montfort, I suppose I'll have to take that under advisement. However, I don't believe that you and I have much else to say to one another. No matter what Silas' motives might be, I'm really not interested in any proposals you might make."

And then I took a breath and began to step away, praying that the presence of all the other reception attendees around us would be enough to prevent Lucius from making a move. Those prayers weren't answered, however, because at once he reached out with a pale hand and wrapped his fingers around my forearm, stopping me from going any further. His flesh was ice-cold, his grip stronger than I could have imagined, given the overall slenderness of his frame.

"I don't believe we've finished our conversation," he murmured into my ear as he pulled me back toward him.

"Oh, I think you have."

Silas' voice. I turned as best I could in his direction, given Lucius Montfort's death grip on my arm, and saw Silas approaching from my other side, his face a mask of cold fury. He came up to the vampire and said, also in an undertone, "Don't make me do it. You know how much you dislike attracting attention."

Thin lips pulling back in a snarl, Lucius at once let go of my arm. His gaze fixed on Silas, he demanded, "You think to intimidate me?"

"If that's what's required, yes. But you should keep in mind that you have a great deal more to lose than I do, should you be exposed."

For the briefest second, the vampire glanced over at me. His eyes narrowed as he returned his attention to Silas. "Oh, I think you stand to lose a good deal as well."

The barest lift of Silas' shoulders. Voice steady, he said, "This is a public place. There could be... questions."

A silence fell. I didn't dare breathe. I could almost hear the thoughts ticking over in Lucius Montfort's head as he pondered whether continuing to pursue me was worth the risk of exposure. Yes, it seemed as if everyone in the crowd was absorbed in their own conversations, their own little worlds, but one whiff of trouble, and there would be a battalion of iPhones pointed in our direction, recording the whole thing.

If you could even capture a vampire's image on camera. I'd have to ask Silas about that. Assuming we all survived our current face-off.

Finally, Lucius let go of my arm. Slowly, though, as if to demonstrate that he was doing so of his own volition. "This is not the last of the matter, Silas."

He didn't blink, his eyes hard as he stared back at the vampire, face so still it might have been carved from stone. "No, I didn't assume it would be."

Turning toward me, Lucius nodded his head slightly. *"À bientôt, cherie."*

Then he was gone, moving toward the pavilion's exit. Everyone in his path automatically got out of the way, as though obeying some unspoken command.

Only then did my heart beat begin to slow down. Chills broke out all over me, as if my body had been too petrified until that moment to allow itself any physical reaction. More than ever, I wished I could run to Silas and have him put his arms around me, hold me close and tell me it would be all right.

Instead, I looked up at him. His jaw was set, his lips pressed together. Was that anger or fear I saw in his face…or perhaps a little of both?

A million questions raced around in my head, so I asked the first one that came to mind. "What was that he said at the end? I didn't quite catch it—I took Spanish in school."

Silas stared down at me, still unsmiling. "It means 'soon, my dear.'"

We slipped out after that. Or rather, Silas waited for me outside while I retrieved my personal belongings from the van that had ferried me and the other models over here to the warehouse for the show. Luckily, my sister was embroiled in a conversation with a stunning black woman whose braids fell to her waist and an older Latin-looking man, maybe more buyers. She didn't even notice as I located the van's driver and had him unlock the door so I could fetch my purse and the clothes I'd worn earlier in the day.

I thanked him, then shoved the bundle under one arm and went to meet Silas over at his truck. Although the day had been mellow enough, now that the sun was down, the air was cool and damp on my bare arms and legs, bringing with it the fog coming off the ocean. I shivered, although I wasn't quite sure whether my shivers were more due to that frightening encounter with Lucius Montfort than the actual air temperature. It didn't help that the parking lot wasn't nearly as well lighted as I would have liked. My imagination conjured legions of vampires lurking in the shadows, ready to pounce. I tried to tell myself that was silly, because Silas had made it sound as if Lucius only had a few true vampires in his cabal. But I didn't have any idea how many of his semivive slaves he had working for him. Right then, my scalp crawled and my skin prickled with goose-bumps at the thought that I might be surrounded by Montfort's half-alive minions, and I wouldn't even know it.

Silas already had the pickup running; a welcome wave of warm air from the heater greeted me as I opened the door and got inside. As soon as I had my seatbelt fastened, we were moving, headed over toward the 10 Freeway for the long drive home.

A minute went by, then another. I sneaked a peek at him from below my lashes, but it was difficult for me to see anything of his expression in the muted glow from the dashboard's instruments. Was he angry?

Maybe. His jaw did look way too tense. I had to hope his anger wasn't directed at me. Not that I was at all responsible for that lovely little encounter with Mr. Montfort. How in the world could I ever have guessed he would be able to wrangle an invitation to my sister's show?

If anyone should be angry, it was me. Shouldn't Silas have figured out that Lucius might have attempted just that sort of gambit?

At last I said, "Is it safe?"

His head swiveled toward me and then went back to facing forward, his gaze intent on the traffic around us. You'd think that at a little past nine o'clock, things would have eased up a bit, but the eastbound traffic on I-10 was still sluggish, barely hitting fifty.

Welcome to L.A.

"Is what safe?"

My fingers tightened on the bundle of clothes and purse I held on my lap. "Is it safe for me to go home?"

"Yes, it's safe. Lucius Montfort does not have an invitation to go to your home." I caught the glint of his eyes as he glanced at me once again, then returned his attention to the road. Voice flat, he added, "Or at least, I assume he doesn't."

"Of course not," I snapped. "You think I'm that stupid?"

Something about the hard line of his jaw softened slightly. "I don't think you're stupid at all. In fact, I think it was rather impressive, the way you were able to face him down."

"You do?"

"Yes. There are not many people who can match wits with a vampire. One of their powers is to confuse and befuddle their victims, making it that much more difficult for ordinary mortals to resist them. But clearly you had no problem with doing so."

No, I didn't. I could recall the encounter very clearly—too clearly, if you wanted to get right down to it. No vampire fog swirling around our exchange, that was for sure. I'd been scared, sure, but my mind had been my own. "I don't think so," I said. "I mean, I was terrified about what he might do, but I still felt like myself."

"I'm sorry you had to go through that. I should have been more careful."

"Careful? How?"

"I should have realized he might attempt that sort of gambit. I did stay close by, just because I couldn't get rid of the nagging sensation that something was wrong, but I should have stayed near you, with you."

So his anger was directed at himself. Since I'd survived the encounter with Lucius unscathed, I couldn't let myself be too upset with Silas. "It's all right. That is, if you'd really come along the whole time, I would've had to explain you to my sister. I couldn't have told her you were my bodyguard, so I'd have to lie and say you were my date or something. The second the reception was over, she would've been on the phone to my mother, telling her that I had a new boyfriend."

I'd purposely kept my tone wry, so he could tell I was trying to make a joke, but he didn't smile. "Perhaps that would be easier."

"What would be easier?"

"If you told your family that I was your boy-friend. At least that way they wouldn't question my being near you whenever you went out in public."

Silas as my boyfriend. My fake boyfriend. He'd made the suggestion as if inquiring whether I'd like to have Thai instead of Chinese for dinner. And even so, my heart made a weird little thump, as if it would be only too glad to have him as a faux boyfriend, even if the real thing was still completely out of reach.

I managed a laugh—an entirely unconvincing one, unfortunately. "I'm not sure that's such a good idea. You have no idea what you'd be letting yourself in for."

"Which is?"

"Well, for one thing, you'd have to give me some kind of last name. My mother definitely wouldn't go for that whole one-name rock-star thing."

"It's Drake."

Startled, I looked over at him. "Silas Drake?"

"Yes."

"So why didn't you tell me that from the beginning?"

"I didn't think it was necessary."

Oh, for God's sake…. I huffed out a breath, then decided it wasn't worth arguing about. "That's a start, but really, I'm not kidding when it comes to my mother. If she thinks someone is at all involved in my life, she turns into a complete bloodhound. You won't have any secrets left. Trust me."

I truly wasn't joking. Somehow she always managed to dig up all sorts of dirt on anyone I was foolish enough to mention to her. Travis, my last serious significant other, had passed muster, but that was because he was the son of one of my father's business associates. The Lindley family traveled in the same circle as ours, so there was no reason to have the CIA dig up anything it could on him. On paper, he was the ideal boyfriend.

So of course Travis Lindley, Mr. Perfect, was the one who dropped me like a hot potato after the accident. Oh, sure, he hung around while I was in intensive care, did the attentive boyfriend thing—my parents thought he was a real gem—but as soon as the visions started in, and there was talk of neurological damage and unending tests and therapy, he was out of there so fast, I was surprised he didn't leave skid marks in his wake. Last I heard, he was engaged to the daughter of a Hollywood producer. Her family didn't have the kind of money mine did, but Travis probably figured the trade-off was worth it, considering the sort of baggage I brought with me.

When Silas spoke next, his tone was thoughtful. "You don't talk about your father very much. He doesn't share the same worries as your mother?"

"Oh, well, Dad is…." I shrugged, since I didn't know how else to respond. "He always left that sort of thing to my mother. His work keeps him busy. That is, I think he was more involved with Jackson, but he let my mother take care of the girl stuff."

"'Work,'" Silas repeated. "Forgive me if this is a delicate question, but I was under the impression that your family's wealth was inherited."

"Oh, it is. When I say 'work,' I mean overseeing his investments, meeting with the people who manage his trust. And there's the foundation…." I trailed off then. It was difficult to explain, since I didn't understand all of it that much. I didn't want to. Yes, I knew that someday I'd have a great deal of wealth to manage, but since my father was only in his early sixties and more fit than a lot of men half his age, I'd been able to push that prospect off into a dim "maybe someday" zone where I didn't have to think about it any more than I absolutely had to.

I also didn't want to admit to Silas that my father had more or less written me off. It wasn't that he didn't love me or want me to be happy, but in his mind, the accident had left me permanently impaired, someone who'd never be able to fulfill her potential. Because of my family's financial situation, I'd never want for anything, and so he considered me a problem that had been handled as best it could, and which could be ignored from now on. Jackson was his shining star—he and his wife Bethany had given my father three gorgeous grandchildren, so not a lot was expected of me. Vanessa had her own success, and so her decision to stay single and not have kids wasn't that big a deal. But I? I was the one my father tried not to talk about.

"It's complicated," I said at last, a total cop-out. But I just didn't feel like getting into it then.

Or ever.

"I see."

Another silence. By that point we'd hit the interchange with the 110 Freeway downtown, and it, too, was still vaguely nightmarish to negotiate, although not as bad as it had been when we were heading in the opposite direction that morning. I stared out the window at the lights in the high-rises and wondered what method Lucius Montfort had used to return to his castle-like mansion perched on the edge of the arroyo. Did he have to drive like a normal human, or could he just turn into a bat and fly away? That mode of transportation would definitely save on gas and insurance.

"Sorry," I said at last. "Talking about my family is a lot like negotiating a minefield. I know you're just trying to help."

"I understand."

"What about yours?"

"What about my what?"

"Your family. Are you natives of Southern California?"

"We've lived in California a long time, but we're not natives."

It was a tiny morsel of information, but better than nothing. "Oh? Where did you come from before that?"

"Here and there."

Talk about your non-answers. Was this just more of his policy of doing his very best to tell me as little as possible, or maybe a little payback for my not wanting to vomit up every last detail about my own family?

I decided to take the high ground. For one thing, the day had been a long and exhausting one, and I really didn't feel like getting into an argument right then. "But you've been in L.A. for a while."

"Yes."

"Doing...whatever it is you do. Making the world safe for democracy."

To my surprise, he actually chuckled a little at that remark. "I suppose you could call it that. Keeping the world safe, at any rate...one bit at a time."

Did that make me one of those "bits"? How exactly I was supposed to keep the world safe, I had no idea, but maybe Silas had a better sense of the big picture than I did.

We were past downtown by then, the highway narrowing down to two lanes in either direction as it looped its way up to Pasadena's soft underbelly. I thought it was better to move on to a more neutral topic, or at least one that wasn't quite as fraught with stories he didn't want to tell. "How did you know to intervene with Mr. Montfort, anyway?"

"As I said, I kept close by...just not close enough. Some sixth sense told me as I dropped you off that I shouldn't return home, so I waited outside your sister's studio, then followed the van when it took you to the warehouse. After that, I stayed in the parking lot."

"You just sat in this truck all day?"

"Mostly. I did take a short break in the late afternoon to go get some food."

Talk about your stakeouts. His dedication impressed me. On the other hand, I felt mildly irritated that he'd managed to get a decent meal in there somewhere. I'd only been able to eat about half of what was on my plate before Lucius Montfort made his appearance, and in that moment, I realized how hungry I really was. Well, I had all that leftover pizza back at my condo. That would do nicely. For some reason, I was reluctant to mention to Silas how starved I was. He might feel compelled to take me somewhere for dinner, and I didn't want that. If we ever had dinner together, it should be because he wanted to, not because his misguided sense of chivalry was telling him that he needed to take care of me.

I had a feeling that day would be long in coming, if ever.

"So did you see him drive up? Do vampires drive?"

"They can. They don't need to. They can travel on the wind, coming and going unseen."

Lovely. No wonder it seemed as if Lucius Montfort had appeared out of nowhere. He literally had.

The creepy crawly feeling returned. "So he turns into a mist?"

"No. That's Hollywood theatrics. He just…disappears, and then reappears where he wishes. Of course, that ability is somewhat limited. He can't travel enormous distances. No more than fifty or sixty miles at best, based on our observations."

Well, I supposed that was better than being able to blip from one side of the world to the other, but still, fifty or sixty miles could easily get you from Pasadena to Santa Monica. Or vice versa. Or pretty much anywhere in the greater Los Angeles area.

"But he can't turn up on my doorstep."

"Oh, he can turn up on your doorstep," Silas replied, his voice grim. "The trick is not to invite him in."

CHAPTER EIGHT

AFTER THAT, THERE WASN'T MUCH LEFT TO DISCUSS. I SAT quietly as the familiar exits slipped past—Monterey Road, Fremont, Fair Oaks—and the freeway finally dead-ended into Arroyo Parkway. Soon we were turning onto Cordova, and then into the driveway for my condo complex.

Silas parked the truck in one of the visitor spots. "Wait for me to come around and open your door."

I knew he wasn't being chivalrous. He literally didn't want me stepping out of the truck until he was at my side. A chill moved down my spine, prickling the skin at the back of my neck. I hated feeling so vulnerable, but that meeting with Lucius had told me that I couldn't let my guard down for a second.

The door opened, and Silas waited as I climbed out, wobbling a little on those damn heels I was wearing. Good thing he was there to watch out for me, because I couldn't have outrun someone on crutches in those stupid shoes.

He offered me his arm, and I took it. Maybe that was a mistake. But I liked the feeling of his strong muscles under my fingers, liked knowing he would be there to catch me in case I stumbled. I could pretend he was there to support me for reasons that had nothing to do with the reality that I was his charge, his duty.

It was easier to make it up the stairs with him there to steady me. And then we were at the door to my condo, and I was fumbling to find my house keys in the bundle of clothes and purse I carried. Eventually I did dig them out, and inserted the key in the lock. As I turned it, I said, "Do you want to come in? You know…to make sure there aren't any vampires lurking."

"I told you…they can't come in without an invitation."

"Oh, right." I paused there awkwardly, wishing I knew what I should say next, the one thing that would persuade him to come inside so our evening wouldn't end here. He seemed very close, his body angled toward the hallway so he would be the first thing any would-be attacker might come up against.

He let go of my arm. "You're safe here. I promise."

I nodded. "I know. Um…thanks, Silas. Thanks for being there."

"It's what I'm supposed to do."

Disappointment coursed through me at those too-formal words, but I made myself nod. Maybe someday I'd stop being so gawky and clumsy around him. It was strange, because normally I really didn't act like some silly seventh-grader, all self-conscious and tongue-tied whenever her crush got near. I was a grown woman. What difference did it make how good-looking he was, how strong and thoughtful, when I clearly didn't matter to him except as a duty that must be carried out?

I said, "Well, good night, Silas. Have a safe drive home." *Wherever that is, exactly….*

"I will." He gave no sign of moving, however, and I realized he wouldn't leave until I was safely inside and had shut the door.

So I made myself cross the threshold and go into the foyer. As I was closing the door, however, my eyes met his. Just for a second…a second that felt as if it lasted forever.

He murmured, "You looked very beautiful tonight, Serena."

Then he turned and headed back to the stairwell, and I barely had the presence of mind to finish closing the front door so I could turn the deadbolt. I

activated the alarm, then leaned against the wall and
closed my eyes.

So he had noticed. Had noticed, and seen.

Damn.

I was basically a mess after that. Yes, any impartial
observer would have thought I was doing all the
things that someone who'd spent a long day out
of the house might do after she first got home—I
kicked off those horrible heels, got myself a couple
of slices of cold pizza, poured myself a very modest
half glass of wine. Just enough to take the edge off,
to help ease the ache in my neck and shoulders.

Through all of those commonplaces, however,
my mind kept replaying those words.

You looked very beautiful tonight, Serena.

What was I supposed to do with that remark?
My somewhat shaky composure around Silas Drake
had been predicated on the notion that he didn't see
me as a woman, only an asset which needed to be
protected. But then his compliment had come out of
nowhere. What had he intended by it?

Maybe nothing at all, I told myself as I put my
dirty plate and glass in the dishwasher. I glanced at
the clock on the stove. Ten forty-two. Was he home
yet, in that place he'd confessed was just outside
Little Tokyo? I didn't know downtown all that well.

His home could be an apartment, or a condo, or one of the area's converted loft spaces.

I wished I could see it. If I were ever able to see where Silas lived, I might get a better idea of who he really was.

My odds of that probably weren't all that good. He'd only just told me his last name.

Drake. It sounded very formal and English. Actually, his whole name did. Like something out of a Dickens novel. Master Silas Drake, Esquire.

I would have laughed at myself, but I didn't find anything all that humorous about the situation. Especially since mooning over Silas and attempting to determine his true intentions should really have taken a back seat to the scary reality that I'd been face to face with a vampire earlier that evening. And lived to tell the tale, but only because of Silas' intervention.

Just what had Lucius really wanted? To sway me to his side? I couldn't see that happening, not in a million years. One only had to look into those cold, cold eyes of his to know that he was evil. Whatever his agenda, his end game, I doubted it was anything for the good of mankind.

I also didn't know what would have happened if Silas hadn't been quite so prescient, if no one had intervened when Lucius Montfort took me by the arm and attempted to remove me from the reception.

For some reason, I had a very strong feeling that no one would have stopped him, that he would have used his vampiric powers of coercion or glamour or whatever it was to walk me right out of there with not a single person—not even my sister—noticing. And then I would have been gone, with no one to report what had actually happened.

A shiver passed over me. I didn't want to think about that. Instead, I repeated the mantra Silas seemed to believe in. It was the only thing that would allow me to go upstairs and get ready for bed, to close my eyes and believe no creature of the night would steal in to interrupt my sleep.

"I am safe here."

It seemed that I was safe, because I slept the night through without any disturbances. Actually, I over-slept; when I blearily opened my eyes, I saw that it was past nine-thirty. Most days I was up by nine at the latest, even though I didn't have a job to go to, no set schedule that would require me to wake up anything close to what was considered a socially acceptable time. But I tried to get up no later than that, partly because I didn't want to turn into one of those people who didn't get out of bed before noon and stayed up half the night because they had nothing better to do. I felt divorced enough from the real world as it was. Most of the time, I had to try to damn hard to make myself ignore what a lonely existence mine was.

I was waiting for my coffee to finish percolating when the vision swept over me.

A crowd of people, cheering. Red, white, and blue bunting hanging everywhere. A stage where a tall dark-haired man stood at a podium.

That was all. Only a flash, but it was enough to tell me that the man who'd stood at that podium was my brother Jackson.

And? I asked myself as I got out a coffee mug with shaking fingers. *That could have been just a memory, not a vision at all. He's in the Senate...I guarantee he's stood at a few podiums.*

Unfortunately, I knew it was a vision, even coming less than forty-eight hours since the last one I'd suffered. A memory wouldn't have had that particular hazy, luminous quality to it, as if I was viewing the scene through a camera lens draped with cheesecloth. I hadn't quite made out the sign affixed to the podium, but I knew the outline was wrong for the logo Jackson had used when he ran for his senate seat four years earlier.

Which meant I must have seen him as he would be in the near future. Making a bid for the White House.

It wasn't unexpected. In fact, it was the very opposite of unexpected. I poured some of the fresh-brewed coffee for myself and sat down at the little table for two by the window, looking outside but not really seeing much. As visions went, this one didn't have anything terribly startling or frightening in it, especially when compared to the vision I'd had of Lucius Montfort's house.

Why, then, did my hands shake so much?

I wrapped them around my coffee mug, hoping its warmth would help to steady my fingers. And maybe their chill would help to cool down the coffee so I could drink it that much more quickly. Because no matter how innocuous that image had seemed, something about it had chilled me to my very core.

Only because you hate the idea of him running, I told myself. *You hate it because of how it might disrupt your life. That's what's got you so scared. There isn't anything supernatural going on here, and you know it.*

That all sounded very sensible. Whether it was true or not remained to be seen.

I blew on the coffee and sipped at it cautiously. The caffeine began to run through my veins, and I could feel myself start to relax. Yes, I knew caffeine was supposed to be a stimulant, but right then it was having the opposite effect.

Midway through the cup, I felt recovered enough to slide a couple of pieces of sourdough bread into the toaster oven. I'd just closed the door to the oven when my cell phone rang.

I wished I could ignore it. My gaze slid over to the clock on the stove. Nine forty-seven. All right, not exactly o'dark thirty, but also not an hour when I really wanted someone calling me, either. Especially not after just experiencing a vision. A minor one, true, but even the short visions knocked me out of myself, made me off balance.

But if it was Silas, then I'd feel awful if I let the call roll over to voicemail.

So I dug the phone out of my purse, which still sat where I'd dropped it on the kitchen counter the night before, and checked the display.

My mother's number.

The temptation to drop the phone back into my purse was so overwhelming, I found myself reaching for the bag before I even realized what I was doing. Then I stopped and told myself to be a big girl and answer. Normally, my mother would never ignore the ten/ten rule—no calls after ten at night or before ten in the morning unless it's an emergency—and so I reasoned that she must have a very good reason for contacting me now.

I should have known better.

"Did you really walk right out of Vanessa's reception?"

"Hi, Mom," I said. "How are you?"

She ignored the comment, as I figured she would. "She said she turned around, and you'd just vanished."

I put the phone on speaker so I could retrieve my toast from the oven before it burned to a crisp. "I didn't vanish. I was tired and my feet were hurting, so I had a friend pick me up and bring me home."

Her tone sharpened. "A friend?"

Funny how Vanessa hadn't asked a single question about how I'd gotten to her studio in West Hollywood, even though she knew good and well that I tried to avoid driving whenever possible. I'd been ready with an explanation for Silas, even though I hadn't needed it at the time.

"Yes, a friend. His name is Sam. He had business to handle out in that area, so he said he'd give me a lift."

"I've never heard you mention him before. How do you know him?"

"He's a friend of Candace's. That's how we met. Anyway," I hurried on, hoping to head my mother off at the pass before she asked any more questions about "Sam" and how he was suddenly a part of my life, "when he texted me to say he was out in the parking lot waiting for me, Vanessa was in the middle of a discussion with two people who looked like investors. I didn't want to interrupt her."

"Yes, well, she was worried sick until her van driver let her know that he'd seen you drive off with a dark-haired man in a black pickup truck. I suppose that was this Sam person?"

Funny how she could make the mere mention of his name sound disdainful. Probably it was the part about the pickup truck that had set her off. People in her circle didn't drive pickup trucks. They had Mercedes and Land Rovers and BMWs and the occasional Audi or Maserati or restored classic car. Never a Rolls, though. They were considered far too ostentatious. "Yes, that was Sam. Anyway, I'm sorry if I worried Vanessa, but you know, I think she would have been even more ticked off if I'd interrupted her while she was talking business."

And how like her, I thought, *to go tattling to Mom instead of giving me crap about it to my face.* But that was Vanessa all over again. I thought that, deep down, she'd felt betrayed when I was born, had thought up until that point she'd get to be the precious only daughter. I was probably a nasty surprise. No matter how successful she was—and no matter how much of a screw-up I turned out to be—she couldn't get past the belief, however erroneous, that they'd had another child after her because she hadn't quite filled the bill.

"Well," my mother said. From the way she hesitated, I could tell she probably thought it was better that I had been discreet, even though she didn't want to admit such a thing. "You could have texted her at least."

"I know. I'm sorry. I was tired and just wanted to get home."

"Luckily, she did make some very good contacts last night, from the sound of it, so at least that's some good that came of the evening."

"I'm glad." And I was. Vanessa possessed the unique ability to irritate the living crap out of me, but I didn't begrudge her the success she enjoyed. She was very talented, and driven. Probably put in a harder day's work than my father ever had, although I knew I didn't dare point out such a thing to my mother. "And I'll make sure I get the dress and shoes I borrowed back to her as soon as I can."

My mother let out an annoyed little huff of a breath. "As if that matters. In fact, she said she had intended to give them as a gift, since they fit so well, but she never got the chance to let you know that."

Ah, my mother's innate gift for heaping coals of fire at exactly the right moment. I had been feeling guilty about the clothes, but it wasn't as if I'd had much of an opportunity to change back into my own things. No, I'd only wanted to get the hell out of there as quickly as possible.

Just as I really, really wanted to get off the phone right now. "Um...thanks for the call, but I was in the middle of getting breakfast together, and if I don't eat it soon, it's going to get cold. I'll call you back later."

I could almost see my mother stiffen, even though of course she was at the house in San Marino, some five miles from where I stood. "Don't worry about that. Your father and I are going up to Santa Barbara for a weekend at the ranch, and we're going to be busy."

The "ranch" was a cozy little hundred-acre spread about fifteen minutes outside Santa Barbara. My father bought it not too long after Vanessa was born and spent a year improving the house and its outbuildings. Some of the happiest times from my childhood had been spent there, mostly because I'd been able to ride and hike and run around without anyone paying too much attention to me. I hadn't been back for several years, though, because I liked suffering my visions in the privacy of my own home, and not someplace where my parents could witness the whole thing.

Now, though, instead of feeling wistful about not being able to get away, I could only be relieved that my parents would be safely out of town for the weekend. My mother would be otherwise occupied, instead of attempting to find out more about this "Sam" person I'd just concocted. And that would give me time to figure out how I really did want to handle the whole Silas situation. If he was going to be my constant companion whenever I left the house, I'd be forced to come up with something. Sooner or later, I'd have to go visit my parents. They expected me for dinner at least once a month…probably to make sure I was still alive. Phone calls weren't quite enough to keep my mother reassured.

And probably sooner rather than later I'd have to introduce Silas to Brian and Lewis. If I put that off for too long, Brian would definitely start to wonder why I was trying to keep my new "boyfriend" away from them. But sufficient to the day the evil thereof….

"Well, have a wonderful time in Santa Barbara," I told my mother. To my surprise, I actually meant it. Just because my own life had been thrown into utter chaos didn't mean other people shouldn't be able to get out and enjoy themselves.

"Do you have any plans this weekend?"

Of course I didn't. I never did. A huge outing for me was going to the movies…and sitting in the back row, so if I did zone out, there wouldn't be as many witnesses to the event. "Not really. I'm due to get a new editing project soon, so I'll probably start on that."

Was that a sigh I heard coming from my phone's speaker? "Serena, you really don't have to make such a martyr of yourself. If you'd only go back to that psychiatrist—"

Oh, yeah, and let myself get drugged out of my mind on a nice combination of antidepressants and anti-psychotics. No, thanks. I'd tried medication several years ago because I was desperate, but it hadn't done anything to stop my visions, only made me feel as if I was walking through a fog all the time. If I had to suffer their interference, then I damn well was going to feel like myself when I was doing it.

"Um, my food is getting really cold," I broke in. "Enjoy Santa Barbara, and tell Dad I send my love."

Then I pushed down on the screen to end the call. For a few seconds, I stood there, tense, wondering if my mother was going to call back. But the phone remained silent.

I didn't let out a sigh of relief. Instead, I picked up my now-cold toast and tried to spread some butter on it. The resulting mess didn't look very appetizing, but I ate it anyway. What else was I supposed to do?

The promised manuscript I was supposed to edit didn't make an appearance, however. After noon had come and gone, I emailed the client. He got back to me right away, full of apologies—but also delivering the bad news that the book wasn't ready, that he was way behind, and that it would be at least a week before he thought he'd be able to send it to me, since he had to squeeze writing in around his day job.

I told him it was no problem, and to let me know the following week if there were going to be any more delays. And then I sat there, staring down at my laptop, and wondering what the hell I was supposed to do with myself now that I had this huge hole in my schedule.

The movies? Maybe, but that would require calling Silas to drive me. Then he'd probably want to sit next to me, just to be safe. While part of me welcomed that notion, I knew it was also fraught with problems. Probably going to see a movie wasn't the best idea. The weather was nice. I could go out on my balcony, take a book, put my feet up and try to unwind.

Although it was tough trying to relax when you knew that there was a nest of vampires only a few miles away from where you lived.

On an impulse, I went to the Google home page on my laptop and typed in "Lucius Montfort." I really wasn't expecting anything—after all, hadn't Silas said that all vampires like to keep a low profile, that Lucius had gone to a good deal of trouble to make sure he remained anonymous?

But there it was, on an online fashion site whose name I didn't recognize. No big surprise there; I wasn't the one who followed fashion. That was my sister's gig.

Vanessa Quinn expands her "Serene" line into new markets, thanks to backing from the Montfort Group.

Yes, she'd named the clothing line after me. In a sort of backhanded way, but still. She argued that it was a great name and one that was easy to remember, but I'd always disliked it. However, I hadn't bothered to protest; I knew I would lose that battle.

As for this "Montfort Group"…my body went tense as I tried to determine what the ever-loving hell that was all about.

I supposed it could be some kind of a hideous coincidence, but "Montfort" really wasn't too common a name. Besides, I did see Lucius' full name mentioned in the text of the article, which went on to explain how Vanessa had just gotten financial backing to move from designing only clothes to shoes and accessories as well, which had always been a dream of hers. She wasn't haute couture; her fashions went into high-end boutiques here in Los Angeles, and also in New York and Chicago and Palm Beach. So expanding into the sorts of areas that might get her products sold in more mass-market stores would only help to make her more of a household name, like Betsey Johnson or Vera Wang.

And all because the Montfort Group had been "impressed" with her fall collection, and stepped in to provide the necessary financial support for such a move. Yes, she could have gone to my father for money, but Vanessa was stubbornly proud about such things. She didn't want to be seen as being successful because of her family's wealth. After my parents had paid for her college education, as far as I knew, she hadn't accepted another dime from them.

Which I supposed put her on higher moral ground than me, although she didn't have the deficit of having to come back from traumatic brain injury.

But because of her independent streak, she was always looking for new financing. Now it seemed as if she'd found it. I had to wonder how Lucius had managed his end run. As far as I recalled, he'd walked into the reception midway through the event, so it wasn't as if he'd been schmoozing her the whole night. The only thing I could think of was that he'd come back after Silas and I left.

For what purpose, though? What did he hope to accomplish by insinuating himself with a member of my family? Maybe he thought I'd be more malleable if the success of my sister's business partially rested on his shoulders. That was the sort of oily trick I could imagine him pulling. The problem was, I really didn't know what to do about it.

Well, except one thing. I picked up the phone and called Silas.

CHAPTER NINE

HE SAID HE'D BE OVER RIGHT AWAY, AND I HAD TO MAKE the embarrassing confession that I had only just gotten up and hadn't showered yet or anything. That revelation made him back off somewhat, although he still said he would come over at ten, which didn't leave me a heck of a lot of time. Luckily, the hairstylist's work from the fashion show the night before had survived mostly intact, so all I needed to do was take a quick shower and get dressed, rather than start from the ground up by washing my hair.

When Silas arrived, he looked grim-faced, which I could completely understand. As I was shower-ing, I kept trying to visualize how exactly Lucius had approached my sister. Had he been serious? Focused? Flirtatious? My sister was single, but she was no nun. Although she very rarely introduced any of them to the family, I knew she had a series of men come in and out of her life, getting companionship from them when she needed it, then kicking them to the curb when she needed to buckle down and focus on her next collection. Frankly, I couldn't quite understand her approach to relationships, but it seemed to work for her. In a way, I envied Vanessa's attitude, the way she could keep herself from getting too attached to anyone. I was just the opposite; when I fell, I fell hard. Which had its own drawbacks.

So I could see how Lucius might have turned on the charm when he went to talk to her. The very idea of his existence horrified me, but Vanessa would have no means of knowing he was no ordinary man. Objectively, I had to admit that he was very good-looking, in an unorthodox way. That quality would have worked for him rather than against him, since Vanessa's taste tended toward the unusual, to men with shaved heads or who had interesting tattoos or who were exotic mixes like Irish and Maori, or whatever. Maybe her choice in companions was her way of rebelling against our decidedly white-bread upbringing. If she'd been serious about any of these men, it was possible that our parents might have had more to say on the subject, but because these companions were in and out of her life so quickly, my mother and father kept quiet on the subject. Bringing attention to it would have caused more harm than good, especially when it came to saving face amongst their circle of friends.

I had to admit that I had a hard time imagining Lucius being flirtatious, but just because I hadn't personally witnessed such a thing didn't mean it couldn't happen. Trying to visualize such out-of-character behavior made me wonder about vampires and relationships, or actually, just sex. Were they even capable of performing that physical act? Movies and TV and books didn't help much on the subject, since vampires had been portrayed as everything from the body-morphing bloodthirsty monsters of *From Dusk Till Dawn* to the sparkly obsessed boyfriend from *Twilight*. Which was the truth? None of it? All of it? Somewhere in the middle?

Asking Silas was probably the best thing to do to satisfy my curiosity, although the mere thought of bringing up the topic of sex with him was enough to make the blood rush to my cheeks. My feelings toward my protector were complicated enough without introducing the painfully awkward subject of vampire sex.

I'd just finished putting my breakfast plate in the dishwasher and closing it up when the doorbell rang. A quick glance around told me that I'd left everything in reasonably tidy shape, so I hurried to the door to let Silas in…after I looked through the peephole and determined it truly was him waiting outside.

This morning he was back in his usual dark T-shirt—this one in a deep wine color—and jeans and boots. I had to wonder what he did in the summer when it got really hot. Somehow I couldn't imagine him wandering around in shorts and flip-flops. But that thought only led me to ponder how long all this would actually go on. Would he be forced to babysit me forever? After all, vampires lived a lot longer than we mere mortals....

Okay, I really didn't want to think about that, either.

As soon as I shut the door, Silas said, "Show me this article you found."

Lovely. No "good morning," or "how are you?" Maybe he was regretting that moment of weakness the night before when he'd told me I looked beautiful. But if that was the way he wanted to play it, fine.

"Here," I said crisply, leading him over to the dining room table where I'd left my laptop. I opened the lid and typed in my password, then maximized the window that contained the article I'd found.

Silas leaned down so he could see the screen more clearly. As he read, his brow furrowed with concentration. Or maybe that was worry, or even anger. When he was done, he glanced over at me. "Have you talked to your sister about this?"

"Of course I haven't," I snapped. "She doesn't discuss her business with me, and I don't ask her about it."

"But she had you model in her show last night."

"Yes, because she was desperate and knew I could do the bare minimum for her. That's all. But she sure as hell wouldn't call me and tell me all about her new investor. That's not how she operates."

"I see." He'd straightened up as soon as he was finished looking at the article, and right then he looked very tall and somehow foreboding as he stood there, a frown still pulling at his dark brows. No wonder he had that crease in between them. "So it would be out of place for you to call."

"Very." I reached past him and shut the laptop. "Do you want some water or something?"

"If you think it will help."

I wanted to laugh. "Right now I'm not sure anything is going to help. But I'm thirsty."

"Then I would like some water, too."

That reply made me want to shake my head, but instead I went into the kitchen and fetched a couple of glasses, then dispensed some water from the refrigerator door. As I handed one of the glasses to Silas, I said, "So…what's the point of all this? Blackmail?"

"'Blackmail' is a crude word for it. Rather, I think Lucius wants to have influence on a member of your family, just in case."

"In case of what? I'm not sure why he even thinks my visions are so important. Half the time, I don't even know what's going on in them, and when I do, it's rarely helpful. Sure, I've had a couple of instances where they did do some good, like locating that kidnapped girl from Altadena or getting the police to that house over in Rosemead before that woman's boyfriend could beat her to death, but...." I stopped myself there and took a drink of my water. It flowed down my throat, cool, somehow reassuring. "The thing is, I haven't had a single vision that would help Lucius with his plans for world domination. Or whatever else it is he wants."

For a moment, Silas didn't reply. He drank some of his water as well, then said, "Let's go sit down in the living room so we can talk more comfortably."

Since I was currently leaning up against the kitchen counter and could feel the edge of the granite surface cutting into my back, I wasn't inclined to argue. "Sure."

We went into the living room. This time, I sat down on the couch, just to see what he would do, whether he would take a seat next to me. I should have known better. After a very short hesitation, he headed to the armchair and sat there, his expression inscrutable.

Great. I'd say that was a pretty clear signal. I was beginning to regret the time I'd spent fussing my hair back into place, applying my makeup. Oh, well.

After an awkward pause, Silas said, "It may not be the visions you've already had. It could very well be the ones that Lucius believes you *will* have."

"That's kind of crazy, don't you think?"

"Not necessarily. Vampires are masters of the long game. They can afford to be."

I hadn't looked at it that way, but Silas had a point. "So...what should I do?"

He set his glass of water down on a coaster on the coffee table, then folded his hands over one knee. His skin was tanned from the sun, except for that pale scar on his right hand; no sign that he'd ever worn any rings, no paler band around one finger. It was stupid of me to feel relieved by that minor detail, but there it was. "Since you don't feel comfortable talking to your sister...."

"No, I really don't." Such feelings might be cowardice, but I wasn't going to lie to him. Besides, what could I possibly say? *Gee, Vanessa, I think you might want to reconsider your new investment partner, since he's a vampire and all.*

I could just see my sister's face. She'd think I'd finally lost it. And then she'd be on the phone to my parents, and off I'd go to some "facility" that had a fancy name and even fancier doctors, and I'd be pumped full of Thorazine and no good to anyone at all.

Except Lucius Montfort. I could see how such a scenario would be enormously helpful to him. It wouldn't be difficult for him to wrangle an invitation inside, and then I'd be at his mercy.

A shudder wracked me, and I quickly lifted my glass to my lips in an attempt to cover up my trembling.

"What is it?" Silas asked.

"Nothing," I replied quickly. "Just imagining worst-case scenarios."

"Good."

"'Good'?" I repeated, shooting him an incredulous look.

"Yes, it's good for you to do such things. That means you're paying attention to contingencies, to everything that might go wrong. Practice in these matters makes you less likely to be a target when the time does come."

He appeared completely serious. Incongruously, I noted how the light coming through the living room window caught glints of dark russet and deep umber in his hair, which normally looked almost black to me. Then I realized I was staring. There didn't seem to be a way to look away without being obvious, so

I made myself utter a half-hearted laugh instead. "I guess that's one way of looking at it."

"Have you had any more?"

"What, visions?"

"Yes."

I hesitated. The vision I'd experienced that morning had been so brief, so inconclusive, that it hardly bore mentioning. On the other hand, I certainly didn't want to withhold information. So I shrugged and said, "Maybe. That is, it *felt* like a vision, but—"

"But?"

"It didn't have a lot of detail. I saw my brother on a stage, with a podium in front of him. People were cheering. But that doesn't mean much. He's been on the campaign trail for the past ten years practically, if you count the mayor's race here in Southern California before he ran for Senator."

Silas seemed to think that it meant something. The frown returned, and he tapped his fingers on his jeans-clad knee. "But you said it felt like a vision. Not a memory."

"I don't think it was a memory. But it was so short, I can't say for sure."

"Is he campaigning now?"

"No. He still has almost two years left in his Senate term, but…." I set down my glass of water, then crossed my arms. "If you know so much about me, about my family, then you probably also know that he's planning to run for President."

Not a single shift in his expression. Silas sat there, mouth still grim, but he didn't blink or react in any other way that I was able to notice. After a brief hesitation, he said, "I had heard the rumors, but nothing concrete. He hasn't announced it formally, has he?"

"No," I replied. "I think it's coming soon, but I don't know exactly when. Sometime this spring, I would guess. That would give Jackson nine months to ramp up to the New Hampshire primary, right?"

"Something like that."

From the taut look on my protector's face, I could tell he wasn't too thrilled by that piece of information. What, had he been hoping that Jackson would decide against a presidential run at the last minute? If that was the case, he didn't know my brother, or his record, very well.

"But as a senator, he has Secret Service protection."

"Well, Jackson does…because of being on the Intelligence Committee or something. He wouldn't really give the family many details as to why he had a Secret Service detail while others didn't." I was about to ask Silas why he was concerned about such a thing, but then it sank in. With government agents watching Jackson all the time, it would be a great deal harder for Lucius or any of his minions to get close enough to do any kind of damage. Congress was in session, and so Jackson and his family were at their house in Alexandria, Virginia. They wouldn't be back in California until the summer, except for—possibly—a quick trip here for spring break. That hadn't been decided yet, or rather, I guessed that he'd prefer to stay in D.C. and strategize rather than spend the Easter holiday hanging out by the pool at his Claremont home.

And since Silas had also told me vampires couldn't travel distances like that except via the same methods we mere mortals could, by plane or train or car, I thought it rather likely that Lucius wouldn't attempt anything with Jackson in the near future. If only I could come up with a convincing argument for why my brother and his family should stay in Alexandria for Easter, preferably an argument that didn't involve bringing vampires into the equation.

"Do you really think Lucius Montfort is going to use Jackson to get at me? Or," I continued, horror beginning to dawn, "use me to get at Jackson?"

"I don't know." Silas shifted in his chair so he could look past me and out the window. What he expected to see there, I wasn't sure. The day was sunny and bright, not a cloud in the sky, exactly the kind of day where you shouldn't have to be worrying about vampires. "Frankly—and I'm not saying this to frighten you, only to prepare you—it could go either way. There's so much we don't know about your visions, about what they choose to show you and why."

"Well, that makes two of us," I said with some bitterness. Restless, I got up from my seat and went to the window. Palm trees waved in the breeze, and I watched as two of the neighbors from my building, an older couple I knew by sight but not by name, walked along the path that wound through the condo complex's grounds. In that moment, I was suddenly, violently, jealous of them, jealous that they'd found someone to spend their lives with, jealous that they could walk outdoors and enjoy the day without having to worry about visions or vampires...or brothers who wanted to be President.

I didn't even realize that Silas had stood as well until he was there next to me, looking down just as the couple I'd so envied disappeared around a curve, presumably going into the complex's recreation room. "It's difficult, I know," he said quietly. "To hold all this knowledge within you, to see aspects of the world that most people will never know even exist."

From the way he spoke, I got the feeling he wasn't just talking about me. He'd also been carrying the burden of secret knowledge...and for much longer than I ever had. "I suppose I'll get used to it."

"Don't."

I looked up at him in surprise. "What?"

"Don't get used to it. Don't get blasé. That's when people inevitably make mistakes. You must always stay on your guard."

That sounded like a hell of a way to live. I crossed my arms and said, "For how long? Forever?"

His gaze moved away from mine. "I can't answer that."

"Well, you must have some kind of an idea. You say the people you work for have been watching the vampires for years. Is there an end game?"

"'End game'?"

From the way he still wouldn't quite look at me, I could tell that he was being deliberately disingenuous. "Yes, end game. You said you don't hunt the vampires deliberately, so it doesn't sound as if your plan is to wipe them off the face of the earth."

"No, that's not our plan." This time he did focus on my face, his dark eyes earnest. It was harder than I'd thought, to stand there so close to him, to look into his eyes and not try to break the contact. Something about the connection felt almost as intimate as a kiss, although of course we hadn't done anything remotely like that, hadn't even held hands. But in that moment, I remembered how strong his arm had felt beneath mine when he steadied me as I stumbled up the stairs the night before. My pulse speeded up slightly, even as he continued, "Annihilation destroys the natural balance that exists in this world. We still don't know for sure why the vampires came to be, but they are a part of existence now. What we do is attempt to make sure they never gain an unfair advantage, never do anything that would shift the balance of power. Do you understand?"

On the surface, it sounded like a noble enough sentiment. Predators had their place in the world. But these predators preyed on human beings.

And? I asked myself then. *Human beings prey on human beings, too.*

That seemed like an overly cynical thought, although I couldn't really come up with an internal argument to counter it. "I suppose I'll try to understand," I told Silas. "Whether I'll actually manage it is an entirely different thing. It's hard for me to be neutral and impartial because we're talking about my family here."

"I know," he replied, his tone gentler than I'd yet heard it. "And I know this must seem grossly unfair to you—that you have to carry this burden in addition to the ones that have already been placed on you."

It did feel unfair. But then, as one of my physical therapists had told me following the accident, "fair" was for little kids. The world was what it was, and we needed to suck it up and face it head on, no matter what happened.

I shrugged. "It is what it is, I guess. Still, I could use some sage advice right about now."

"I think you're handling the whole situation as well as anyone could be expected to. And you're doing the right things—you're letting me protect you, and you're keeping yourself hidden away as best you can."

"I should have said no to my sister," I protested, thinking again of the way Lucius Montfort had approached me so casually, as if there was nothing so terribly strange about him waltzing into Vanessa's reception.

"And if you had, that would have caused trouble in your family. You had no way of knowing Lucius would exploit that small weakness. If anyone should be blaming themselves, it should be me. I also didn't think he would be so bold. I thought you would be safe at an event with so many people attending. Now we both know better." His jaw tightened as he added, "It won't happen again."

No, I supposed it wouldn't. Good thing I was already such a recluse; hiding from vampires would fit neatly into my lifestyle. If only my sister hadn't given Lucius such an opening. Even though it would be awkward in the extreme, I felt as if I had to ask. "Silas, this is going to sound like a very strange question, but…."

"Ask it. I'll do my best to answer."

A flush heated my cheeks, but I managed to keep my tone even as I said, "Do vampires have sex?"

His eyebrows lifted, but at least he wasn't blushing furiously the way I knew I was. "It is not their primal drive, but yes, they can engage in physical intimacy, if it suits their purpose." A narrowing of the eyes, so much that his lashes nearly obscured his gaze, as he went on, "You think your sister and Lucius…?" The words trailed off there, as though at last he was too embarrassed to say more.

"It would make sense," I said. "My sister loves her man-candy."

"Man-candy?"

"Good-looking guys. She never gets too serious about any of them, but I know she's also not averse to mixing business with pleasure. Some of her former…." I stopped, floundering for the right word to use for the men who went in and out of my sister's life. If I'd been talking to Candace or even Brian, I probably would have just said "lays" and gotten on with it, but I couldn't see myself being quite that crass with Silas. "Some of her former lovers have also been investors, or models, or… well, I guess any interesting man who crosses her path. So I could see that happening with Lucius… if such a thing was even a possibility. That's why I asked."

"As I said, it's not a primary drive, because of course vampires don't reproduce the way humans do." He paused, then seemed to correct himself, saying, "The way we do, that is. But when confronted with a situation where it might give him more bargaining power, I can see Lucius doing such a thing."

Great. I'd asked because I needed to know, but the thought of my sister being in bed with Lucius Montfort in more than purely a business sense made my stomach churn. I swallowed, willing the nausea away. Feeling sick wasn't going to help the situation at all. "Do you think talking to her will help? I mean, has he cast some kind of a spell over her or something?"

Silas gave a grim chuckle. "He's a vampire, not a warlock. His kind do not cast spells. They possess certain powers, true, but it's not as if he's turned your sister into a semivive."

"Why hasn't he? I mean," I hastened to add, since I knew the question sounded terrible, "it seems as if that's what vampires do when they need willing slaves."

"Because the semivives lose their sense of self. They exist only to follow the will of their master. Subjecting your sister to Lucius' power would make her unable to perform her design work, and then it would clearly be obvious to everyone involved that she was not herself."

"And yet Lucius wants to control my brother Jackson? How is that any different?"

"Because being a politician is not the same as being an artist. Lucius possesses the intelligence and the cunning to convincingly manipulate your brother from behind the scenes, but he is not creative, at least not in the way that your sister is. There's no way he could take over her mind and still have her create at the level the world expects from her."

Was that supposed to be reassuring? All right, yes, I was glad to hear my sister was safe from being turned into Lucius' mindless minion, but at the same time, I couldn't help feeling somewhat offended that Silas considered my brother much easier prey. Jackson was absolutely brilliant, and charismatic and intuitive to boot. All those qualities couldn't be terribly easy to fake, could they?

But then I thought of how Silas didn't even know exactly how old Lucius was. Three centuries at least, maybe more. That was a hell of a lot of time to learn how to play politics, or anything else, for that matter. Maybe Silas had a point.

"Anyway," he went on, "we still don't know for sure that Jackson is the target. Lucius has made it clear that he wants you, and Jackson may only be leverage."

"So my sister isn't enough?"

"'Enough' is not a concept that Lucius Montfort understands very well."

I could well believe that. "Should I talk to her?"

"Do you think it will help?"

"I don't know," I answered honestly. "But I guess I'd better try."

CHAPTER TEN

SILAS LEFT NOT TOO LONG AFTERWARD, SAYING THAT HE
thought it better if I had some privacy when I talked to
my sister. At the same time, though, he reminded me
to call if I should have another vision, or if I needed
him for anything else.

As I said goodbye and watched him walk down
toward the stairs that led to ground level, I thought
I definitely did need him for a lot of other things.
Number one, to pull me close and hold me and let me
know that I'd somehow get through all of this.

Since I didn't see that happening anytime soon, I
shut the door and went back to the kitchen, where my
cell phone still sat on the little table by the window. I
picked up the phone and held it in my hand for a long
moment, staring down at it, wondering what in the
world I could say to my sister.

Not the truth, that was for sure.

Well, not all of it, anyway. Maybe a distorted version of it. I'd been so focused on Lucius during our conversation that I hadn't been paying much attention to what was going on with the rest of the people at the reception, my sister included. It was possible that she'd seen me talking with him, however. So what if I told her he'd picked up on me first, then moved on when I made it clear I wasn't interested?

I hated to play those kinds of mind games, but that sort of gambit might just work. All three of us Quinn offspring were good-looking people, but my parents had always thought of me as the beauty of the family—probably because I didn't have any other outstanding skills or talents to distinguish me. And while Vanessa had always shrugged off that sort of thing, I could tell it bothered her. Somewhere deep down, it bothered her that she wasn't the "pretty one," even though she was an enormously talented designer.

So if I made it sound as though Lucius had been more interested in me, then moved on to her after I gave him the cold shoulder, there was a possibility, however slight, that she'd be offended by her second-place status and would kick him to the curb. Of course, if I'd misread the situation, and it turned out that nothing physical had happened between her and Lucius, I'd sound like a complete idiot. Well, I'd gotten sort of used to my family thinking I had more than a few screws loose, so it wasn't as if I had much to lose.

And also, I knew that my plan was a long shot, but it was all I had right then. After all, I couldn't come right out and say Vanessa's new business partner was a centuries-old creature of the night.

I hefted the phone in my hand, then went to the living room and sat down in the armchair. A delaying tactic, but I hoped being in my favorite spot in the house would give me some much-needed courage. And it was probably just my mind playing tricks on me, but I fancied I could still feel some residual warmth in the seat cushion, left behind from when Silas had been sitting there.

Because I knew I'd lose my nerve if I didn't go ahead and get it over with, I went to the contacts screen on my iPhone and touched the entry for my sister. Her phone began to ring, and I tensed, even as I hoped, as was often the case, that she'd be busy elsewhere and the call would just go to voicemail.

But of course I couldn't be that lucky. She picked up almost immediately, saying, "What is it, Serena?"

Clearly, she was still annoyed by the way I'd slipped out of the reception the night before. While I could see why she'd be irritated, I knew this whole conversation would be that much harder, just because she was already predisposed to be ticked off at me.

I cleared my throat. "Look, I'm sorry I bailed, but it seemed like you were busy, so I didn't want to bother you. I'll try to get the dress back to you somehow—"

"I don't care about the dress. It was one that just went into production. I have hundreds more."

Well, that figured. I should have known she wouldn't waste one of her precious couture gowns on me, but instead got me something that could have been bought in a local boutique for a couple hundred bucks. Bickering about it would only be counterproductive, however, and so I told myself to push the slight aside. I had much bigger things to worry about. "Okay, then," I said. "Anyway, like I was saying, it seemed as if you were otherwise occupied. And my friend showed up earlier than I'd planned, so I didn't have a lot of choice. I didn't want to make him stand around and wait when he'd done me a favor by coming all the way out to Santa Monica to get me."

"Your friend," Vanessa said then, her tone flat. "This Sam person."

News sure got around quickly. But then I supposed that my mother had called Vanessa to give her more details. Yes, my parents were supposed to be on their way to Santa Barbara, but my mother would always find the time to pass on some intel. "Yes, Sam,"

I replied, trying not to sound impatient. "Anyway, I heard the good news about your new investor...."

My sister didn't even bother to ask where I'd picked up that particular piece of information. She probably figured that our mother had passed it along, and I wasn't going to disabuse Vanessa of that notion. "What about him?"

I hesitated. "Lucius Montfort, right? The man with the light-colored hair in a ponytail?"

"Yes," she replied, a cautious note entering her voice. I could tell she wasn't happy I'd mentioned him.

"Had you been courting him previously?"

"Excuse me?"

"You know what I mean. You're always looking for more backing. So I was just wondering whether he'd crossed your radar before, or whether that was the first time you'd heard of him."

A pause. Then Vanessa said, "It was the first time I'd heard of him...or seen him. I would have remembered running into him before that."

Of course she would. As I'd told Silas, my sister was a connoisseur of man-candy. But my heart sank. Because if she was speaking of Lucius in such an approving way, that meant there was probably a good chance the two of them really had already been intimate. No doubt the vampire would consider that to be a nice little bonus fuck-you. The mere thought made the bile rose in my throat, and I had to choke it back, try to take in a breath so I wouldn't be sick right there.

Since I didn't reply right away, she inquired, tone even sharper than before, "Why do you ask?"

Oh, boy. I'd embarked on this crazy plan, so there wasn't much I could do except continue with it. "Nothing. It's just—well, he approached me earlier, paid me all sorts of compliments, asked why he hadn't seen me at one of these functions before. I told him I was your sister, not really a model at all, and that was why. He kept pressing me for more information, and it was kind of creepy. I sort of had to tell him point-blank that I wasn't interested before he finally took the hint and left me alone."

An even longer silence this time. I could practically feel pulses of rage coming through the phone, and I held my breath. All I could do was wait and see who she was angrier with—Lucius Montfort, or me.

At last she said, "I don't think he's creepy. He seems like a perfect gentleman...one with very deep pockets. So I think you need to stay out of it, Serena."

Great. She might as well have told me point-blank that she'd slept with him. If this had been a normal case of her just being with a guy I didn't much like, I would have let it go. Vanessa never hung with any man long enough for any real damage to be done. In this case, though, I couldn't be quite that blasé. "I wasn't aware I was in it," I retorted. "I just thought you should know that he seemed like kind of a player."

My response actually made her laugh out loud. "Well, of course he is. A guy with those looks and that kind of money? I wouldn't expect anything else. But right now it seems like we both have something the other person needs, which means that once again I'm going to tell you to stay the hell out of it."

I'd definitely hit a nerve, because normally Vanessa wasn't anything close to that rude. Brisk and businesslike, which might be construed as brusque by someone who was overly sensitive about that kind of thing, but she was my sister. I was used to the way she dealt with the world. So I thought she wasn't too thrilled about the story of Lucius Montfort hitting on me first, but she also wasn't going to do anything about it. I doubted there was anything I could say that would make her back off from her arrangement with him.

Except that whole bit about him being a vampire, but again, I wasn't quite ready for an express ticket on the Thorazine train. I'd have to try to figure out some other way to disentangle her from his clutches. What that might be, I really had no idea. Possibly Silas could help me out there, but I wasn't too sanguine about those prospects. Direct intervention wouldn't work, and he didn't know my sister at all. If I couldn't win this particular round of psychological warfare, how could I expect him to do any better?

"Okay, fine," I said, hoping I sounded appropriately hurt. "I just thought you should know what kind of person he is. Might be, I mean."

"I'm a big girl," Vanessa replied. "I can handle it. And the last thing I need is my little sister interfering in matters she knows nothing about. So I think we're done here. I need to go—I have a meeting at one."

She hung up then, leaving me to stare down at the phone in my hand and mutter a curse under my breath. What I was supposed to do next, I had no idea.

The one thing I resolved firmly *not* to do was phone Silas. Even though he'd told me to call whenever something came up, I really didn't feel like talking to him just so I could let him know that yes, my sister apparently was boinking an undead creature of the night. And taking his money as well. For investments in her business, of course, but even so, the whole thing made me feel downright squicky. The only comfort I could take from the whole situation was that Lucius probably wouldn't do anything to hurt my sister. Killing her or turning her into a semivive would only ensure that I'd be his enemy forever.

Right now she was just…leverage. An insurance policy that would probably never be cashed in.

Also, while Silas wanted to offer whatever protection he could, I knew I needed to sort out exactly how I felt about him. It wasn't like me to get all moony and swoony about a guy, like some thirteen-year-old sending texts about her latest crush to her BFF. On the other hand, I couldn't deny my physical reactions to him. Something about the guy definitely made my heart go pitter-pat.

It's just that tall, dark, and mysterious thing, I told myself as I went into the kitchen to pour myself an iced tea. *Sure, you're grateful for the help he's giving you, but if he looked like Truman Capote, I doubt you'd be quite so interested.*

True enough. But also…even on our short acquaintance, Silas had proven to me that he would be there when I needed him. I couldn't say as much for the other men in my life. My father was like an absentee landlord; he might check in every once in a while to make sure the ceiling hadn't caved in or the toilets hadn't backed up, but that was about all I could expect from him. Certainly not a listening ear or a shoulder to cry on. Ditto for my brother Jackson. He definitely had far more important things to worry about than his little sister's neuroses.

And in the wasteland that was my love life, there sure wasn't anyone else around.

So…handsome and dependable and understanding. No wonder I was having such a hard time keeping my feelings for Silas Drake purely platonic. It had been a long while since such a paragon had crossed my path.

It sounded like a good time to get in touch with Candace and see if she was available for drinks tonight so we could have a girl-to-girl talk, but the problem with that scenario was that I'd have to call Silas to drive me. And then I'd have to explain to him why I had such a sudden raging urge to have drinks with a friend…and then I'd have to introduce him to Candace….

Never mind. She'd sent me an email the day before, just checking to make sure that I was okay. Which I was, mostly. At least I hadn't been attacked by any random strangers lately. One day at a time.

No, it was time to be quiet and still, and be a good little hermit, here in my luxury condo. Time for that Netflix binge, or maybe some reading, although I knew I'd do better at just watching TV, something where I could disengage my brain for a while.

So I took my iced tea into the living room, turned on the television, and started going through my "saved" list on Netflix, attempting to decide which of the series I'd bookmarked to try next. But just as I raised the remote to give the *Gilmore Girls* reboot a try, the world went hazy around me, the remote falling from my fingers onto the coffee table with a clatter.

This wasn't the vampire's mansion in Linda Vista. I saw a shabby one-story house with faded beige stucco, tired-looking day lilies lining a cracked cement walkway. No place I knew, but its analogue could be found in half the cities in the San Gabriel Valley, including right here in the poorer parts of Pasadena.

The scene shifted, to a room inside the house. A bedroom, I supposed, although there wasn't a bed to be seen. Boards covered the window. A thin mattress sat on the floor. And on that mattress was a young woman, probably a few years younger than I. Her hands had been cuffed behind her back, and her feet were bound with bright yellow nylon rope. Dark hair spilled over the mattress and onto the floor. A thick gag in her mouth did a good job of distorting her features, but I could tell that her dark eyes were large, terrified.

Another flash, of a green street sign with the words "Daines Dr" on it. And then the vision was gone.

I'd been sitting on the couch with my feet on the cushions, but I sat bolt upright then, heart pounding, cold sweat trickling down the back of my neck. Even though I'd experienced these sorts of visions before,

I still wasn't used to them. But at least I did know exactly what I had to do.

My phone was also sitting on the coffee table, so I didn't have to get up to fetch it. The number I needed was already programmed in. It rang twice, then a third time.

Please God, not voicemail, I prayed, although I knew that even if I had to leave a message, it would be returned almost immediately. But in my mind's eye I saw that girl's terrified face once more, and I knew that even minutes were precious.

A crisp voice came through the iPhone's speaker. "Detective Ortiz."

"Detective Ortiz, it's Serena Quinn."

Even though I couldn't see him, I almost felt the way he straightened in his office chair. "What did you see?"

I loved that about him. Yes, the first time he'd been skeptical, but ever since, Raoul Ortiz had taken my visions seriously. I didn't have to waste valuable time trying to convince him of anything. "A house, on Daines Drive, according to what I saw. I don't know where that is, though."

"Not in Pasadena. El Monte, I think."

"Can you do anything if it's not in your jurisdiction?"

"Sure. I'll make a call, say I'm acting on an anonymous tip. Give me the details."

The vision hadn't faded, was still clear in my mind. I described the unobtrusive beige house as best I could, the drooping day lilies on either side of the front walk. "I didn't see a house number or anything," I told him, my tone apologetic. "There's a girl being held captive in one of the bedrooms. Early twenties, dark eyes and hair. I think she might be Hispanic, but the gag in her mouth was distorting her features, so I can't say for sure."

"I'll check if the description matches up with anything from missing persons. Did you see anything else?"

I shut my eyes, hoping I might see more details that way. And although I couldn't find anything more to say about the house, I did notice one thing—a tattoo on the back of one of her hands, intricate, tribal. I described it as best I could to Detective Ortiz, saying it seemed like something that could have been done in henna, although the pattern had looked like an actual tattoo, not something painted on.

"That will help," he said. "I'll get right on it." A pause, and he added, "Thanks, Serena."

"Don't thank me," I told him. "Just find her."

"We will." He hung up then, and I set my phone back down on the coffee table.

The adrenaline that had surged through me was now gone, and in its place had come a sort of drained sensation. This wasn't the first time I'd suffered that kind of aftermath, but I still didn't enjoy it much. At least I knew it would go away soon.

And I knew I should be grateful that this was something I could handle over the phone. Calling for Silas to come drive me to Raoul Ortiz's office at the civic center would have wasted far too much valuable time.

I wondered then if I should contact Silas after all, though. He'd told me to phone him if I had any more visions. So I had, but this one didn't seem to have any connection to my family, or to Lucius Montfort and his local vampire gang. Instances like these were the only times I didn't resent my gift—or curse—times when I could actually use it for something good.

If only they could all be like this. I didn't want to think about a dim, hazy future that involved dodging vampires for the rest of my life. All I wanted was for these visions to help people, instead of making things somehow worse for me, turning me into a pawn to be manipulated by someone like Montfort.

In the end, I didn't call Silas. I waited there on the couch, only paying partial attention to the television. One episode bled into another, and about two hours later, my phone rang.

The display told me it was Raoul Ortiz calling back. I grabbed the phone, heart pounding. The short time frame didn't necessarily mean good news. I could only pray that it did.

"Serena."

"Detective Ortiz."

"We found her."

I sagged against the sofa cushions, relief making me limp. "And she's all right?"

"She's safe. She'd been assaulted multiple times, and she's on her way to the hospital for observation, but we got there in time."

"Who...?"

"An ex-boyfriend. I can't say anything more than that."

"Of course." I understood; just because I was in a unique position to provide him with these tips didn't mean that I could be privy to sensitive information. As horrible as the ordeal that girl suffered had been, I couldn't help being slightly relieved that at least this appeared to be a one-off crime. I didn't have to worry about a serial killer working in the San Gabriel Valley, on top of everything else.

"Thank you, Serena." Ortiz's voice was calm, but I could hear the gratitude in it. "Because of you, that girl has a future. You keep calling me whenever you see something. Please."

"I will. Trust me on that."

"I do. You have a good afternoon."

He hung up, but I held the phone in my hand for a moment longer, staring down at it until the screen began to grow dim and fade to black. I'd just helped to save a girl's life. That had to give me some additional good karma, didn't it?

I just wasn't sure if it would be enough to help me prevail against Lucius Montfort and his minions.

CHAPTER ELEVEN

I slept well that night, better than I had in a long time. No dreams disturbed my slumber, nothing to prevent me from getting the rest I so desperately needed. And when I awoke, I also felt better than I had since that semivive had attacked me on Marengo Avenue. The future was still uncertain, but I didn't feel quite so hopeless. I'd saved someone else's life.

Maybe I'd be able to save mine, too.

Or my sister's.

The worry about Vanessa returned, although I did my best to push it aside as I made my morning coffee and some toast. I'd done everything I could to remind myself she wasn't in any immediate danger, but how could I know that for sure? Yes, she was well-known in fashion circles and had kind of a cult following amongst the fashionistas, but I honestly had no idea whether that minor level of fame was sufficient to make her immune to an assault by Lucius Montfort.

To reassure myself, I opened up my MacBook and went back to the blog where I'd first read about the connection between the vampire and my sister. Yes, I could have simply called or texted her to make sure she was still among the living, but I knew Vanessa. She was probably still angry over what I'd said about Lucius Montfort, and there was a high likelihood that she wouldn't respond to a phone call or a text, would want me to stew a good long while before she got back to me. Anyway, I supposed it was too much to ask for her to be featured two days in a row on the same blog, because I didn't see anything else mentioned there. Fine, well, Google was my friend. So I typed in "Vanessa Quinn" and "Montfort," just to see what would pop up. Yes, there was the original article I'd found, but I also saw a mention of the financing deal on another industry blog, along with the projected date for the launch of her spring line. Both entries had today's date on them.

As far as I could tell, things seemed to be humming right along. All that could change on a dime, of course, but I figured I had enough time to shower and get ready for my day, and decide what I needed to do next. The impulse that had kept me from speaking with Silas seemed childish now, and I resolved to call him as soon as I was done with my morning prep.

I didn't rush, though, but took a leisurely shower, and spent more time than I normally would on my makeup and hair. Why, I couldn't exactly say, only that the last time Silas had seen me, I'd still been sporting an expertly styled coif, courtesy of the hair magicians who worked for my sister. I wanted to do what I could to measure up to that standard.

It was almost as if I considered it a given that Silas would come over once I had called him.

Which, as it turned out, wasn't completely ridiculous, because after I did make the phone call, letting him know about what was going on with my sister, and also about the vision I'd had, he immediately said that he wanted to come over and discuss matters with me. While I was starting to get used to the way he never wanted to talk about anything important over the phone, I couldn't help being a little startled.

"You're sure?" I asked. "I mean, it's all's well that ends well in terms of the vision, and my sister seems to be okay—"

"For now," he responded, his tone grim.

What in the world was I supposed to say to that? Since I knew he didn't want to get into any detail over the phone, there wasn't much I could say. "All right," I told him, then added, sparked by a sudden impulse, "But let's go out for lunch. It's a beautiful day, and I'm getting stir-crazy."

A pause. For a few seconds, I wondered if he was going to refuse, but then he said, "Of course. I'll be there in a half hour."

He ended the call then. I stared at my phone's screen for a moment, then shrugged and put it in my purse. It didn't exactly take a rocket scientist to figure out he wasn't thrilled about the lunch thing. Why, I wasn't sure. Because he didn't think it was a good idea for me to go out any more than I absolutely had to, or because he felt that going out for lunch veered a little too close to "date" territory for his liking?

I couldn't know. Actually, I wasn't even sure what whim had driven me to make the suggestion, except that I really was starting to have a bad case of cabin fever. It was one thing to stay inside for days when doing so was my own choice. Being driven to do the same because of trying to avoid vampires and their slaves? That was something else entirely.

Because I didn't have anything better to do, I went in the bathroom and fussed with my hair a bit more, then scrutinized my appearance in the mirror. I'd put on one of my long skirts and a fitted tee with a denim jacket over it. Ballerina flats because it wasn't quite warm enough to go around in sandals…at least not for me. My feet tended to get cold easily, residual circulatory damage from the accident. Anyway, the whole ensemble was fairly casual, but not as casual as jeans. Would Silas think I was trying too hard? That my styled hair and light makeup and silver hoop earrings meant I'd dolled myself up for our "date"?

I really didn't know. True, if I knew I wasn't going to be leaving the house, then I'd gladly flop around in yoga pants, my hair pulled back in a pony-tail and no makeup on at all, unless you could count lip balm. But my mother had trained me far too well—I didn't dare go outside without being "done." After all, roaming around town looking like a com-plete slob would reflect badly on her, on the family. And it would only get worse if—when—Jackson for-mally announced his candidacy. I could only imagine paparazzi lurking outside Whole Foods, trying to get a snap of the candidate's sister with a bare face and wearing a tank top or something.

The doorbell rang, and I hurried out of the bath-room so I could answer it. Silas stood outside, once again in one of his inevitable dark T-shirts and a pair of jeans. Since I'd seen him in a dress shirt the other night, I knew that he must have other items of cloth-ing in his wardrobe, but sometimes I still couldn't help wondering. Maybe all he had was that single button-down shirt.

Luckily, Southern California was casual pretty much all the time, unless you were trying to eat at a five-star restaurant or something. I certainly didn't have designs in that direction; I figured we could go up to Slater's 50/50—I was hungry, and one of their burgers sounded great right about then—or maybe over to Green Street if Silas wanted something a little more refined.

As soon as I shut the door, he said, "Tell me about your vision."

"I thought I did."

"You said it wasn't important."

That sounded awful. "What I meant was, it wasn't important in terms of being connected to Lucius Montfort, or my family. Obviously, it was hugely important to the girl who was rescued."

Silas nodded. "Perhaps, but I'd still like to hear it."

It would take more time to keep protesting than it would to simply tell him the story. So I did, doing my best to include every detail, even the ones that didn't seem significant. He listened, expression grave, but he didn't try to interject. At the end of my recitation, though, he asked, "How many visions like this do you have in relation to the ones that seem to be hinting at some sort of possible future?"

I'd never really analyzed my visions in that way. A shrug, and then I replied, "I'm not sure. Maybe… twenty percent? I haven't kept count. I'd have to go through my journal and try to crunch some numbers."

"But you also keep a record through your drawings."

"A partial record," I allowed. "Some visions lend themselves better to that kind of recollection than others. The other ones I try to write down, because they don't always stay with me for very long. This one was very sharp and brief and vivid…and urgent. I knew in this instance, it was more important for me to contact Detective Ortiz right away rather than try to commit any of it to paper. The same with the other visions I've had where I knew immediate action was needed."

"And you can always tell the difference?"

"So far."

Silas was quiet then, one hand absently rubbing his chin, which as usual was covered in a few days' worth of scruff. "Well, that's a good thing, clearly."

"I think so." I went to retrieve my purse from where I'd dropped it on the dining room table. "So… are you more in the mood for burgers or something a little lighter?"

"Whatever you want," he replied, which I supposed I should have expected.

I made a spur-of-the-moment decision. Yes, the burgers at Slater's were awesome, but at Green Street we could sit outside on the patio and enjoy the bright day. I was starting to feel like a cave-dweller. "Have you ever been to Green Street?"

"I've driven down it," Silas said, looking slightly mystified by my question.

"Not the road, the restaurant. They have a salad that's truly divine. And we can eat outside."

"Well, then."

That seemed to settle it. Luckily, no one was around when we emerged from my condo. I knew Brian was on some kind of deadline, and his partner Lewis worked in downtown L.A. and wouldn't be home for hours, so I avoided having to make any awkward introductions. Not that I thought they would be awkward, exactly, because of Lewis and Brian's overwhelming cheerfulness, only that I really had no idea how to even explain Silas to them. It seemed better to avoid the meet-and-greet until it was truly inevitable.

The big black Dodge truck waited for us in the visitor parking area. I thought about asking Silas how he always managed to get one of those premium spots, no matter what time of day it was, then decided maybe I didn't want to know.

"So is Green Street actually on Green Street?" Silas asked as he pulled out of the parking space.

"Not exactly. I think it used to be, years ago. You can head east here on Cordova, then turn on Shoppers Lane. There's a parking structure, and the restaurant is next to that."

He nodded, and we drove along in silence. It really was a fairly short hop, one that might have been walkable…except for that old joke about how no one walks in L.A. Or Pasadena, for that matter. Anyway, I could see why staying safely inside a vehicle was probably a better idea. Although I couldn't imagine a semivive being bold enough to jump both me and Silas in broad daylight, I also didn't want to put that belief to the test.

By that point it was close to one-thirty, and the lunch crowds had begun to thin out. We didn't have to wait long for an outdoor table, where the hostess took our orders for a couple of iced teas and told us our server would be along shortly.

Even as I sat down, I could feel myself begin to relax. Until that moment, with the warm sun just beginning to slip toward the west and a gentle breeze blowing across my face, I hadn't realized how much I needed to get out of my condo. True, I'd gone to model in my sister's show, but that wasn't quite the same thing, since I'd first been cooped up in her workspace getting pins stuck in me, and then had been at the warehouse in Santa Monica working the show itself.

"Better?" Silas asked.

I blinked, and realized he'd been looking across the table at me, his gaze steady. Those dark eyes met mine for a moment, and then I lifted my shoulders and smiled, a smile that probably wasn't terribly convincing. Oh, it wasn't that I didn't feel better. I did. But I realized it was getting more and more difficult to act normal around him, to pretend that his presence didn't affect me in a way I wouldn't have thought possible a few days earlier.

"Yes, better," I replied. Because it was too awkward to maintain the eye contact, I turned away and made a show of rummaging in my purse for my sunglasses. I set them on my nose and added, "It's bright out here. I'm not used to it."

"I suppose it is." Maybe that was the faintest suggestion of one eyebrow lifting, as if he wasn't quite sure he believed my excuse, but he didn't call me on it.

And in the next moment, we were interrupted by the waitress, who brought our iced teas and then asked if we knew what we wanted. I promptly ordered the Dianne salad, because it had been a while since I'd had one. Silas hadn't even glanced at the menu, but he asked for the same thing, probably so he wouldn't hold up the show.

After the waitress was gone, he picked up his iced tea and squeezed the lemon into the glass. A brief glance around, as if making sure that no one seated in the outdoor area could overhear what we were saying. Not much chance of that, as by that point only two couples remained sitting there, both of them on the far side of the area designated for *al fresco* dining.

"And your sister?"

"All quiet on the western front, as far as I can tell." I sipped some iced tea through the straw provided. Even though I'd slept well, right then I thought I needed the extra boost of caffeine. "She was not happy when I told her my story about Lucius coming on to me before he ended up with her."

"No, I suppose she wouldn't be. That sort of thing must be a blow to the ego." Silas straightened in his chair. The metal legs scraped against the concrete ground, and I tried to keep from cringing at the sound. "But the real question is, did she believe you?"

"Maybe. I'm not sure. But it doesn't really matter, because even if she did believe me, deep down, what I said didn't deter her one bit. It sounds like she's determined to work with Mr. Montfort. I hoped she'd get angry...which she did, only at me rather than him." I didn't quite sigh, but I did let out a small breath before I took another pull on my straw. "So I think that plan backfired."

"It's all right. While I don't think she's in any immediate danger, I asked someone to watch over her."

That news made me raise an eyebrow. "So now she has a guardian angel, too?"

"In a manner of speaking. That is, this is some-one who will look out for her, but he won't make himself known. There won't be any direct interventions unless absolutely necessary."

I thought of the way Silas had "directly intervened" to save me from that semivive, and tried to imagine my sister's reaction if something so completely outside her experience happened to her. One might say I was already primed to be more accepting of the supernatural, simply because the experience of my visions had taught me that the world was a much stranger place than most people believed. But Vanessa was so down-to-earth, so hard-headed in her own way, that I really didn't know what she would do.

It wouldn't come to that, though. Whoever was looking after her, he was just a safeguard, "a break glass in case of emergency" sort of thing. What I sincerely hoped was that she'd gracefully move on from Lucius the same way she'd moved on from every other man in her life.

Except for the minor little detail of them all being men, not vampires. Not unnatural creatures intent on an end game I couldn't begin to imagine.

A feeling of hopelessness began to rise in me, one I wished I could ignore. What happened to my expression because of it, I didn't know, but Silas must have seen something in my face. He said, "It's far too early to despair. Your sister is safe, and will remain that way. It's entirely possible that Lucius will determine she has little worth as a point of leverage, and will give up that aspect of the game."

"But not the game itself."

"No," Silas responded. His voice was calm, but I could see the way his jaw set slightly, the slightest furrowing of his forehead. The bright sunlight showed all too clearly the line between his brows. Not that I minded. I liked that he wasn't some perfect pretty boy. I'd had enough of that with Travis. Voice lowering, Silas went on, "I fear he won't give that up easily. Which is why I am here with you."

And the only reason, I reflected, although I didn't want to acknowledge such a self-pitying thought. "I thought we were here because we were hungry," I quipped lamely, and he shook his head.

"Yes, there's that, too."

The waitress showed up then with our salads and their accompanying bread, asked us if we needed anything else, and then departed when we said we were fine. Although some of my pleasant mood from earlier had evaporated, my stomach still wanted something to satisfy it. I lifted a forkful of salad and chewed, and then realized this was just what I wanted. Some people might say salads couldn't really be comfort food, but I'd argue that they just hadn't tried the salad Dianne with its nutty-sweet

Asian dressing and slivers of almonds and chunks of chicken. It was divine.

"This is very good," Silas said, after he'd taken a few bites.

"Isn't it? They've been serving it for more than thirty years. My parents used to come here on dates. Or rather, the original location, the one on Green Street."

"Ah."

And that was all he said. I realized it probably hadn't been very politic to mention the subject of dates. We weren't on one, of course not, but I had asked him out to lunch. Some people would consider that only a friendly gesture, while others might look at it as something more. Judging by the way Silas was acting, I guessed he was in the "friendly gesture" camp, if even that.

More eating in silence. One of the couples who'd also been sitting in the outdoor dining area got up and walked past us. They looked to be a little older than I, probably in their early thirties. I noticed the way the woman's gaze flicked toward Silas and paused there for a second before she kept moving. Nothing major, most likely just someone taking extra note of a person they found attractive, but it still made my hackles go up.

Which was a ridiculous reaction. I had absolutely no claim on Silas, except perhaps to expect him to keep me alive. He'd been doing a pretty good job of that so far.

Because I could feel my neck tensing up, I cast about desperately for something to restart the conversation. "So…how do you know the people around us aren't semivives?"

"They aren't."

"But how do you *know?*"

"They're not attacking us."

Point taken. I set down my fork and reached for my iced tea. "They're that aggressive?"

"Not always." Silas also put down his fork, but in his case, it was so he could break off a piece of the zucchini bread that had come with our salads and take a bite. "Actually, they're quite passive when they're not acting on orders from their masters. But if any were in the vicinity, they would be there in an attempt to capture you. Which is why I said they would be attacking."

"The vam—" I broke off then and cast a furtive glance toward the one couple that remained on the patio with us. They were chatting animatedly and didn't appear to be paying any attention to what Silas and I were saying, but that didn't mean I still shouldn't be careful. "The ones who control them don't use them as spies?"

"No, because they're not very good at processing information. A good spy reports on what he sees and offers analysis to go along with it. The semivives are mainly muscle."

Well, that was something. At least I wouldn't have to worry about thralls of the undead hanging out in unlikely places, trying to catch me in a compromising position. Not that I was ever in a place to be in a compromising position, so to speak, unless that included trying on bras at Victoria's Secret or something. I couldn't feel much relieved, though, because Silas went on, "The vampires do their own spying. Their ability to become invisible stands them in good stead when it comes to that sort of thing."

"*Invisible?*" The word came out as almost a squeak. This time the couple on the other side of the patio did pause to shoot a curious glance in our direction. I quickly reached for my iced tea and sipped at it, trying to appear as if I didn't have a care in the world.

"Well, invisible to mortal eyes. It's more that they can move so very quickly that they might as well be invisible."

"This just keeps getting better and better."

Silas shook his head. "It's not as bad as it seems. Because you are safe in your own home, and when you're not, you're with me. They won't try anything."

"How do you know that for sure? If they're as fast as you say—"

"They operate in stealth, Serena. Even if Lucius—or, more likely, one of his counterparts—were to slip in here one night and grab you and steal you away, do you realize what that would look like? One moment a woman would be sitting at a patio table at a restaurant, and the next she would be gone. It would cause far too much of a disturbance. Yes, the…person…who took you wouldn't have been seen. But he would have to reappear somewhere—and somewhere close by, because their kind can't travel nearly as far while burdened with the weight of a human. It isn't worth the risk."

That made some sense. I was glad to hear that, for all their supernatural abilities, vampires had their own limitations. They were still scary as hell to me, just maybe not quite as scary.

Even so, I couldn't help glancing over my shoulder before I returned to my salad. Silly, I knew, because even if any vampires had been lurking in the vicinity, I wouldn't have been able to see them. And then I realized I was being doubly silly, because of course it was bright blazing daylight on a clear day as February was just about to bleed into March, and if I couldn't be safe sitting out here in the sun with Silas across from me, then I couldn't be safe anywhere.

After I'd taken a bite of my zucchini bread, I said, driven by a sudden impulse, "Let's go to the Huntington."

"'The Huntington'?" Silas repeated, brows lifting.

"You know, the Huntington Library. It's only about fifteen minutes from here."

"I thought you didn't want to be inside."

"I don't. I want to walk in the gardens. Just for an hour or so, before we go back to the condo."

He hesitated, then gave the briefest of shrugs. "If that's what you wish."

"I do."

The waitress came by and asked if we were done, and I said yes, even though I'd eaten only about half my salad. She offered to box it up for me, and since I knew this particular salad traveled much better than most, I said yes.

When she came back with the check, I grabbed it before Silas could even attempt to reach for the little leatherette case that held the bill. "This was my idea," I said sternly.

"If it makes you happy," he replied, settling back in his chair.

"It does." I put a couple of twenties inside the case, then closed my wallet and stuffed it into my purse. As I stood, Silas got up as well. We were both quiet as we headed toward his truck. Once I was inside and fastening my seatbelt, though, I asked, "Do you know how to get to the Huntington?"

"Refresh my memory."

So I gave him directions, and he pointed us south on Lake Avenue before jogging to the east on California. We passed Caltech, as tall trees closed in overhead and large Craftsman homes built during the boom of the teens and early twenties filled the streets on either side.

Since it was a weekday afternoon, the parking lot at the Huntington wasn't very full. When Silas and I got to the entrance, I flashed my platinum membership card, and the gal on duty there waved us in. We were descending the steps that led from the building which housed the gift shop and museum offices when Silas asked, "How long have you been a member here?"

"Forever," I replied. I veered to the right, following the path that would take us to the Japanese gardens. It was still too early for the world-famous wisteria to be in bloom, but I thought the tranquility of that section of the property was just what I needed right then. The sun glinted down from overhead, bright and warm, reassuring me that as long as it rode in the heavens, I didn't have to worry about Lucius Montfort or any of his vampires popping up in the vicinity.

"Your family took you here?"

"All the time. We all have lifetime memberships. My great-grandfather was buddies with Henry Huntington."

That revelation made Silas tilt his head down toward me. "He was?"

"Oh, yeah. Great-grandfather Jonas Quinn was a railroad man, too. Not quite as big a deal as Mr. Huntington, but still enough that he did very well for himself, and then expanded his fortune when he came to California and started buying up property wherever he could. He knew it would be worth a ton one day."

"I had no idea."

I paused on the path and looked up at him. Because of the bright sun beating down on us, I wore my sunglasses, but Silas didn't seem to be in need of such protection. "They didn't fill you in on the Quinn family's wealth when you were briefed about me?"

He sent me a wry glance. "Not all the details. The extent of the Quinn fortune wasn't of that much concern."

His reply made me chuckle. "Well, you're the first person to have that point of view about it. The Quinn fortune is certainly important to a whole lot of other people."

"So what is your family worth?"

From anyone else, such a question would have been cause for immediate indignation. You simply didn't ask how much money someone had, just like you weren't supposed to ask a woman how old she was or how much she weighed. In Silas' case, though, I was almost positive he'd done so out of pure curiosity, not because he was attempting to think of a way to leverage the information.

"Around a billion, give or take," I said carelessly. Somehow it sounded so much more awful when I uttered that figure aloud.

"Ah." He was quiet for a moment, his eyes not meeting mine, but apparently fixed on some point in the distance. "That sort of fortune confers a great deal of responsibility."

Once again he'd surprised me. Most people would be thinking of what they could do with that kind of money, instead of contemplating the burden that came with so much wealth. I offered him a smile, then said, "You and my father think alike, then. His foundation does a lot of charity work, offers grants and scholarships. That kind of thing. He's not really into consumption."

"Is that why your brother went into politics?"

"Maybe. Jackson always did want to do something more than sit around and count his money. Of course, having that money made him much more able to do whatever he wanted. He never had to worry about whether the profession he chose would buy a decent house or put food on the table for his family."

"I can understand that, but still, it sounds as if he wants to serve because of his duty to this country, and not because of what a position of power might do for him."

"True." My brother always was very patriotic—not the rah-rah kind who thought patriotism ended and began with wearing a flag pin on his lapel or something, but someone who truly believed in the institutions of this country. "And he's kind of unbribe-able because of it. Some people found that out the hard way when he first was elected. But the voters love that about him."

"As they should."

We began walking again, following a path that meandered its way into the Japanese garden. It was very quiet here, the only sound the rustling of the leaves and the quiet murmur of the stream that flowed under an enormous arched wooden bridge. Silas and I came to a fork in the pathway, but instead of heading up the hill toward the tea house, I took the other branch, one I knew would dead-end near a pond. Most people went to the tea house—not that I'd seen many visitors out and about on the grounds so far—and so I thought Silas and I would be undisturbed here.

He didn't say anything as we walked down the path. At the spot where it ended stood a stone bench, and I sat there, glad for a chance to rest. The pin in my left leg—another artifact from my accident—had begun to ache somewhat, which told me that more weather was probably headed our way, despite how clear the skies might be right now.

"You're tired?" Silas asked, his expression almost surprised. I suppose it might have seemed sort of strange that I'd need to rest so soon, when I'd walked a lot farther with him that day he'd rescued me from the semivive.

"Not exactly tired," I replied. "But I've got a pin in my leg, and sometimes it gives me a little trouble."

Concern entered his eyes, and he nodded. "I didn't know that. From your accident?"

"Yes. Compound fracture." I didn't bother to go into any details other than that. He should be able to fill in the blanks.

"I'm sorry."

"It's really not a problem. Most of the time I don't even notice it."

Those words didn't seem to convince him, however. A small frown tugged at his brows, and I couldn't help noticing the way his gaze shifted to where my legs were covered by the long skirt I wore.

"Wondering where the scar went last night?"

He looked almost ashamed, as if he hadn't thought I would figure out that he must be recalling the way my legs had looked in the short cocktail dress I'd worn at the reception the evening before.

"Dermablend," I explained, then went on, "thick makeup for covering up scars, birthmarks, that sort of thing. Vanessa's makeup artist put some on my leg while she was prepping me for the fashion show, and also on the scars on my left arm. That one was just a regular break, but it left me with some road rash that's never going away."

A nod. "Do you mind if I sit?"

Of course I didn't. Or rather, part of me wanted him sitting next to me, even though I knew such proximity was fraught with issues. "Go ahead."

He settled himself on the stone bench beside me. Not super close, but there was only so much distance he could put between the two of us before it became patently obvious that was what he was trying to do. Even so, I was acutely aware of everything about him—the faded areas on the knees of his jeans, the old, pale scar in the tanned skin on the back of his right hand...the way the breeze caught at his overlong hair, the wayward strands around his face somehow calling into sharper relief the fine bones of cheek and chin.

"Usually I don't wear dresses that short," I went on. "It's easier to stay covered up than to keep trying to explain my scars. Vanessa hates these skirts, though—whenever she sees me wearing one, she always goes out of her way to remind me that the sixties were a long time ago."

"What does that have to do with your skirt?" Silas asked, looking confused.

"I guess she thinks skirts like this one look like something a hippie would wear. I don't know. I just think it's comfortable."

A little pause, and he said, "I like it. I like the way the wind catches it as you're walking."

It was an innocent enough remark, and yet my cheeks flushed. Maybe because it was just flirting with the edges of being a compliment. "Thank you."

He went quiet then, as if he'd just realized that he'd said something a little too intimate. His gaze moved toward the path we'd just traversed to get to this spot, but it was still empty. A couple of jays scolded one another in a nearby tree, but otherwise, that was the only sound I could hear. We might have been all alone in the world.

Then, so carefully that he might have been touching porcelain instead of human flesh, he reached over and laid his hand on top of mine where it rested on the bench. My breath caught. Then I turned my head to look over at him. Those dark eyes, in their ring of long lashes, looked so deep that I was sure I could drown in them.

And in the next moment, he was bending toward me, his lips touching mine. A thrill moved through my body, followed by a rush of warmth, the kind of heat I hadn't experienced for far too long. Our mouths opened, and then we were tasting one another, even as he reached over to pull me closer to him so he could put his arms around me, his fingers tangling in my loose hair.

The only sound in the world was the thudding of my heart, the heavy pulse of my blood echoing in my ears. I'd hoped for this moment, but I truly hadn't thought it would ever actually come to pass. What had brought Silas to this point, I had no idea. I didn't want to question his motivations, though. I just wanted to thrill in the sensation of his lips on mine, those strong arms around me. From somewhere, I caught a drift of jasmine.

Eventually, though, he did pull away. Desire seemed to struggle with shame in his expression, although I didn't know why he should feel ashamed. It wasn't as if he'd had to force me. I wanted this. Oh, I'd wanted it badly, and had only realized how badly in these last few precious minutes.

"I am sorry," he said, his voice pitched so low that it was hardly more than a murmur.

"Sorry for what?" I asked. "Did you think I didn't want you to do that?"

A long silence. Then he adjusted his position on the stone bench so he wasn't sitting quite so close to me. "I believe you did. That's not the problem."

"Then what is?"

"The problem is that we should not have this sort of a relationship. I've been assigned to protect you, not...." The words trailed off there, as if he couldn't quite bring himself to say the words.

"You *are* protecting me," I told him. "I don't see how kissing me gets in the way of that. All right, maybe you were a little distracted, but what is there to protect against here? It's broad daylight, and even a semivive would think twice about attacking us at the Huntington Library. There are actually a lot of security guards at this facility, even if they're not immediately obvious."

"No, it's not that. It's...." Again he stopped himself.

"What, have you taken a vow of celibacy or something?"

Despite the serious expression he wore, he chuckled. "No, not exactly. But—"

"But nothing." He'd moved away from me, but that didn't prevent me from shifting so we were now sitting very close to one another, our legs almost touching. "If it makes you feel any better, I've been mooning over you like some high school girl crushing on the quarterback."

Although I would have said he had the kind of warm-toned skin that didn't flush easily, I couldn't help noting the flare of color on his high cheekbones. "You have not."

"Yes, I have. And I will not allow you to beat yourself up about this."

Just a small twitch at the corner of his mouth, hardly enough to be called a smile. "Oh, you won't?"

"No." To prove to him I meant it, I leaned over and kissed him again. I wasn't given the chance to deepen the kiss, however, because a second or two later I heard the crunch of gravel, and pulled away from Silas, startled.

A couple maybe around my parents' age stood a few paces away, looking decidedly embarrassed. "So sorry," said the woman, and they quickly turned around and headed off in the opposite direction.

The spell was broken. Silas reached out to touch my hair briefly, then stood. "I should get you home."

I didn't want to go home. I wanted…what did I want? To stay out with him, to let this day continue so we could spend it together. But I knew I shouldn't protest. While I didn't see anything wrong about sharing that kiss—or taking things further—I could tell that Silas needed some time to process the change in our relationship. It was better to allow him that time rather than forcing things.

So I got up from the bench, and followed him out to the main path. As we walked along, not speaking, his hand stole its way into mine, the pressure of his fingers warm, reassuring.

Right then, vampires were the furthest thing from my mind.

CHAPTER TWELVE

As much as I wanted to ask Silas to come inside the condo, to sit down and have a glass of wine, I restrained myself, and only offered a quick kiss on his cheek as he said goodbye. I watched him walk away, then shut the door and leaned up against it.

I never would have said I was the overly romantic type. It wasn't that I hadn't cared for the men I'd been with—even when they didn't deserve it, thank you, Travis—but I'd also never really understood all that swoony sunset-and-roses stuff, either. Then again, I'd never met anyone like Silas before. Just remembering the kiss we'd shared made me go hot, then cold with shivers, followed by a rush of desire so unexpected and overpowering that I actually had to stop and take a breath.

That was so not me.

Even with Silas returned to his loft in Little Tokyo—or wherever he'd headed after we made our goodbyes—I thought that a glass of wine sounded like a damn good idea. I headed to the fridge and got out a partially drunk bottle of chardonnay, then pulled out the little rubber stopper and poured myself some. Not a lot, but just enough to take the edge off. Because clearly kissing Silas had given me a hell of an edge.

It was Friday night. I wished I could have thought of the right words to convince him that we should keep the party going, so to speak. But he needed his space. I understood that…on an intellectual level at least. Physically…well, right then I was hornier than a fifteen-year-old who'd just been banned from making out with her boyfriend on the couch.

Instead, I took my wine to the living room and turned on the TV. I still had one episode of *Gilmore Girls* to get through. What I'd do after that, I wasn't sure. Find something else to watch, I supposed. Nothing remotely romantic, though. That would only make things worse.

My phone pinged, and I quickly set down the glass of wine I held and hurried back to the kitchen, where I'd left my purse. I pulled out my phone, heart pounding, hoping that the alert was from Silas trying to reach me.

No, it was a FaceTime request from Candace. I'd answered her email, so she knew I was still alive, but apparently she wanted visual confirmation. I pushed the button, and her face appeared on the screen, looking tired. Behind her, I saw bookcases filled with volume after volume of case law, and so I knew she must still be at work, even though by then it was past six o'clock.

"Exciting Friday night, huh?" I asked as I took the phone back with me to the living room.

"Almost as exciting as yours, looks like," she said. "No hot date with your bodyguard?"

"Actually, that was earlier," I replied, trying to sound casual but—I assumed—failing miserably.

"Do tell. I have to live vicariously through you right now…which is even more tragic than it sounds."

Candace did have to work insane hours much of the time. Despite that, she'd managed to keep her relationship going with a full-time boyfriend, right up until the time she discovered the Tinder profile on his phone and ongoing text chats with at least three other women. Clearly, he'd been taking advantage of all those long nights she spent at the office.

"Silas came over to talk," I said. "And we went out for lunch."

"Sounds relatively harmless."

"It was. But then we went to the Huntington afterward so I could get some fresh air. I was starting to feel pretty fried and just needed to get out for a while."

She raised an eyebrow. "Still sounds pretty harmless."

"It was…right up until the moment he kissed me."

Her eyes widened, and she settled against the back of her chair, as if she needed its support to help her process what I'd just said. "Hold on. Did he kiss you…or did you kiss him?"

Good question. I thought back to that moment, recalled how he'd bent toward me, initiating the embrace. Yes, he'd definitely been the one who had started things. I wouldn't have had the guts.

"He kissed me," I admitted. "But I definitely wanted him to."

"Oh."

Her response was so noncommittal that I knew it had to include a ton of subtext. "What is 'oh' supposed to mean?"

She didn't answer me right away. I saw her pick up a pen and tap it against something just outside the FaceTime camera's field of view. Maybe the desktop, or maybe a pad of paper. She still liked to take notes longhand, said it helped her retain details better. "It's just…how long have you known this guy?"

I had to stop and think. So much had happened— especially in contrast to the monotony of my usual life—that it felt as if I'd met Silas weeks ago. In reality, though, he'd only stopped that semivive attack on Monday. "Five days," I replied, my tone cautious. Even though she'd only asked that one question, I didn't know if I liked where our conversation was going.

"And how much do you know about him?"

"Is this going to be a cross-examination?" I snapped. Way to take the bloom off a moment that had been the highlight of the past few months.

Actually, if I wanted to be perfectly honest with myself, that kiss was more like the highlight of the last year.

She tucked a strand of loose blonde hair behind one ear and let out what sounded like an exasperated breath. "Listen, Serena…I want to be happy for you. I really do. But you need to be careful. I mean, how do you know for sure he didn't stage that attack on you, just so he could get close?"

Of course I knew for sure, because I'd had the misfortune of meeting Lucius Montfort. I knew vampires were real.

Only…did I? Did I know for absolutely sure? I hadn't seen Lucius drinking anyone's blood, after all. Yes, he'd disappeared apparently into thin air, but that could have been just another trick. I lived in the land of illusion, after all. What if this had all been an elaborate setup?

"He didn't stage the attack," I said, but my voice didn't sound terribly convincing even to me.

"Look." Candace paused there, as if she was carefully choosing her words so they would have the most impact and cause the least offense. "I certainly don't want to dissuade you from seeing someone if you really think you might have a chance…but you have to admit that the circumstances of your meeting this Silas person were pretty strange. And you know you have to be on the radar of some unscrupulous people."

I didn't want to admit it, but she was right. I lived a very quiet existence, but that didn't mean someone who was sufficiently determined couldn't track me down. Growing up, I'd been in a safe little cocoon in San Marino, a place where most of the people I went to school with and associated with were very wealthy, if not quite on the same level as my family. I'd gone to a private elementary school, but public schools for the rest of my pre-college career. It didn't matter, because the playing field there was pretty level. All the same, my parents—my mother especially—had always told me to be careful of who I dated, to make sure they weren't interested simply because of my family's background. They'd liked Travis because Travis was safe. His family traveled in the same circles as ours.

But now…with a little careful investigative work, anyone could figure out that the Serena Quinn on Cordova Street in Pasadena was the same Serena Quinn whose father had inherited the Quinn fortune, whose brother might very well be the next President of the United States. Yes, I had an excellent security system at the condo, the kind that would summon an armed guard if necessary, but it wasn't as if I had a private security detail who followed me everywhere.

Unless you counted Silas, of course.

I remembered then how my father had told me about the way his parents were so unnerved by the Patty Hearst kidnapping back in the 1970s, of how they'd made sure he went everywhere with a body-guard for about the span of a year and a half. They'd relented finally, but still. And even though my family couldn't really compare with the Hearsts when it came to sheer wealth, I still might provide a tempting enough target.

"Silas isn't like that," I said, after a long pause. "I know that makes me sound like every misguided woman on *Maury Povich* or something who's trying to defend her asshole boyfriend, but in this case it's true. He's a good person. If he really wanted to kidnap me and hold me for ransom or something, he would have had ample opportunity before now."

"Kidnapping is a little splashy," Candace replied. "I wasn't really thinking of anything that drastic.

More like…getting close so he could have access to your money. It's not as if that sort of thing hasn't been tried many times before, whether it's a guy going after an heiress, or a gold-digger trying to get her claws into a rich man."

I couldn't argue with her about that. It was a natural impulse to think someone was after you simply because of your money. Lord knows I'd entertained that thought enough times myself. I hadn't worried about it so much with Travis because he didn't need my money. But every time I'd gathered enough strength to try and see other men after Travis and I broke up, the thought had crossed my mind. Between those concerns, and managing my damn visions, I hadn't dated very much. It was easier to simply stay alone, rather than question someone's motives every time I began to be even a little bit interested.

"I know it's been tried—and been successful. I just don't get that vibe from Silas, though. He seems pretty…self-sufficient."

"In what way?"

"I don't know." I shifted my phone to my other hand and wished Candace had initiated the FaceTime call when I was on my laptop. It would have been easier to manage. "That is, I don't get that sense of neediness about him. He drives an expensive truck, but it doesn't really seem as if he has a job." *Other than watching me,* I added mentally, but I really didn't want to get into that aspect of the relationship with Candace. "He has a place somewhere near Little Tokyo. That couldn't have been cheap, what with the way they've been gentrifying downtown lately. I get the feeling that he must have an alternative income source."

"Hmm."

Which could have meant anything. While I appreciated my friend's need to watch out for me, I thought her concern was misplaced. She might have planted a seed of doubt there, just for a minute, but the more I thought about Silas, about my interactions with him, the more I knew his motives were pure. Candace hadn't met him, and so she didn't have any way of knowing that my trust in him wasn't merely wishful thinking.

"Look, I get it," I told her. "You want me to be careful. I *am* being careful—this isn't my first rodeo. But I know that Silas isn't another Travis. Not that Travis was a gold-digger. But still…someone I shouldn't have trusted."

"A world-class jerk is what he was." She set down her pen and shifted her weight in her chair slightly. "Okay, I'll back off. If you think Silas is a paragon, then he must be."

"I don't know about a 'paragon.' Just…someone who's solid. I might have only known him for a few days, but he's already proved that he's there when I need him to be. That goes a long way for me."

"I know." Her expression showed me she was still worried, though. There wasn't much I could do about her concern, except hope with time she'd come around to trusting Silas the way I did. Then she sighed and said, "Well, I need to get back to these briefs. But maybe we can get together for lunch next week? Wednesday doesn't look completely crazy."

"Sounds good. Lucky Baldwin's again?"

"Sure. And this time I can have a beer, because I don't have to be in court that day."

"It's a date."

We said our goodbyes, and she ended the FaceTime call. I set down my phone, wishing that I had the courage to reach out to Silas. I wanted to hear his voice. It would reassure me that any doubts I'd entertained were no more than fancies, momentary hesitations brought on by Candace's line of questioning. I knew he was a good person. He was.

I touched my fingers to my mouth, just for a moment. Just so I could remember how his lips had felt, touching that same sensitive skin. With any luck, I'd be able to experience one of those kisses again very soon.

In the meantime, I needed to turn on the TV and turn off my brain for a while.

He did call the next day, but only to check to make sure everything was still all right, that I hadn't had any visions or gotten any bad news from my sister. I wasn't brave enough to ask him to come over, and so I told him I'd spent a quiet evening the night before, and didn't have any plans to go out this weekend. My comment should have been enough of an opening for him to suggest that we see one another, but he didn't say anything along those lines. All he did was tell me he'd call again the next day, wish me a good afternoon, and hang up.

So where the hell was my tortured lover of the day before, the man who had kissed me because he simply didn't have the willpower to prevent himself from doing so?

Apparently, that man was nowhere to be seen at the moment.

Scowling, I took on the one task I always resorted to when I was pissed off at the world—I cleaned the condo from top to bottom. No doubt my mother would have been horrified to see me scrubbing toilets, since she paid for a service to come in and do that every other week, but housework was a good way for me to focus on something outside myself. True, because of the aforementioned cleaning service, it wasn't as if I had to scrub very hard, but it was the intention that mattered.

By the time I was done, my left leg was complaining loudly, and the condo practically sparkled, it was so clean. I threw the last used paper towel in the trash and poured myself a glass of iced tea to celebrate. Actually, what I really wanted was a drink, but starting to drink at four in the afternoon felt like admitting defeat.

I'd just sat down in the living room with my tea—making sure to use a coaster so I wouldn't mar the freshly cleaned surface of the coffee table—when the doorbell rang. For a second, I contemplated not answering. After all, I wasn't expecting anyone. But if it was either Brian or Lewis, the most likely suspects, they'd want to know why the hell I didn't come to the door when I was clearly home. Anyway, the door had a peephole; I would check before I opened it. Since the sun was still up, if muted by thick clouds that promised rain, I knew I didn't have to worry about any vampires lurking out on the landing. And I doubted a semivive would knock.

Fighting back a sigh, I got up from the couch and went to the door, then got on my toes and squinted so I could look through the peephole.

That wasn't Brian or Lewis out there. It was Silas.

I didn't quite gasp, but I did look down at myself in dismay. Because I hadn't been planning to go anywhere, my hair was pulled back in a scrunchie, and I had on yoga pants and an old faded USC T-shirt. Not exactly glamour girl material.

For just a second, I had the wild impulse not to open the door at all. I really didn't want Silas to see me like this. But then I realized I was being cowardly, and if we were going to have any kind of a future together, sooner or later he'd end up seeing me in crap clothes and no makeup.

So I punched the code into the alarm panel by the door, then undid the deadbolt and looked out, doing my best to smile. "Silas!"

He didn't smile in return. "I'm sorry I didn't call. I should have. But did you see this morning's *Los Angeles Times?*"

Of course I hadn't. I subscribed to the digital version, since I hated to have physical papers stack up, but I hadn't looked at it. Usually I did skim the top articles when I had a chance. Today, though, I'd been just a bit distracted. "Um, no, I hadn't looked at it yet. Come in."

He entered the foyer, and I shut the door behind him, locking the deadbolt and rearming the alarm out of force of habit. I didn't even know what I'd been expecting from him—a hug, a quick kiss on the cheek?—but he didn't do either of those things. Instead, he moved past me and headed into the dining room, where he paused to unzip the leather jacket he wore before pulling a folded-up front-page section of the *Times* from somewhere within its recesses. The headlines were dominated by the usual internecine warfare going on at City Hall and an article about a five-car crash that blocked the eastbound I-10 right at rush hour the day before, but I couldn't miss the story at the bottom right-hand corner of the page.

Senator Jackson Quinn Formally Announces White House Run.

I'd been expecting the news any day now, but seeing it in print like that suddenly made the scenario feel far more real. Actually, what it really felt like was a punch to the gut, not the least because I'd expected Jackson to call all of us to give us a heads-up before he made his announcement. For all I knew, he had contacted my parents in Santa Barbara, and expected them to pass on the pertinent details.

"It's not really that much of a surprise," I said as I looked up from the paper. My voice sounded almost too calm, but that was better than the alternative. "Do you think it changes anything?"

"I'm not sure." Then, his eyes narrowing slightly, he added, "This is the first you've heard of it, though."

The words weren't phrased as a question. My shoulders lifted. "In this family, I'm usually the last one to hear anything. I suppose my mother would have been in touch after she and my father were back in town." Silas still wore a faint frown, so I said, "Obviously, no one thinks I'm that important. I haven't had reporters camped out on my doorsteps or anything."

It might have been my imagination, but I thought I detected a softening of his expression. "I think you're important."

"Oh?" I managed, but I didn't have the chance to say anything more, because he'd moved toward me, his arms going around my waist so he could bring me closer to him, could bend down and touch his lips to mine.

This was what I'd been hoping for, to feel the strength of his body, taste the richness of his mouth. I let myself melt into his embrace, lost myself in him. It was even better than the day before, if such a thing was possible. We kissed, and I forgot about the news the paper contained, the worry about my sister—everything except the way I felt in his arms.

At last, though, he lifted his mouth from mine, even as he pushed back a stray strand of hair that had escaped the scrunchie and fallen across my cheek. "I should have stayed away," he whispered. "But I couldn't."

"I don't think you should've stayed away," I replied, a thin thread of worry moving through me at the pain in his voice. "I'm glad you're here. I want you to be here. Why should there be anything wrong with that?"

"Because…." He let go of my waist and took a step back. "Because if I'm this close to you, then I might make mistakes. I might allow my judgment to become clouded."

"You don't seem very cloudy to me," I quipped, but the joke fell completely flat. He stared down at me, unsmiling. "Anyway, if we're—if we're involved, it seems to me that would make you even more concerned about protecting me."

"It's not concern that's the problem." He stopped there and made an odd gesture with one hand, as if he'd intended to wave it in denial, then stopped himself partway through.

"Then what is?" I tilted my head up at him, trying to read something more of the expression he wore. Yes, he appeared troubled, but I still couldn't quite figure out exactly what was the source of his worry. "Are you going to be in some kind of trouble with the people who assigned you to protect me?"

"Not the kind of trouble you think," he remarked cryptically.

"Silas, you're not making much sense right now."

"I suppose I'm not." He shoved his hands in the front pockets of his jeans, his gaze moving away from me to the front-page section of the *L.A. Times* where it still lay on the dining room table. "This—this just adds an extra layer of concern, though. Suddenly, you've become that much more valuable."

"To Lucius Montfort."

"Yes, but also to others who are very mortal."

"I really don't think I have that much to worry about," I protested. "Like I said, I haven't seen a single reporter. No one cares about the siblings of a candidate, or even really the President. Okay, if Jackson tried to make one of us Attorney General or something, maybe, but—"

This time Silas did actually crack a smile. "No, I suppose he wouldn't do something like that. But still, there's far more visibility involved with being the immediate family of a presidential candidate rather than a senator."

I couldn't really argue with that statement. When Jackson was running for Senate, I actually was tracked down by a few reporters, ones who were doing more lifestyle sorts of pieces, who wanted the skinny on what it had been like to grow up with my brother. Problem was, with such an age gap between us, I didn't have a lot of those stories to tell. By the time I was old enough to really engage with Jackson, he was off to college. I'd given a few feel-good anecdotes that might have been true, and that was the end of it. But now? I really didn't know what to expect.

Struck by a sudden thought, I said, "Well, if you're really that worried about them tracking me down here, why don't we leave?"

"Leave?"

"Yes, get out, go somewhere else. Maybe you could show me your place?"

From the way his brows pulled together, I could tell he wasn't terribly thrilled by that suggestion. "My place?"

"Yes. Let's go downtown. Take me out for sushi or something. You're right next to Little Tokyo, aren't you?"

"Well, yes, but—"

"I'd need to change, though. I spent most of the day cleaning the house, and—" I broke off there and sort of waved at my ensemble of T-shirt and yoga pants. "Anyway, it was just a thought. If you really don't want to—"

"It's fine," he said. "You're right. You should come over. It's certainly no place that a reporter would come looking for you."

"Just give me fifteen minutes," I told him, even as I mentally added, *Or twenty….*

"However much time you want. It looked like it wanted to rain, though, so you might want to bear that in mind."

My leg had already given me advance notice of the approaching storm. "No problem." I flashed him a smile, then hurried upstairs, already plotting out what I should wear. Downtown Los Angeles on a Saturday night. A good pair of jeans, probably, and the knee-high lace-up Børn boots I'd gotten on clearance but hadn't had much of a chance to wear. A thin black sweater, my favorite dark green leather jacket. That would get me through the rain, if it arrived after all.

I hurried with my preparations, putting on quickie nighttime makeup of lots of mascara and a dark-stained mouth and not much else. The increased humidity had kind of fluffed up my hair, so once I shook it out of the scrunchie and ran my fingers through my wavy locks, they looked more or less presentable.

By the time I headed downstairs, it was nearly five and the world outside was growing dark, daylight saving time still a few weeks away. Silas stood at the dining room table, staring downward as he read an article in the front-page section of the Times— although not the one about Jackson. As I entered the room, Silas looked up. While he didn't exactly smile, I thought I saw a spark of admiration in those dark eyes.

"I hope this will work," I said.

"Oh, it will. Shall we?"

I nodded and went to retrieve my purse, then followed him to the front door. I set the alarm for "away," and locked up.

Yes, I truly was going "away." I couldn't wait to see Silas' place.

CHAPTER THIRTEEN

Rain began to fall as we were halfway down the 110 Freeway. I didn't mind; there was something cozy about the weather, about being together in the cab of Silas' truck as the raindrops pattered against the windshield. He turned on the wipers, then said, "It's a little early to eat. Should we go to my place first? We can have a drink there and head out after that."

"Sounds perfect."

Which it did. Maybe a little loosening-up time at his loft, just so he could get used to the idea of me being there. Dinner, and then...? I wouldn't lie to myself—I wanted to go back to his place afterward and have him make love to me. His kisses were divine, so I could only imagine what it would be like to feel him against me, *in* me.

The wave of heat that passed over me then was so intense, I was surprised it didn't fog up the truck's windows. I swallowed, and told myself that I needed to back off until I could know for sure which way the evening was trending. It wasn't like I'd packed an overnight bag or anything, although I always carried a little travel toothbrush in my purse, just in case I wanted to freshen up after a meal out. Something my mother had taught me, although I didn't exactly go out on the town very much.

Well, I was definitely going out on the town tonight.

L.A.'s skyscrapers grew larger, shimmering, blurred through the rain. We jogged onto the 101 Freeway briefly before getting off at Alameda. This was an area I didn't know very well. I'd been downtown, of course, but to places like the Disney Concert Hall and the Ahmanson Theatre. Little Tokyo lay south of there, in an area of mixed high-rises and what looked like warehouses but could have contained lofts.

We passed what I thought was a museum of some sort, although I didn't have time to read the signage, and then headed down a narrower street. It wasn't as well lit here, the sort of place I wouldn't have felt comfortable going if I didn't have someone as obviously capable as Silas with me. However, when he pulled up to what must have been his building, a sprawling multi-story structure that looked fairly new, I felt myself relax somewhat. We entered a parking lot with a remote-controlled gate, then headed down into an underground parking garage. This might have been a loft complex, but it obviously wasn't some converted warehouse.

After he parked in a numbered space that must have been assigned to his loft, Silas got out of the truck, and I followed suit. We went up a flight of stairs, then through a sort of courtyard, with pathways leading to the front door of each unit. His was down at the end of the row, which meant he would have corner views. And, as we entered the loft, I realized how spectacular those views were, since the unit faced north and west, so I could see a good chunk of downtown, lights shimmering in the rain. On a clear day, Silas could probably see all the way to West Hollywood.

He flicked on the lights. The place seemed all hard angles to me, concrete walls and huge banks of windows, although the pale oak floor did warm things somewhat. And although I didn't go for that ultra-modern kind of style, I still was impressed, both by the spaciousness of the loft and the realization that a place like this had to have cost a chunk of change. So much for Candace's theory that Silas was after me for my money.

"You like sake?" he asked as he pulled a small bottle out of the gleaming stainless refrigerator.

"Sure," I replied, although I'd only drunk it a handful of times. Regular wine worked better for me, but if we were going out for Japanese food, it was probably better to stick with the same kind of alcohol all night. I tilted my head at him, watching curiously as he poured some of the sake into a pair of small ceramic cups he'd retrieved from one of the cupboards. "Aren't you supposed to drink it warm, though?"

"Not this kind of sake," Silas said. He came over and handed one of the cups to me. "You might find that you like this kind better."

"Did I sound that lukewarm about drinking it?"

"Possibly." While he didn't exactly smile, I noted the way his eyes crinkled at the corners as he looked down at me.

I lifted the cup of sake to my lips and allowed myself a cautious sip. The liquid was cold and slightly tangy, and yet at the same time smooth, slipping easily down my throat. Much better than the stuff I'd tried at a few frat parties in college, where, if memory served—some of those parties were now a little hazy in my mind—the sake had been nuked in someone's microwave.

"Good?"

"Yes," I said. "You were right, of course."

Some guys might have tried to rub that fact in. Silas only asked, "Why don't we sit down?"

I nodded, and followed him into the living room area, where a large leather sectional faced the huge window that took up almost one wall. Off to one side was a large metal staircase that clearly led to the second floor.

"It's an impressive place," I said, my gaze moving toward the window. The view outside was so mesmerizing that it was hard to keep from staring at it—even when I had someone as stare-able as Silas Drake seated on the couch next to me. "How long have you lived here?"

"A few years. The central location is useful."

I supposed it would be. Living here in the heart of L.A., he could head out in almost any direction and be there soon enough—or at least as soon as the dreaded Southern California traffic would allow. Even when the freeways were clogged, any local worth their salt knew all the goat paths to get around town. It might take a while, but I knew how to travel all the way from San Marino to Santa Monica without ever getting on a freeway.

Or I used to, back when I wasn't afraid to drive.

"I like it," I said. "It has an interesting energy. And I love the feeling of space."

He seemed to consider me for a long moment, cup of sake held in his hand, although he didn't seem terribly interested in drinking any of it right then. "I'm curious—your family has a great deal of wealth. But your townhouse seems rather modest, in the grand scheme of things."

That it was. Oh, it was certainly adequate for my purposes, and I'd redone the kitchen and the bathrooms before I moved in, but I could have afforded a lot more. That is, my parents could have…and wanted to. "My choice," I replied after I'd taken another swallow of sake. "We had quite the battle about it, actually. My parents wanted to buy me a house in San Marino, someplace where I wouldn't be too far from them. But I didn't want them to do that. I already felt completely beholden to them, knowing that these visions, these episodes, would keep me from ever having a real job, any way to support myself. So I put my foot down. I didn't want a million-dollar house somewhere. And the condo has actually been a very good investment—its last appraisal put it at about fifty thousand more than my parents paid for it, so they can always pass it off as an asset, instead of the place they bought for the daughter who'll never amount to anything."

"Serena." Silas' tone was gentle, but reproving. He set his cup of sake down on the slate and iron coffee table, then moved closer to me. "You shouldn't say such things about yourself."

"It's true, though. I'm not looking for sympathy," I added. "The last thing I want to be is some clichéd poor little rich girl. But don't try to tell me that the accident didn't prevent me from doing what I wanted with my life."

"I wouldn't presume to do that." His hand settled on my knee, and, despite the turn our conversation had taken, a thrill of desire went through me. It felt so good to feel him touch me like that—even through my jeans, I could sense the warmth of his touch. I wanted more of that.

So much more.

"But," he continued, "I also think it's very possible that you were thwarted in your initial goals because you had an even more important destiny before you."

"'Destiny'?" I repeated, not bothering to keep the disbelief from my voice. "You don't really believe in such a thing, do you?"

"Of course I do," he said calmly.

"So you don't believe in free will?"

"That's not what I said."

I raised an eyebrow and took another sip of sake. Even though the liquor was cool, it did have the slightest pleasant burn as it worked its way down my throat.

"You think having a destiny and possessing free will are two mutually exclusive things?" Silas settled against the back of the couch, removing his hand from my knee as he did so.

Was that a sign he was displeased by my question? I couldn't tell for sure, since his expression was almost studiously neutral, as if he didn't want to influence my reply in any way. "I—" I floundered for a second or two, then said, "I suppose I never really thought about it. Destiny to me always seemed like it must be a guiding force, one that puts you on the path it's already chosen for you. How does free will fit into a scenario like that?"

"Because it's actually the choices you make that drive you along that path. The end may be predetermined, but how you get there is entirely your own doing."

He looked so serious and handsome sitting there, his eyes focused on me, his hands folded loosely in his lap. What I really wanted to do was lean over and kiss him again, but I somehow realized that was the wrong thing to do right now. Later…sure. Absolutely.

"That does make me feel a little better about it. I don't really like the idea of some otherworldly force pulling the strings." I took another sip of sake, then put down the cup. "But hey—I think we might be getting a little too serious for a Saturday night."

A smile pulled at his lips. "You might be right. Hungry?"

If asked half an hour earlier, I would have said no. But the liquor seemed to have woken up my stomach, so I nodded. "I could eat something."

"I'll take you to my favorite place."

That sounded promising. Not only because Silas preferred the food there, but also if it was his favorite restaurant, that meant he probably went there frequently, and so they would know him. I doubted he would take a casual date to someplace like that. At least, I hoped that was what the suggestion meant.

We went back out to his truck and emerged into a downpour once we cleared the underground garage. I was beginning to question my failure to bring an umbrella, although there wasn't much I could do about it now. Hopefully, it wouldn't be too long a slog from wherever we'd have to park to get to the restaurant.

We actually didn't travel very far before Silas pulled into a parking structure—maybe seven or eight blocks. In decent weather, we could have walked. Now, though, I was glad we drove.

The restaurant itself didn't look that impressive, not much more than a storefront in a strip mall in Little Tokyo. When I saw the line out the door, though, huddled as close to the wall as possible so people could stay out of the rain, I began to wonder how great an idea this actually was. My leather jacket and thin cashmere sweater wouldn't do that much to keep me warm if I had to stand outside for any length of time.

To my surprise, though, Silas cut past the crowd and went on inside, while I trailed in his wake, wondering exactly what he had planned. He paused at the hostess station, where the girl on duty, who barely looked old enough to be in high school, smiled at him, and said something in Japanese. I was even more surprised when I heard him reply in the same language. Then the girl gathered up two menus and led us through the packed restaurant to a small table set up against the back wall.

As we sat down, I murmured to Silas, "What, do you own part of this place or something?"

His eyes glinted with amusement. "No. I did a favor for the owner a few years ago, however, and so he repays me with a table that's always available—as long as I call or text to give them a heads-up. So I called while you were getting ready."

It was good to have friends in high places. There were several restaurants in Pasadena where my parents could walk in at any hour and get an awesome table. I always struggled with the concept, just because I didn't think it was fair to people who had reservations or who were waiting to be seated that someone else could breeze right past them. Unfortunately, money talked. At least in Silas' case, he was being granted these favors because he'd done a good turn for the owner.

The menu was printed in both English and Japanese. Since my Japanese was nonexistent—just where the heck had Silas learned to speak Japanese, anyway?—I glanced over the English side of the bill of fare.

"The albacore tataki is very good," Silas said. "Do you want to start with that?"

"Sure," I replied. I'd never had tataki, so I had no idea what I was signing up for, but this was not the time for food cowardice. Anyway, I'd had sushi and sashimi, so I wasn't a total novice. All the same, I was probably going to get a combo plate for my main meal, one with some tempura included, just so it wasn't all raw fish, all the time.

We placed our orders, and Silas ordered a bottle of sake as well. Fine by me; if it helped to loosen things up a bit, then maybe I would get to stay over tonight. Was that rushing things? For the old me, maybe. But it had been a very long time, and my body's response to his slightest touch was enough to tell me that I thought this was right. What was the point in delaying things?

Unless he put on the brakes when we got back to his loft, in which case I'd have to go along with his wishes. Right then I was having a hard time reading him. Mixed signals for sure, kissing me one minute, drawing back the next. I still couldn't figure out what had him so conflicted, but I knew better than to pressure him into confidences he wasn't willing to give. I'd learned from Travis that the best way to start a full-blown argument was to keep poking when a man clearly wanted to be left alone.

The place was loud, filled with both couples and large groups out to enjoy their Saturday night, and all of them apparently chattering away all at once. It wasn't the sort of atmosphere that was conducive to sharing confidences, and so Silas and I talked about harmless things—house hunting, and dealing with contractors while making home improvements. The possibility of it being a wet spring. We didn't bring up vampires, or their half-living slaves, or anything we might worry about having overheard.

Despite the care we took to keep the topics light, the conversation moved along easily, and I found myself relaxing, letting myself enjoy the different flavors and textures of the food, the delicate tang of yellowfin, the buttery, comforting taste of the acorn squash tempura. Plates were brought and taken away, and the people at the tables that surrounded ours changed as one group finished their meals and others came in to begin theirs.

At last, though, we were done, and Silas had paid the bill. I'd tried to reach for it when it arrived, but he just shook his head at me. "This was my idea," he said.

"Coming to this restaurant, but not going out tonight," I protested.

"Still. You took care of lunch. Let me take care of this."

Since I didn't want to have an argument there in front of everyone, I subsided. Luckily, the restaurant wasn't overly expensive. Not cheap, either, but it wasn't like he'd had to drop a couple hundred bucks to pay for the two of us.

We emerged from the restaurant to find that the rain had stopped, although the streets and the sidewalks shone slick and wet. A gibbous moon peeked out from a bank of clouds before being obscured again. I stood on the sidewalk and breathed in the damp air, relishing the scent of the rain and the gleaming asphalt. It wasn't even that cold, now that the rain had cleared out.

"Let's walk," I said, and Silas lifted an eyebrow.

"Walk where? We drove here."

"Just walk. Stretch our legs a little. It's safe to walk around here, isn't it?"

"Yes, as long as we don't stray too far off the main streets."

"Okay. Then let's walk for a few blocks, then come back and get the truck. I don't want to waste all this nice fresh air."

He lifted his head into the breeze, inhaled deeply, and nodded. "It's true—you can't even smell any exhaust right now."

"Well, then."

Silas looped his arm in mine and began to head south on Alameda, although he turned onto a smaller street not long afterward—4th Place, read the street sign. However, even though it wasn't the main drag, there were obvious signs of life here. Cars lined the street, and lights glowed from storefronts, even if the stores themselves had been closed for the night.

From a building down toward the end of the side street, right before it jogged to the right, I heard music playing. Not pounding hip-hop, or deafening electronica, but something hard-edged and bluesy, the kind of thing I would have expected to hear coming from a honky-tonk deep in the French Quarter in New Orleans. Then again, this was L.A. You got a little bit of everything here.

"Let's go," I told Silas, tilting my head toward the source of the music.

"To that bar?" he asked, not looking terribly thrilled by my suggestion.

"Sure. The music sounds great."

He hesitated. "We can go look."

It wasn't exactly a rousing response, but at least he hadn't said no. As we approached the bar, I saw that it had a neon sign over the entrance proclaiming it to be the Spirit Lounge. That also sounded very New Orleans-y, and I wondered if the owners might be transplants who wanted to bring a little of their hometown to the City of Angels. The music was louder here, but still not overwhelming. You could sit and listen to it and still be able to hear yourself think.

Silas stopped right outside the door, expression wary. "I'm not sure we should go in."

"Why not?" I asked, trying not to let my annoyance show in my tone. "It's a public place. Otherwise, they wouldn't have left the door open...or be advertising a cover charge."

Because there was a sign next to the door, one that stated the cover was $10 Monday through Thursday and $15 on Friday and Saturday nights. That sounded reasonable enough to me.

"I can pay it," I added. "This was my idea."

But he'd already pulled out his wallet and was handing over a ten and a twenty to the large customer who guarded the front door. Judging by his impressive size and the jet-black hair he had pulled into a ponytail at the back of his neck, I guessed he was probably Samoan.

"Thanks, man," said the bouncer, who stepped out of the way so we could enter the bar.

Luckily, my eyes were already adjusted to darkness, or I would have had a hard time seeing clearly inside the place. Pendant lamps hung overhead, but they'd been dimmed down to almost nothing. Most of the illumination came from the neon Pacifico and Budweiser signs placed above the bar, with the remainder provided by the spotlights focused on the stage. A trio played there, two guys on lead guitar and standing bass who looked like ZZ Top's long-lost brothers, with gray beards and gray hair worn in ponytails, while the drummer was a woman who might have been in her forties. It was hard to tell for sure, due to the lighting, but it seemed to me that her face was weathered in a way you didn't see much in Los Angeles, lines deep as scars bracketing her mouth. The one on lead guitar sang as well, in a hoarse whiskey-roughened voice that suited the blues-tinged music they played. I didn't recognize the song; I didn't need to.

Silas and I went up to the bar. He ordered beers for both of us; this was obviously not the kind of place where you ordered chardonnay or sake. While he was handling the transaction, I shot a surreptitious look around the room. There were four or five small tables, all of them occupied, some by people who looked as if they might have wandered in off Skid Row, and others around my age or a little younger, hipsters who were trying to find the latest cool thing that no one had heard of.

Since there wasn't any place left to sit, Silas and I took our beers and retreated to the far end of the bar, closer to the stage. It was too loud to talk, so I swallowed some beer and listened to the music, to tales of back roads and rundown towns and secrets buried too long. All exotic to me, so far from where we stood now, from anything I'd ever known or experienced.

Then a trio entered the bar, two men and a woman. I noticed them because they looked far too perfect to be in that kind of a dive, the men in long black trench coats, dark-haired, model-handsome. The woman was flaxen blonde, wearing a black patent leather motorcycle jacket, tight jeans, and black over-the-knee boots.

"Someone's out slumming," I murmured to Silas, knowing full well that a lot of people probably would have said the same thing about the two of us.

He shifted so he could see past me…and stiffened, his whole body going rigid. At the same time, the man in the lead of the little group locked eyes with Silas. A small, mocking smile touched the stranger's lips, and he began to walk straight toward us.

Under his breath, Silas told me, "Let me do the talking."

Startled and suddenly off-balance, I stared up at him. "Do you know them?"

"Yes," he replied.

"They're Lucius Montfort's fellow vampires."

CHAPTER FOURTEEN

I FROZE, THE LITTLE BIT OF A BUZZ I'D GOTTEN FROM THE sake at dinner evaporating as if it had never existed. Beside me, Silas was as tense as I'd ever seen him, his jaw set, eyes going to slits as he watched the trio of vampires approach. They sauntered up to us, the leader still wearing that little smirk of a smile, as if he hadn't a care in the world. The three of them stopped a few feet away. To someone who didn't know better, they probably looked like people who'd just spotted a pair of acquaintances and so were going to talk to them. But they certainly weren't friend of ours. Hell, no.

The vampire who stood in front of the other two surveyed me for a moment. His smile broadened. "Aren't you going to introduce me to your friend, Silas?"

"You know very well who she is," Silas replied, voice tight, gaze locked on the otherworldly creatures who stood in front of him.

"Oh, of course." The vampire chuckled and directed his gaze toward me. Unlike Lucius Montfort, whose eyes might have been chips of ice, this particular specimen had eyes that looked—in that bad lighting, anyway—like they'd been carved from jet. "How are you, Ms. Quinn? Since it seems that your friend here doesn't want to make the introductions, allow me to do so. I'm Michael St. John, and this is Tristan McVey and Leticia Carver."

The two other vampires barely inclined their heads. But I could feel their eyes locked on me, cold, hungry. Did I look like a particularly juicy piece of steak to them? I really had no idea how a vampire's mind worked.

"Charmed," I muttered, and Michael laughed.

"Oh, I doubt you are. But—"

"What do you want, St. John?" Silas broke in.

"'Want'?" Michael St. John repeated, as if such a concept was completely foreign to him. "Why should I 'want' anything? As your pretty little psychic said earlier, this is a public place."

My mouth dropped open. He smiled—a smile that revealed the same slightly sharp canines I'd noticed in Lucius Montfort.

"Didn't Silas tell you? Our kind have very good hearing."

"Apparently," I said, forcing myself to stare right back at him, even though I wanted nothing more than to find the back entrance to the bar and run right through it.

Silas crossed his arms. "I'm surprised to see you here, St. John. I would have taken you more for a smooth jazz man."

The female vampire—Leticia Carver—almost appeared as if she wanted to snigger, but then her features smoothed themselves back into supermodel perfection, complete with a blank stare off to some-where in the middle distance. The third vampire, the one called Tristan McVey, didn't seem to react at all, his gaze fixed on us, unblinking.

"Well, we are creatures of the night," Michael St. John said. "So we're out for a little nightlife. Sometimes one must seek out the more esoteric entertainments"—for some reason, his gaze flicked to me for a moment before returning to Silas— "when the usual amusements pall."

"I see," Silas replied. "In which case, we'll leave you to your 'amusements.' If that's all right with you, Serena."

"Oh, it's fine," I said. Yes, I'd only had three swallows of my beer at the most, but right then I thought I might throw up all the lovely sashimi I'd eaten earlier if I tried to drink any more. It wasn't the beer's fault; it was just hard to keep it together with three vampires staring at you if you should have been on the buffet. "I'm ready to go."

Silas put his hand on my arm and guided me past the trio of vampires. I avoided making eye contact, although I couldn't help but hear Michael St. John laugh as the two of us moved away. The whole time, I kept waiting for them to leap out and attack us, but for some reason they didn't move, and instead allowed Silas and me to safely exit the bar and begin walking down the rain-slick sidewalk. A thin, miserable drizzle had started to fall, but I ignored it. Who cared if my hair turned into a frizzed-out mess? All I wanted was to get to Silas' truck and out of there, back to the safety of his loft.

"Are you all right?" he asked in an undertone.

"I'm fine," I replied. "A little shaky, but okay. It was just…they're kind of overwhelming, aren't they?"

"They can be. Usually they don't move in groups like that. Two at a time, possibly, but three?" He shot a quick glance over his shoulder, as if he expected to see them emerge from the club and follow us, but the sidewalks remained empty, the damp clearly driving any casual pedestrians inside.

"So what were they up to?"

"I don't know." In the uncertain light from the street lamps, his expression was hard to read, but I could still see the tension in his jaw, the rigid set of his shoulders. "And that's what bothers me. Perhaps their only motivation was to put us off balance, but—"

He stopped there, his hand clamping down on my arm. Under other circumstances, I might have protested such treatment, but not then. Not when I saw what was ahead of us on the sidewalk.

A group of men, of various heights and ages and builds. I counted nine, maybe ten. It was hard to tell because of the way they were milling around. But then they all stopped, their dead eyes fixed on Silas and me.

And I realized who they were. What they were. A pack of semivives. Maybe all that Lucius Montfort had in his arsenal; I couldn't say for sure. Not that it really mattered at that point. I knew Silas was tough and competent, but I honestly didn't see how he could possibly prevail when he was outnumbered ten to one.

"Get behind me," he said, his tone low but cutting.

"Silas, I—"

"Get behind me."

I did as I was told, even though I still didn't see what he could do to protect me. Not when faced with those odds. No wonder Michael St. John had been smiling at me in such a malevolent way. He and his cohorts could keep their hands clean, because their master had sent his half-living army to take us out.

The semivives advanced. They were a motley group, some in jeans and T-shirts, some in bedraggled-looking business suits. None of them seemed to pay any attention to the drizzle, which had now turned into a light, stinging rain.

Silas faced them, his chin up, shoulders squared. Very slowly, he reached into his pockets and pulled out a pair of long knives. How he'd managed to keep them hidden, when they seemed far too big to be concealed by a set of jeans pockets, I had no idea. The knives glinted in the ghastly pinkish-orange glare of the streetlights, gleaming, deadly.

"You can't win," said the semivive in the lead, a stocky man wearing the remnants of what originally looked to have been a thousand-dollar bespoke business suit.

"Try me," Silas replied.

The semivive ran at him. *Snick!* went the knives, and the possessed man fell in a heap to the ground, his head rolling away from his body. I put my hand to my mouth, but there wasn't enough time for me to even gasp, because, just like the first semivive Silas had dispatched on that Monday which seemed so long ago now, the corpse shivered down into a pale, oily substance before disappearing entirely.

Instead of discouraging the remaining members of the horde, the loss of one of their own just seemed to enrage them. Faces contorted with fury, they rushed at Silas in silence, as if they knew that to cry out would only attract attention. He struck out again with the knives, felling another of them, but there were so many, and he was doing all he could to shield me with his body, so his blows weren't landing as often as he needed them to.

Then a cold hand grabbed me by the arm, and I screamed. At once Silas whirled and began to move toward me, but the pack of semivives crowded around him, blocking him from getting any closer. Even though I knew my own puny strength wasn't enough to prevail against my attacker, I struck at him as best I could, swinging my heavy purse so it connected with his jaw in a heavy crunch, then stomping down on one foot with the high, blocky heel of the boot I was wearing.

I might as well have been attacking a bag filled with sawdust for all the effect my assaults had on the semivive. He began to drag me away from Silas, back toward the bar, where no doubt Michael. St. John and his vampire friends waited. I knew they would take me to Lucius, and what would happen after that, I really didn't want to find out.

But then I heard Silas say, "I'm sorry, Serena."

Protests bubbled to my lips—I wanted to tell him I knew this wasn't his fault, that he was completely outnumbered. This wasn't the movies, after all; I couldn't really expect him to fight off eight or more assailants at once, especially when they seemed to feel no pain whatsoever, would only keep coming unless their heads or limbs were lopped off.

But the words I'd been about to say died before I could speak, because in the next moment, I saw why he had said he was sorry.

A shredding sound, followed by—no, I couldn't believe what I was seeing, but I knew it had to be real, just as vampires were real, just as my crazy visions were apparently real as well. From the back of Silas' jacket emerged a huge pair of black, leathery wings, even as his jacket and T-shirt fell to the sidewalk, looking as if they'd been torn to pieces by a pack of wild dogs. His skin turned dark and leathery as well, features transforming into a nightmarish visage that wasn't quite human or canine, but somewhere in between. Amber eyes glowed from that nightmare of a face.

A scream rose to my lips but got caught somewhere in my throat. Even the semivive holding me seemed taken aback, because he hesitated for a moment, staring at this frighteningly transformed Silas as if he didn't quite know what to do.

That hesitation proved his downfall, because in the next second, my protector had taken to the air, those heavy bat-like wings propelling him upward while at the same time scattering any of the semivives near him like they were ninepins. Then he launched himself toward me and my attacker. One enormous clawed hand came out, talons gleaming like burnished silver. They caught the semivive across the throat, and it fell to the ground, writhing as it melted away into nothingness.

And then Silas—or whatever he was—caught hold of me and bore me away, rising higher and higher until the rooftops of 4th Place were at least a hundred feet below. The needle-like rain drove against my face, and I winced. At the same time, though, I realized I wasn't cold, even though I should have been. His flesh was very warm, so warm that I thought I saw steam from it rise as the raindrops hit his body.

Los Angeles passed below us, and all around us, glittering and surreal in the rain, like something out of a dream. This definitely felt like a dream, or a nightmare. I couldn't decide which, and didn't know if I even wanted to decide. Silas had saved me...but for what? I trembled in his inhuman arms, and wondered what in the world would come next.

We flew among the skyscrapers, his wings propelling us forward, taking us back toward the outskirts of Little Tokyo. I realized then that he must be headed for his loft, to a place I hoped must be a sanctuary from the vampires and their servants.

His building approached, grew larger. Then he touched down, landing on the roof with hardly even a bump. Before I could even begin to struggle to get away from him, his arms opened, releasing me. I staggered a few paces away, then stopped, my breaths coming in huge, panting gasps. Where was I going? There had to be a way down somehow, but….

"Serena."

Reluctantly, I turned toward him. I didn't want to see that—that thing again. Not until I could gather my thoughts, try to figure out just what the hell was going on.

To my surprise, the Silas I knew stood there, not that enormous winged creature. His shirt and jacket were gone, and rain slicked the impressive muscles of his arms and chest. Otherwise, though, he looked entirely the same, like the man I thought he was.

I knew better, though. I'd seen the creature he'd become. He wasn't a man at all.

"I can explain," he said.

"That's going to be one hell of an explanation," I returned, my voice shaking.

"I know that. But please, Serena—come inside so you can get dried off and warm." He extended a hand, but remained where he was, as if he knew that to approach me would only make me retreat.

Did I dare reach out to him, take that proffered hand? The sensible side of my mind was telling me to turn and run, to find the stairs or fire escape or whatever I could to get off that roof, and down to the street so I could call an Uber. Throughout the whole ordeal, my purse had remained looped over one arm. I had my phone, my I.D. I could get away if I wanted to.

But....

There was the not-so-sensible part of me, the part that had visions and believed in vampires. It was telling me I needed to know the truth, whatever that truth might turn out to be.

Time seemed to stand still as I remained where I was, staring at Silas Drake. His eyes pleaded with me, but he remained silent. He knew I had to make this decision on my own.

"All right," I said at last. "I'll come inside. And then you'd better start talking."

Underneath my jacket, my sweater was more or less dry. After blotting my hair with a towel, and doing the same with my damp jeans, I decided I could air-dry the rest of the way, especially since Silas had turned on the gas in the freestanding fireplace in one corner of the living room. Instead of fake logs, it had a flat floor covered with chips of heat-resistant glass. They glowed blue in the dim light of the loft, almost as blue as the gas flames themselves.

Silas had covered himself with a fresh T-shirt but didn't seem too worried about drying his own hair. As I sat at the far end of the sectional, the one nearest the fireplace, he came toward me, a glass of red wine in either hand.

"I thought you could use this."

I took it from him, although I was careful not to touch his fingers. They looked human enough now, the same fingers that had stroked my hair, cupped my face.

Oh, God. I'd kissed him. Multiple times.

Maybe I made some sort of despairing sound. I didn't know. But Silas' mouth tightened, right before he moved past me and settled himself on the sectional as well, although several feet away from where I sat.

"We call ourselves the *gula*," he said, after a long pause.

"Demons?" I asked. I couldn't think of another explanation for the monstrous creature he'd turned into.

"No," he replied immediately, sounding almost offended. "What I suppose you would refer to as gargoyles."

My brain still wasn't working very well. I said the first thing that popped into my head. "Those funny-looking creatures that sit on the roofs of buildings?"

"Not exactly. Those representations aren't very accurate. We are...." He stopped there and swirled the wine in his glass for a moment, all the while staring down into it as if he could divine the future in the deep, garnet-colored liquid. "We're a breed of shape-shifters."

"Like werewolves?" After all, if vampires existed, why not werewolves? And while we were at it, we could throw in a couple of reanimated mummies and some swamp creatures, too. Then again, swamps were in fairly short supply in Southern California. But mummies would definitely fit in our dry climate, the current rain notwithstanding. My brain was running away with itself, trying to focus on anything except the impossible transformation I'd just witnessed.

"No. Werewolves are a legend, nothing more. And in that legend, one isn't born a werewolf, but has to be bitten by one in order to turn. We *gula* are born this way."

For the first time, I lifted my wine glass to my lips and took a large swallow. I needed the alcohol if I was going to sit there and continue to listen to this. "So the world is full of people who look like people but aren't? They're gargoyles?"

"Unfortunately, no. There are very few of us." His gaze slipped past me, to the blue-hued dancing flames in the fireplace. Even in the dim lighting, I could see the sadness in his dark eyes.

As shocked and scared and worried as I was by the events of the past hour, I couldn't help but experience a twinge of compassion at the sorrow in his expression. In fact, I had to fight back the urge to put down my wine glass and go to Silas, slip a comforting arm around him.

Which was patently crazy.

"Why so few of you?"

Another swirl of the wine within his glass. This time he did take a drink, although a much smaller one than what I'd just swallowed. "We don't reproduce easily." He met my gaze and paused, as if steeling himself to make the necessary revelations. "The *gula* are only male. Our mothers are all human. Even when conception occurs, and the child is male, there is only a ten-percent chance—give or take—that the child will be *gula*. So you see, we don't have much chance of filling the world with more of our kind."

I had to sit there and absorb those words for a moment. It did make sense why there weren't more of these gargoyles. *Gula*, I reminded myself. Then something Silas had said finally sank in. Voice tight, I asked, "So you always have to be with human women? Is that why you were cozying up to me?"

"No." He set down his wine glass and moved closer, while I did my best to stay where I was and not shrink away from him, even though my first instinct was to get up from that couch and run like hell. "In fact, I knew I shouldn't get involved with you. You are my charge, the one person in the world I must protect above all others. By allowing my emotions to complicate things, I could very well have compromised your safety."

"So that's why you were trying so hard to stay away from me." His words helped me to relax, but only a little. Because he hadn't stayed away, had he? In fact, tonight's mishaps only proved that my safety had been put in jeopardy. Silas-the-bodyguard probably would have made sure I stayed far away from downtown. But Silas-the-sort-of-boyfriend had caved to my request.

"Yes. I had to confess to the Conclave—those who assigned me to you in the first place—that I had not been able to keep my feelings separate from the matter at hand. Now they are trying to decide whether to remove me from this duty and assign someone else to watch over you."

He related this information with a face that was nearly expressionless, but I saw the way he pulled in a breath and wouldn't quite look at me. Clearly, I was more than a little conflicted on the matter, because the mere thought of having someone else as my bodyguard made my body clench slightly. I didn't want someone else. I wanted Silas, hard as it was to admit such a thing to myself.

"Can they do that?"

"Of course. They're the Conclave. They were the ones who gave me this assignment in the first place, and so they have the ultimate authority in deciding what will happen next."

"Well, they can't do that!" I protested. "Where are they? I can go to them, tell them that you have to stay with me—"

"Serena." His voice was calm, but now it also sounded strangely gentle, as if he'd recognized from my heated words that I wasn't quite as frightened by him as I had been not even a half hour earlier. "I'm afraid that's impossible. For one thing, the Conclave is located in Paris."

"Paris?" I replied, the word coming out as not much more than an indignant squeak. "Why Paris?"

"All those gargoyles on Notre Dame," he said, a hint of a smile playing around his mouth.

I refused to be taken in by that smile. If I looked at his lips for too long, I knew I'd be in a lot of trouble. "I thought you said you weren't that kind of gargoyle."

"No, we're not, but we do enjoy our little jokes."

"So when will you know what they've decided?"

"Soon." That bit of a smile was gone now, his expression brooding. "They will not be pleased when I make my report as to what happened tonight."

No, I supposed they wouldn't. The whole thing had been pretty much a shitshow from the time Silas and I left the sushi restaurant. The only bright point was that the street had been deserted when the semivives attacked. Angelenos hated rain, and everyone had taken refuge inside. There hadn't been any spectators to see the melee on 4th Place, or witnesses to Silas' transformation. Maybe some of the stores had security cameras, but those would have been focused on shop windows and doors, not the middle of the sidewalk. And even if those cameras had been aimed toward the sidewalks or the street, with the dark and the rain, how much could they have really caught on tape?

"Still," I told him, "no harm, no foul. I'm fine, and I doubt your Conclave will care too much whether or not you forcibly retired a few of Lucius Montfort's semivives. No one saw anything."

"That we know of," Silas said darkly. "Just because that one street was empty doesn't mean there might not have been witnesses the next street over. A winged monster taking to the sky isn't the sort of thing that happens every day, even in Los Angeles."

I couldn't argue with that. Then again, I knew if I'd seen such a thing, I would have thought someone was filming a movie or TV show. Location shoots happened on a daily basis in various places around the Southland. Most people probably would have guessed the same thing. It was a lot easier to believe you were getting a glimpse at some practical special effects rather than actually witnessing a legendary creature flying overhead.

But I wasn't sure if I could convince Silas of that argument, so I lifted my wine, took a sip, then said, "True, but with that rain coming down, it would have been hard to see anything all that clearly. Especially once we were up above the buildings. In my experience, most people don't spend a lot of time looking up. They're focused on what's ahead of them."

"I hope you're right. We do our best not to transform in populated areas. It's far too great a risk. But I didn't have much of a choice."

"No, you didn't. And you need to tell your Conclave that." I set down my wine glass, then slanted a look up at him through my lashes. "So, your…transformations…are completely voluntary?"

"Not completely. We have to train to be able to control them. But we're not allowed to live and move amongst you until we're absolutely certain there won't be any mishaps. Even then, there have been a few incidents when one of us is under duress and loses control. That's very rare, though."

"So where do you live? That is, those of you who aren't out living amongst us mere mortals."

Silas didn't exactly sigh, but he did release a breath, as if slightly annoyed by my remark. "The *gula* are as mortal as you, Serena. Different, but mortal. We're born and live and die, just like anyone else. We're not vampires. Our lifespans are much the same as yours. As for your other question, we have several compounds where we grow up and train to use our abilities. The largest, and oldest, is in the countryside outside Paris. One is on the East Coast, in Virginia. And there is another here in California, but in the northern part of the state, outside Humboldt."

Humboldt sounded like a good place to put it. That part of northern California wasn't nearly as populated as it was down here in SoCal, and besides, from what I'd heard, the residents of Humboldt and its environs spent so much time cultivating and smoking weed that if they did see any gargoyles flying around the countryside, they'd probably just chalk up the vision to getting some bad bud that week.

"Where are *you* from?" I asked.

"Here in California, just like you." His dark eyes glinted in the odd bluish reflection from the fireplace. Or at least, I hoped it was only a reflection. But it had to be. When he transformed, his eyes were a dark, baleful amber. "In general, we're given assignments near our home regions. If you had been from New York, for example, then you would have been assigned someone from the Virginia compound."

"But you have this loft," I said. "And you said you'd lived here for several years. So how could you have come from the Humboldt compound?"

"I was assigned to you three years ago, as soon as we learned of your visions. You only met me recently, because it wasn't until then that it was required for me to do anything but watch over you."

I had to let that remark sink in for a moment. So, ever since my accident and the visions that had haunted me after I came out of my coma, Silas had been there, watching, waiting. It was a distinctly strange feeling, realizing that all the time I'd felt so desperately alone, I really hadn't been. He had always been looking out for me, even if I hadn't known about his presence in my life.

An uncomfortable silence filled the room. I reached for my glass of wine and drank again, noting that it was already more than half gone. Would Silas refill it? I wasn't sure whether a single glass of wine was enough to help me cope with everything I'd just heard.

What I'd just seen.

"This troubles you."

"Of course it troubles me," I retorted. "It's just a little disturbing to realize you've been stalking me for the last three years, and I knew nothing about it! I never saw you, never got a single clue that this was going on."

"It was not stalking," he said, still in that too-calm tone of voice. But I saw how the fingers of his left hand clenched on his knee, as if he did so to keep himself from responding in anger. "I was assigned to you to protect you. Only when you went out into the world, understand. You were safe when you were home, as I've told you. I never looked inside your condo, never pried into your emails or phone calls."

"*Could* you have?" Somehow that notion annoyed me more than anything else he'd revealed so far.

"I myself couldn't, because technology isn't my strong suit. But yes, someone in our group could have, if they thought it was necessary to preserve your safety."

Wonderful. Was I supposed to feel honored that he and his masters had shown such forbearance?

"Look, Serena," he said, "I understand that this is a lot to take in, especially coming after everything you've experienced tonight. Maybe it's better if I take you home."

"No," I said immediately, then stopped. Where the hell had that come from?

Clearly, Silas was just as confused, because his brow wrinkled as he looked over at me. "I would think you'd want to go home."

Surely that was the sensible thing to do. I should go home, climb into my warmest jammies, and burrow into bed and forget this all happened. For some reason, though, I didn't want to do that. Going home and hiding was the coward's way of coping with all this. I'd spent the last three years hiding. Was I all right with doing that for the rest of my life?

"I don't want to go home," I said, then paused again. What *did* I want? To figure out what I really thought about him. What I really felt about him. The longer we'd sat there, the more the creature he'd transformed into had begun to fade from my thoughts. This was Silas with me, here, now. He didn't look any different from the man I'd become increasingly attracted to. When I'd asked him to take me to his loft, in the back of my mind I'd hoped I might spend the night here. Did I still want him?

Only one way to find out.

I looked him in the eyes and said, "I want you to kiss me, Silas."

CHAPTER FIFTEEN

He started, then went very still. When he spoke, his voice was so quiet that I had to strain to hear his words. "Are you certain?"

Of course I wasn't. Less than half an hour earlier, I'd seen him transform into a demonic-looking creature with enormous bat wings. But the man I saw before me now, the man who gazed into my face with such trepidation—I had kissed him before. All I'd seen was another aspect of him. He was still Silas. I needed to believe that.

"I will be in a minute," I replied.

Gingerly, as if he thought I was a soap bubble he might break, he reached out to touch my cheek. Just a feather of a caress, so light I almost could have imagined it, but even that brief touch was enough to make my breathing quicken, my heart begin to pound.

Oh, yes, I wanted him.

We both leaned in at the same time, mouths touching, then opening. He tasted of the wine we'd been drinking, nothing more. The scent of his skin was warm, human. His hair brushed against my face, and I shivered.

"Are you still cold?" he whispered.

I shook my head. "Not now."

That must have been enough reassurance, because then he was kissing me even more deeply, pressing me down onto the leather of the couch, the weight of his body on mine. It was my turn to tangle my hands in his hair, to press myself against him, feeling his warmth, the reassuring solidity of him. His hand slid up under my sweater, then pressed flat against my stomach. I loved the warmth of his fingers, but I didn't want him to stop there. I shifted slightly, causing his hand to move upward, and then he was closing on my breast—but only for a second. He went still, and he murmured again, "Are you sure, Serena?"

"Yes, Silas," I replied. "I've never been more sure of anything."

He needed no more reassurance after that— obviously, because he grasped my sweater and pulled it up and over my head, then undid the front clasp of my bra. It slid away, revealing me to him.

Scars and all. They'd had to remove my spleen after the accident, and although I was fair-skinned enough that I didn't scar too badly, the T-shaped incision lines on my stomach would be there until the day I died.

I looked up into his face, into those dark, depthless eyes. "I wish I could be perfect for you."

"You are perfect, my splendid, brave Serena," he said. "Wear your scars as medals, because they prove that you survived a great battle."

And then his mouth closed on my breast, suckling, and I gasped and closed my eyes. It had been so long, *too* long—and yet I was fiercely glad I hadn't been with anyone since Travis, hadn't thrown myself away on casual hook-ups to fill the emptiness of my days. Now I could give myself to Silas wholly, without regrets, knowing there had been a real and true reason why I'd waited.

I didn't know who started fumbling with whose jeans first, only that in the next few seconds they'd been pulled off, along with boots and socks and everything else in the way. My fingers wrapped around him, feeling the size and the heaviness of his shaft, of how ready he was for me, even as he reached down to stroke me.

Oh, God, that was amazing. I'd relieved my own tension from time to time, when the pressure had built up enough, but that couldn't compare to the way Silas was touching me now, the way those strong fingers seemed to know exactly what to do. The heat was building in me, and I wondered if he was going to make me come right then and there. Not that I would mind, but usually it took a little more effort than that.

Ah, yes, *there.* I convulsed against him, body spasming as he stroked me to orgasm and I held on to him, having to abandon his cock for a moment while I clung to him with both hands, letting the climax flow through me, the world spinning around and around. He held me, his lips pressed against my neck, kissing me until I was able to return to myself.

"Good?" he asked.

"Amazing. Where—?" I cut myself off there. Did I really want to know what his past sexual experiences had been? Shouldn't it be enough for the two of us to be here now?

Silas seemed to guess where I'd been going with that abortive question, however, because he kissed me again before saying, "We're not encouraged to have casual sexual relations. Too many complications. So…." He didn't say anything more; he didn't have to.

The words popped out anyway. "You're a virgin?"

"Does that bother you?"

Did it? I only had to ponder the issue for a few seconds before I decided that no, it really didn't. If nothing else, the way he'd touched me just a minute earlier seemed to prove that he knew what he was doing. And I thought I liked the idea of being his first…for everything.

"Not at all," I replied. I reached down and took him in my hand again, running my fingers up and down his shaft. He moaned, his eyes closing, and I shifted so we were lying side by side on the couch. From there it seemed the most natural thing in the world to bend down and take him in my mouth, to taste the faint saltiness of his sweat, to breathe in his scent. Oh, yes, he was human enough then, everything that I needed.

His breath quickened, but I kept at it slow and steady, wanting to pleasure him for as long as I could without actually getting him off. But he was getting harder and harder, and I knew I'd have to stop. Not a problem, because as soon as I let go of his shaft, I moved so I was straddling him, letting him plunge into me.

As I did so, however, his eyes flared open in alarm. "Protection—"

"No worries," I said sweetly, rocking my hips so I could bring him even deeper inside me. Ah, sweet lord, that was amazing. Big, but in a delicious way so he filled me perfectly. "I have an IUD. It's all good."

That information obviously was enough to satisfy him, because afterward I could feel the way the tension went out of his body, how he focused on moving with me, slowly at first, then faster, deeper, harder. This time I was the one with the eyes closed, my entire being seeming to close down to this one moment, this one overwhelming set of sensations.

And then he let out a groan as he spasmed into me, the warmth of his seed filling my very center. I clung to his arms as he let go, because then it was my turn, this orgasm harder, more intense than the last, carrying me with it, flooding through every limb. Our mingled cries echoed against the cement walls of the loft, until I didn't have the strength remain on top of him anymore and collapsed at his side, the leather of the sofa sticking slightly to my sweat-dampened skin.

For a long time, neither of us said anything. I was content to lie there next to him, to listen as his breathing gradually quieted. His hand passed over my hair. "Serena, my love," he whispered.

Was that my heart skipping a beat? *Calm down,* I told myself. *He just called you "my love." He didn't come right out and say he loved you.*

Still....

I snuggled against him, knowing that soon enough we'd need to get up and get ourselves sorted out. For now, though, I just wanted to feel his body, feel that smooth skin and the heavy muscles beneath it. "I hope I'm not going to get you in trouble. Because of that 'casual sexual relations' thing."

His eyes opened, held mine. "This wasn't casual. At least, not for me."

"Or for me," I told him. "This was probably the least casual thing I've ever done."

His hand reached out, catching a lock of hair. He wrapped it around his finger, the gesture almost reverent. "I always knew I would wait until the match of my heart entered my life. I love you, Serena."

This time I knew my heart skipped a beat. "I love you, Silas," I whispered. "But what do we do now?"

"Whatever we must," he replied.

Afterward, he led me up to his bedroom. Like the rest of the loft, it was spare, industrial, with exposed pipes overhead, although the bed itself was luxurious, king size, with a heavy down coverlet. It felt amazing to sink down into that bed, to pull the warm comforter over us before we made love again, this time more slowly, savoring each moment, each sigh, each taste.

And then I fell asleep in his arms, his heavy, steady heartbeat guiding me into a deep, dreamless slumber. I realized that I'd never asked him if he needed to sleep as well....

That question seemed to be answered, though, when I awoke early the next morning and saw him still apparently passed out next to me, his hair a shaggy mess on his pillow, his lashes a sooty fringe against his cheeks. A wave of fierce tenderness went over me then as I gazed at him, at the proud profile and scruff of dark hair on his cheeks and chin.

I'd never felt this way before.

About anyone.

How crazy was that? How insane was it that I apparently didn't have a problem with him being a shape-shifting monster?

No, not a monster, I corrected myself. *Something different, something extraordinary. Lucius Montfort and his vampires and semivives—they're the monsters, even if they look human.*

Silas stirred, then rolled over on his side. His eyes opened, met mine.

"Good morning," I said.

He smiled, looking drowsy and relaxed and oh, so sexy. "Good morning."

"It's still raining."

His gaze moved from me to the filtered, gray-tinged light coming through the blinds. "So it is. A good morning for staying in."

That sounded like a wonderful idea to me. To be here with him, enjoying some of the afterglow from the night before…I never wanted to go home.

"You don't have anything important on the docket today?"

He propped himself up on his elbows so he could look down at me. "Only you."

Who wouldn't want to hear something like that? I sat up, too, although I hugged the covers against my breasts. It was one thing to be wild and abandoned in the depths of the night, when everything was communicated by a touch, a caress, the sweetness of a shared kiss. Now, though, I could feel my self-consciousness begin to creep back, even if Silas had told me that he didn't mind my scars.

Clearly, he noticed, because he glanced away. Something about his posture became more business-like, his back and shoulders straighter. He sat up all the way, and pushed himself out of bed, thus treating me to an enticing view of his sculpted thighs and butt. Still facing the wall, he said, "Do you regret this?"

Oh, damn, talk about giving the wrong impression. I got up, too, forced myself to ignore my nakedness. I had to make sure he knew this was about me, not him. "No, of course I don't. If I hadn't wanted to be with you, I would have stopped things last night before they got out of hand."

He stood there quietly, though, and didn't respond. Neither would he look at me.

A crazy idea began to take shape in my mind. I had to convince him that I did want him…all of him.

"Silas, I want you to shift. To change."

This time he did turn in my direction, his expression shocked. "What?"

"Show me. Last night I told you I loved you. I want you to know that I meant it. I'm not afraid."

"Serena, this isn't necessary—"

"I think it is. Please."

He hesitated for so long that I was sure he would say no, would find some other reason to protest. But then his shoulders squared, and he walked away from the bed, into the open part of the room.

Of course. He'd need the space to accommodate those wings of his.

I saw him take a breath, followed by another. And then his skin darkened, changed texture. The wings grew from his back, huge, nearly touching the ceiling. His features shifted, the nose becoming larger, hooked, his lips thinning. And then his dark eyes shifted to shimmering coppery orange, the pupils elongating at the same time.

Even though I'd asked him to do this, I still experienced a stab of fear. He looked so much more real now than he had last night. The darkness had shadowed him, had hidden some of the details that were now revealed in the light of day. It took everything I had to remain standing where I was, to not back away. But I couldn't. I had to accept this—no, I couldn't call him a creature. He was still Silas, no matter what he looked like.

"Is this what you wanted?"

His voice was deeper, harsher. A different set of vocal chords, a larger chest. But the intonation was still his.

"Yes," I said. "This was what I wanted."

I took a step toward him, then another. He didn't move, only stood there, watching me with those alien eyes.

Not completely alien. I could still see Silas in there somewhere.

A few more breaths, and I paused directly in front of him. It was the strangest thing in the world, to stand in front of him naked, although my hair had fallen over my breasts, partially obscuring them. Last night when he transformed, he had broken out of his shirt and jacket but not his pants, wasn't completely revealed as he was now. Definitely male.

I made myself take that final step, pressed my naked body against his. A shudder went through him. "Serena—"

"Kiss me, Silas. Kiss me as you are now."

Dead silence, except the soft patter of the rain outside the window. What would be worse—if he denied me, or if he said yes? I'd been brave up until that moment, but my body was tense, as if it didn't know if it was prepared for what I'd just gotten it into.

Then his arms, corded with muscle, went around me, and he was pulling me close, was bending his head so he could claim my mouth with his. He tasted the same, although his tongue was shaped differently, longer, more pointed. A few impure thoughts crossed my mind as to what he might do with that tongue in the future, and a delicious shiver went through me.

And oh, I could feel him hardening against me, his thick cock pressing against my belly. A wave of desire so intense it was almost cramping in its urgency flowed over me, and I pushed myself against him, knowing I wanted that too, wanted him to make love to me this way, just so he would know that I didn't care, that he was everything I needed, no matter what form he took.

He seemed to understand, because he made a growling sound deep in his throat, right before he lifted me from the wooden floor and supported me with his arms as he pushed himself deep inside. I cried out, clinging to him, hanging on as he thrust in and out, going deeper, filling me, his great wings steadying the two of us as we came together in a joining even more intense than our lovemaking from the night before.

I couldn't help screaming as I came. It was a primal sound ripped from my throat, something I couldn't hold back, even as my body shook with the intensity of an orgasm that thundered through me with the force of a shockwave. A few seconds later, he climaxed as well, his heat exploding into my core. I couldn't do anything except hold on to him, and let him hold on to me, until at last he staggered over to the bed and laid me down on it. Almost immediately afterward, he became the Silas I'd first met, human, his face sheened with sweat, his breathing labored.

"My God," he said at last, right before he collapsed on the bed next to me.

I reached out with my left hand and took his right. His fingers tightened on mine. "So that was okay?"

"So much more than okay." He pushed himself up to a sitting position, then leaned over so he could brush a lock of hair away from my face. "I never imagined—I never thought—"

I rolled onto my side so I was looking up at him. "Never thought what?"

"Never thought that you…." The words trailed off. His hand still lingered on my hair, and he ran his fingers through its length, as if by doing so, he could gather the courage to continue the sentence. "Yesterday you said you thought it was stalkerish for me to be watching you these past three years. In my heart, I never saw it that way. You needed to be protected. But as time went on, I realized my feelings for you might have been something more than merely taking pride in carrying out my duty. It made me happy to see you walking in the sunshine, the wind blowing in your hair, to see you smile at one of your Uber drivers or wave goodbye to your friend Candace. I even...."

"You even what?" I asked softly. These revelations didn't bother me as much as maybe they should have, because I knew he'd only stepped in, had only approached, when Lucius Montfort sent one of his minions to attack me.

"I even hoped that if I ever did have the chance to speak to you, maybe we could learn to be friends. Or more." He stopped there and trailed his fingers along my cheek, and I closed my eyes at the tender brush of skin against skin. "It was a foolish dream, or so I thought. But in all that time, never did I think that you would be willing to be with me as you just were now. It is a very rare thing."

"Really?" I pushed myself up from my elbow so I was upright next to him. "I'd think that the women who are with the other *gula* would want to accept that part of them as well."

"Yes, you might think that, but it does not happen very often. Or so I've been told."

I was quiet then, gladder than ever that I'd been able to find that courage within myself. And, lest I sound too noble, the sex had been mind-blowing.

Those women who were with the other *gula* didn't know what they were missing.

"Silas," I began, then paused. His eyebrows went up, as though encouraging me to continue. "Tell me something about these women, about how all this works. What about your parents? Do you have any siblings?"

"How it works? That depends."

"Depends on what?"

"Depends on whether the women who are with us can bear to live with so many alterations in their lives. They have to leave everything behind—family, friends, career—to stay at one of our settlements. Some can only manage a few years before they go back to their lives."

"What happens then?"

He gave me a sad smile. "We have to remove their memories of their time with us, of our very existence. We can't let the world know anything about us. So...."

"How on earth do you do that?" I asked, aghast. I could just begin to understand the need for such secrecy, but my mind and soul rebelled against it. "Would you do the same thing to me?"

"If I must. Or rather, the task wouldn't fall on me. The Conclave handles such things. But not all relationships between humans and *gula* end in such a way. My parents are still together, and live in the compound outside Humboldt. They're happy. But I didn't want to lie and tell you that these things always go perfectly. And then there are the children."

Maybe we were getting ahead of ourselves when it came to that sort of thing. After all, Silas and I had been intimate for less than twelve hours. Still, I needed to know what I was letting myself in for. "What about the children?"

"I mentioned that it's difficult for humans and *gula* to conceive at all, and even when conception happens, only a small percentage of male children turn out to be shape-shifters. But when children are born who are completely human, they can't remain part of the community. Our secret is too important to be trusted to those who have no true vested interest in keeping it. So all the girl children, and the boys who aren't *gula*, are sent away to be adopted."

I stared at him, open-mouthed. "That's—that's inhuman."

"No, it's necessary. I know it's difficult for an outsider to understand. They are all sent to loving homes. In most cases, they will have better lives than they would if they'd remained in a *gula* compound. Life there is comfortable, but certainly not luxurious."

Was I really hearing this? Shaken, I got up from the bed and started looking around for my discarded clothing, just before I remembered that it was all lying on the floor downstairs in the living room.

"Here," Silas said. He went over to the dresser on the other side of the room and pulled out a pair of boxer briefs and a T-shirt, then brought them to me. "Use these."

"Thanks." I climbed into the underpants, which just barely fit, and pulled the T-shirt over my head. While I was doing that, Silas had apparently gotten another set out for himself, since he was more or less dressed by the time I'd finished pushing all my hair through the crew neckline of my borrowed shirt. He stood by the window, but he wasn't looking outside. His gaze was fixed on me, his expression pleading.

"I know this is difficult to understand. And it must sound like too much, after everything we went through yesterday. I would have had this conversation with you at some point, only not so soon."

"It's all right," I said, even though I really didn't know if it was or not. "I'm glad you told me."

It seemed my reply wasn't terribly convincing, because he crossed his arms, his eyes narrowing slightly. "Are you?"

What could I say? If nothing else, I thought it was probably a little premature to be worrying about a future and children. Yes, we'd slept together…multiple times…and so our relationship would be forever altered. He'd told me he loved me, and I'd told him the same. I knew I did love him, but I'd leaped without looking, without thinking about what I might be getting myself into.

"Yes," I said firmly. "I'm not saying we shouldn't talk about it more at some point, but right now we have Lucius Montfort and his vampires to worry about."

"True." His expression remained troubled, though, and so I went to him and put my arms around his waist.

"I meant everything I said, everything I did," I told him. "You have to believe that. What you've just told me…well…that's a lot to absorb all at once. But it's not going to stop me from loving you, Silas. Not one bit."

For the first time, his mouth lifted slightly. He bent so he could press his lips to the top of my head, bestowing the lightest and sweetest of kisses there. "I'm glad, Serena. More glad than I can say. And now…."

"'Now'?" I repeated.

He pulled away just a little so he could look down at me and smile. "Now, let me make you breakfast."

CHAPTER SIXTEEN

WHICH HE DID, FIRST BREWING UP A POT OF DELICIOUS Italian roast, and then making a simple but tasty breakfast of buttery scrambled eggs and whole wheat toast made of bread so delicious, I asked him if he'd baked it himself.

"No, I can't take credit for that," he replied. "There's a bakery over on 3rd Street that makes it."

"Well, it's amazing."

"Do you want me to put another slice in for you?"

"Better not. Those carbs will sneak up on you."

That comment earned me a shake of the head. "Serena, I've seen you naked. I don't think you need to worry about carbs."

"I knew you were a man after my own heart."

He grinned and kissed me, and after that we went upstairs and shared the large shower with its rain-shower head and built-in tiled seats. In fact, we ended up on one of those seats, with me straddling him as he plunged into me once again. The whole time, though, I couldn't help but be inwardly grateful for my IUD. There were complications ahead, complications we would have to address, but for right now I wouldn't have to worry about the whole *gula* baby thing. Yes, Silas had told me that it was harder for his kind to reproduce than it was for normal humans, but I still didn't want to take any chances.

After we got out of the shower and had dried off—and I'd climbed back into my old clothes, since I didn't have anything else to change into—I pulled my phone out of my purse, just to make sure I hadn't missed any important calls or texts. There was only one voicemail, though, from my mother.

I sighed, wondering if I should put off listening to it until I was back home. As much as I really didn't feel like going back to Pasadena, Silas felt it was best, and so he was going to drive me home that afternoon. My being out for one night was enough of a break from my routine, but if I was gone for too long, someone was bound to notice.

But he was on his computer, checking what he called his daily briefing from the Conclave. I figured I might as well listen to the message from my mother. She should still be up in Santa Barbara, which meant she couldn't be calling about anything too terribly disruptive, like trying to get me to come over for Sunday dinner that evening.

It turned out she only wanted to talk about Jackson's announcement, to tell me that he really had wanted to call me and inform me about his presidential run himself, but that his schedule had gotten away from him.

Yeah, right. He'd had time to call my mother, and I would've bet the fifty-odd bucks in my wallet that he'd probably called Vanessa as well, but, as usual, I was the afterthought.

A week ago, such an omission would have really bothered me, as much as I would have tried to hide it, since leaving me out of those calls just reinforced my belief that I was the family outcast. Now, though, all I could do was give a mental shrug. What with lurking vampires and attacking semivives and falling in love with a guy who just happened to be a gargoyle—sorry, *gula*—worrying about any real or perceived slights from my brother wasn't too high on my list of priorities.

My mother ended the call by saying she would be back in San Marino late Monday, and that she would try to get in touch with me once she was home. Whether her words were a promise or a threat, I didn't know. And right then, I didn't much care.

Silas came downstairs from the office area up on the second floor. He was frowning, brows pulled together and mouth tight. As I caught his gaze, I hoped his expression would lighten somewhat, but if anything, he appeared even more brooding.

"What's wrong?" I asked.

"The members of the Conclave aren't very happy about my involvement with you. They've summoned me to discuss the matter with them in person."

"In person?" I repeated blankly, setting my phone down on the sofa next to me. "You mean they expect you to go to *Paris?*"

"Yes."

That didn't sound good at all. I worried for Silas, for what the people in this Conclave might say to him. And I worried about what I would do, left on my own in Pasadena without him to watch out for me. Even if he caught the first flight out of LAX and didn't linger in France, he would still have to be gone at least two days, maybe more. It was that concern I decided to voice, since I already knew him well enough that I guessed he wasn't overly concerned as to his own fate.

"But that would leave me here without a protector, wouldn't it?"

"No. They would never risk such a thing. Emanuel, one of the Humboldt group, is already here in Southern California and ready to take over for me. You won't see him, of course, but he'll be here to watch over you and make sure Lucius Montfort doesn't try anything. Don't worry—Emanuel is very capable. You'll be safe. "

Was that supposed to be reassuring? I didn't want a substitute, no matter how "capable" he might be. I wanted Silas. But I had a feeling my thoughts and wishes didn't matter too much here. "Are you—are you in much trouble? I mean, it's not like the military or something, is it? I don't want to be responsible for a dishonorable discharge."

At my remark, he almost smiled, then came to me and folded me into his arms. He smelled clean and reassuring, some of the scent from the lemongrass soap he'd used still lingering on his skin. "No, it's not like that at all. It's more—they'll want to know how serious things are between you and me. They'll want to know why I put you at risk."

"You didn't put me at risk," I protested. "For one thing, it was my idea to come down here."

"I could have said no."

"And sounded like a jerk. So it wasn't your fault."

"I'm afraid they probably won't see it that way."

Of course not. I had no idea who was on this Conclave, but I envisioned a bunch of bitter older *gula* who'd either never hooked up at all, or whose lady loves had bailed out because they couldn't handle living such an isolated existence. But then, I realized I might one day be one of those women. Sure, I liked to complain about my family, but I also knew it would be hard for me to walk away from all of them, and Candace, and Brian and Lewis, and the small number of people I could count as part of my circle.

I looked up at Silas. His expression wasn't quite as somber as it had been when he descended the stairs, but he also didn't appear exactly cheerful, either. This might not have been the right time to ask the question, but I couldn't leave it hanging out there, not when he was being summoned to Paris to discuss this very topic.

"So...how serious are we?"

His arms tightened around me. "That depends on you, Serena. I know my feelings. But I also know we haven't been together for very long. These are the kinds of decisions that should only be made after a good deal of deliberation."

He might have been right, but I wished he hadn't made the situation sound so...clinical. "And I know how I feel about you. I know I've never felt this way about anyone else. So I think I could get used living in the compound in Humboldt, even if that pin in my leg might complain about the damp."

I'd said the last bit of that remark with a slightly teasing tone to my voice, just to show him that I didn't want to be all doom and gloom about things. He didn't smile, however, but said, "You would have to deal with a good deal more than damp, which is why we shouldn't have to make this decision now. And I plan to tell the Conclave that."

Even though I knew I wanted to be with Silas, I couldn't help being somewhat relieved by his words. He wasn't like any other man I'd ever known, and sex with him was spectacular, but even so, this wasn't the sort of thing to rush into. We needed more time to get used to each other.

"How do you think they'll respond?"

"I don't know for sure. They may say that my judgment when it comes to you is impaired, and that I can't be your guardian anymore. They may demand that you go live up there if you and I continue to be...involved." His shoulders lifted slightly, even though he still held me in his arms. "It's hard to say for sure, simply because this situation doesn't have any precedent. The jaded part of me thinks they will probably urge me to take you to Humboldt, just because that way you'll be safely ensconced in the community there, and therefore far less easy prey for Lucius Montfort."

That thought hadn't even occurred to me, but it made sense. If Silas and I were going to be together anyway, better to make the move in the near future, removing me from any further attempts on my life... and also having me handily nearby so I could share my visions with the *gula* community. Would those visions change once I was there? Most of my visions so far had involved situations and scenarios that took place somewhere nearby. It wasn't as if I'd had visions of Russia, or Africa, or even New York City. If locations could be identified, they were always some-place in the greater Los Angeles area.

"Well, I can think of worse fates than living with you in Northern California," I said. "Especially if they'll let us slip out from time to time and go on tours of wine country."

"Serena, this isn't a joke."

"I'm not joking." I went on my tiptoes so I could give him a quick kiss on the lips. "I want you to know that as long as I'm with you, where I am doesn't mat-ter so much."

He held me close then, his lips touching the top of my head. "You continue to amaze me, Serena."

"I do my best."

A chuckle, and then he let go of me so he could step back a pace. "I know you do. But for now, I need to take you home. I have to be in Paris by this evening."

"Are you flying, or...." I let the words trail off and sent a significant look toward his upper back, where his gargoyle wings would sprout.

"My wings can't carry me nearly that far. In a pinch, I might be able to fly to Northern California, but traveling overseas is out of the question. I'll catch the earliest flight I can to Paris. The Conclave will send a car for me that will take me to the settlement outside the city."

"How…ordinary."

"We must always utilize the most useful tools."

I supposed that made sense. Silas was a shape-shifter from a race I didn't even know existed before last night, but even he had to obey the laws of physics…up to a point. I assumed there must be a rational, scientific explanation for how he was able to alter his entire form and turn into a completely different creature, but I sure as hell didn't know what it might be. But even the supernatural creature that he was couldn't exactly travel halfway around the globe on his own power.

"How long will you be there?" I tried not to sound pitiful, although I knew I wasn't being terribly successful at it.

"At most two nights in the settlement. I'll be back as quickly as I can. And remember, you are not being left unprotected."

"I know." Despite my best efforts, I couldn't help sighing, just a little. "But it won't be you protecting me."

He reached out and took my hand, gave it an encouraging squeeze. "You'll be fine."

All I could do was give him a wan smile. I knew it didn't matter what I said—he had to go, and I had to endure his absence.

Thank God it would only be for three or four days.

As usual, Silas walked me to my door and saw me inside. The condo looked exactly as I had left it—and why shouldn't it? I hadn't been gone even twenty-four hours, and yet the world had changed forever.

One long, impassioned kiss, and then he was gone. A selfish part of me had thought about coaxing him up to the bedroom so he could make love to me one last time. But I knew he had to go, and trying to delay him wouldn't change his plans. Better to get this over with quickly. Anyway, I didn't want him to be in any more trouble than he already was. So there was only that kiss, a murmured goodbye, and he walked away.

I watched until he had disappeared around the corner. Immediately afterward, I shut the door and locked it, and engaged the security system. Yes, it was broad daylight, and after that melee on 4th Place the night before, I figured Lucius Montfort wasn't in any hurry to send his goons after me—if he even had any goons left—but I knew better than to take any chances.

The house felt quiet and empty. I was used to solitude, or at least I thought I was. And yet now the silence seemed to pound against my eardrums. After spending the night with Silas, I knew I never wanted to be alone again. I wanted to fall asleep next to him, and awake at his side.

And you will, I told myself. *He'll be back in three days, or four at the very most. It's not even a week. Stop being a drama queen.*

I wondered who this Emanuel was that the Conclave had sent to look out for me. Did he have a mate, for lack of a better word, or was he a free agent? Did the Conclave have a rotating pool of free-lance *gula* guardians in case one of their regulars had to take time off for some reason?

So many things I still didn't know. I supposed I'd find out eventually, if I did end up in Humboldt, in the *gula* settlement there. I tried to imagine what it was like. Some sort of enclave hidden in the redwood forests, or a huge ranch with the houses of its members scattered around the property? Silas hadn't given me any details, and so I couldn't begin to guess.

My gaze fell on my purse, which I'd set down on the dining room table. God, I wanted to pull out my phone and call him, which was just ridiculous. He hadn't even been gone ten minutes. All I'd succeed in doing was show him what a needy twit I was.

But maybe I could text Candace. If she wasn't doing anything—and I sort of doubted she was, except working when she should be trying to relax— maybe I could convince her to come over so we could eat takeout and watch some silly girly movie.

Or better yet, some kind of courtroom drama or police procedural, so I could listen to her talk about everything the screenwriters had done wrong and we could laugh at it together.

That sounded like a great way to pass the time. It would be one evening down, and then Silas might be back two days later. And if not, at least I'd only have one more night to get through after that. Three nights was nothing, right?

I picked up the phone and sent the text.

My hopes were dashed, though, when she responded a few minutes later.

Sorry, hon. I'm up to my eyeballs in briefs, and if I get to bed before midnight, it'll be a miracle. Rain check?

Sure, I typed back. *I totally understand. Maybe next time.*

Absolutely. If we can get the other side to settle this coming week, then I'll have a life again. Keep in touch.

Will do.

Damn. But there wasn't much I could do about it. I might be selfish, but I wasn't selfish enough to ask Candace to get behind in her work just so she could come over and hold my hand.

My phone rang, and I startled, because I was still holding it. I looked down at the screen, but I didn't recognize the number. Definitely not Candace calling back, or Silas reaching out to see if I was all right.

Usually, I let calls like that roll over to voicemail. If I didn't know who you were, then I wasn't about to pick up. For some reason, though, I pressed the "accept" button. Maybe it was just that the call had caught me off guard, coming so soon after my text exchange with Candace.

"Hello?"

"Is this Serena Quinn?"

At least I was in enough possession of my wits to counter that question with, "Who's calling?"

"Ms. Quinn, I'm Lora Stiles, from the *Washington Post*. I was hoping you could give a comment on your brother formally announcing his candidacy?"

Damn it. I was tempted to hang up right then and there, but I knew that kind of reaction wouldn't play well in the article this Lora Stiles was planning to write. I supposed I should be glad that I'd gotten a call, rather than having a reporter ambush me as I was going to check my mailbox or something. But how had she gotten my number?

I told myself not to be too surprised; everything could be bought and sold these days.

"Well, Jackson let the family know that he planned to make the announcement in the very near future," I lied. "So it wasn't a surprise. But of course we're all very happy that he's decided to run for President. We think he can do a lot of good. Now, if you'll excuse me, there's someone at the door."

Before the reporter could even interject, I pressed
the red button to end the call, and then touched the
tiny switch on the side of the phone to mute the
sound. That way, Lora Stiles could call back as many
times as she liked, but I wouldn't have to listen to the
phone ring until it flipped over to voicemail. I didn't
want to turn it off all the way, just in case Silas called
me from the airport or something. He hadn't told
me which flight he was taking, but I knew he would
be catching the earliest one that was available. And it
was LAX; I hadn't been to France since high school,
but even ten years ago, flights from Los Angeles to
Paris had been fairly frequent.

My phone vibrated. I looked at the number, and
saw it was the reporter's. Persistent, but I supposed
that was her job. Still, she wouldn't get any satisfac-
tion out of me.

I dropped the phone back inside my purse, then
went upstairs to change into some fresh clothes. And
maybe another shower, just a quick one to give me a
sort of reset. That sounded like a good idea.

That short shower turned into a long one, followed by more than a half hour of blow-drying my
hair and putting on some makeup. Why I was wasting my time, I wasn't sure. Silas was gone, and I certainly didn't expect any other company. But it was
something to do, something to use up a spare hour.
By the time I was walking down the stairs, thinking

maybe I should make myself a snack, the day had already begun to grow darker. Not sunset yet, but it felt gloomy enough, since the clouds from earlier hadn't dissipated, although the rain had stopped.

I was headed to the kitchen to get some water when the doorbell rang. Great. Were reporters now going to start camping out on my doorstep? True, Lora Stiles' area code indicated that she'd been calling me from the East Coast, but that didn't mean some of the local journalists hadn't decided to begin stalking me in person. A hell of a time for Silas to abandon me, although I knew I was still protected, that the other *gula,* Emanuel, was on guard duty now.

When I looked through the peephole, I saw my neighbor Brian standing outside. I relaxed slightly when I saw his face; no doubt he'd noticed me missing, and had come over now that I was home so he could make sure everything was okay. True, he could have texted me, except that he hated texting. He liked to talk in person.

So I turned off the alarm, then opened the door. "Hey, Brian. Come on in."

"I just wanted to check on you—you didn't come home last night, but then I thought I heard you come in a few minutes ago."

"I was out," I said, and he blinked, then lifted an eyebrow.

"Out? The agoraphobe went out?"

"I do leave my house sometimes, you know."

"Not all night."

I couldn't really argue with that statement. However, I also wasn't in the mood to kiss and tell, especially with Brian. If Candace had come over the way I'd hoped, I might have confessed something of what had happened between Silas and me the night before, even while making sure I didn't relate any of the more supernatural aspects of the evening. As much as I wished I could discuss what had happened with my best friend, I knew that was impossible. No matter what happened, I had to keep Silas' true nature a secret. Since I could tell Brian was waiting for some kind of explanation, I said, "I crashed at Candace's. We went to the movies, and it got late."

A strange glint entered his blue eyes. His lip curled, and he said, "Come, come, Serena. I saw you leave with that Sam person. I know you weren't with Candace."

Something off about Brian's expression…and his words…sent little flickers of doubt through me. Not that he wouldn't press me for info about a "hot date"—Brian loved to gossip. But his responses some-how didn't feel quite right, even though I couldn't put my finger on exactly why.

"Okay, I went out with Sam. I stayed at his place. End of story. I don't really want to talk about it."

A satisfied nod, as if Brian was pleased with himself for getting me to confess the truth. "Did he tell you who he really is? *What* he is?"

I stared at my neighbor, alarm bells pinging in my head. There was no way in the world Brian could have known anything about Silas, about the secrets he kept, unless....

The condo's temperature was comfortable enough, but right then I went so cold, I might as well have been standing in a meat locker. "No."

"Oh, yes," Brian said. He wore a loose-fitting chambray shirt, untucked, which I knew his partner Lewis hated but was Brian's standard attire when he was working. The shirt had large chest pockets, pockets that always had a variety of pens and pencils tucked into them. They were just as full today, only I realized, as I began to back away from him, that one of those "pens" wasn't a pen at all.

It was a hypodermic needle.

CHAPTER SEVENTEEN

Somehow I managed to stammer, "W-what are you doing, Brian?"

"I don't want to use this on you," he said, his tone reasonable, although that weird glint was back in his eyes, a glint that told me this really wasn't Brian standing in front of me. I didn't know when it had happened, or how, but my neighbor was now a semivive. And I'd invited him in because I had no reason to suspect he was anyone—or anything—more than the man I'd known for the past three years. "I've heard you'll wake up with a hell of a headache."

"Then don't use it."

"I won't, if you cooperate. Mr. Montfort wants to talk to you. You just have to come along with me."

"Come with you where?" I asked, desperately trying to stall for time.

"Does that really matter? He wants to talk to you…and he wants to show you something."

I didn't know which option sounded more ominous. For a desperate moment, I wondered if I should try to fling a chair at Brian, do something so I could make a break for it. After all, he wasn't the world's most impressive physical specimen. Yes, he was taller than I, and bigger, but he spent most of his days in a desk chair and had a slight paunch—something I knew Lewis nagged him about on occasion, telling him he should use the exercise room at our condo complex. It wasn't as if I'd be taking on one of Montfort's fellow vampires, all of whom looked like perfectly toned specimens of humanity, despite not being human at all.

But then I remembered how unnaturally strong that first stringy-looking semivive had been. That guy had appeared as if I could have broken him over my knee, and yet he'd been able to fight back against Silas for a good moment or two before eventually being overpowered. I had no reason to believe I'd get very far if I tried to take on Brian, no matter how sedentary he'd been when he was still human.

I crossed my arms. "Maybe I don't feel like talking to Lucius Montfort."

Brian laughed. Or rather, his mouth opened, and a sound that should have been a laugh came out, but it was completely false, a counterfeit of laughter made by a creature that no longer understood what humor was supposed to be. The sound made me go even colder than I already was.

"Serena, you need to understand that what you want or feel doesn't matter right now. You will come with me…one way or another."

"Okay," I said at last. "Let me get my purse."

"You won't need it. Come along."

Of course he wouldn't want me to bring my purse. It contained my cell phone, which could be dangerous. The handbag also held a few items that would be completely useless when it came to trying to get away, like my lipstick and sunglasses, but my purse was my security blanket. It would feel so much worse to walk out of here without it, almost like going out barefoot.

However, I knew arguing wouldn't do me any good. "Can I at least get my sunglasses?"

He considered that request for a moment, even as he directed a sideways glance at the window and the gray gloom of late afternoon outside. There wasn't much day left, and he probably thought my request a foolish one. Still, he only lifted his shoulders slightly and replied, "I suppose so."

My hope was that I'd be able to get out some kind of text under the pretense of fumbling in my purse for the sunglasses. Unfortunately, Brian—no, he wasn't Brian anymore—*not-Brian* followed me into the dining room and watched me through narrow eyes as my fingers closed on the soft leather case that held my glasses. There was no way in hell I'd be able to get any kind of a message out, especially since the phone would have already locked itself down, and I would have had to enter the security code before I did anything else.

So I didn't even bother, but got out my sunglasses, then asked, "What about my house keys?"

"I'll take care of that. Give them to me."

Not so much as a by-your-leave, but then, I'd already sort of realized that the semivives were a little short on social niceties. With shaking fingers, I got the keys from the inner pocket of my purse where they resided, then handed them to not-Brian.

He took them from me. "All right. No more stalling. We're leaving."

Crap. Crappity crap crap. Right then I really wished I hadn't lived such a solitary existence. If only I'd made friends with more people in the building. Maybe that way I'd have a better chance of someone dropping by unexpectedly. Problem was, even if I had been more social, anyone coming by the condo really wouldn't have seen anything out of the ordinary. Just Brian over for a visit, which happened several times a week. Anyway, the last thing I would have wanted was to put anyone in danger, just to try to save me.

No, it really looked as if there wasn't much I could do.

Don't lose hope, I told myself as I went to the door, and waited in the hall while Brian locked up the condo. He didn't mention the security system, and I didn't ask. I wasn't sure what good it would do me to have the alarm on, but maybe if someone broke in and the security company was forced to answer, that would get the police on my trail.

Unless the would-be robbers stole my purse. It was kind of a target, sitting exposed on the dining room table like that. No, they wouldn't take the purse, just the cash and credit cards it contained.

And I realized that my thoughts were babbling away because I was scared shitless and didn't know what I was supposed to do. A superhero I most definitely was not.

Or even an ordinary hero, come to think of it.

As we headed down to the garage level, I found myself glancing around at my surroundings without trying to appear as if I was looking around. Silas had said he'd left Emanuel to watch over me, but I didn't see any evidence of such observation. Surely this Emanuel should have known I wouldn't be leaving my condo except under duress, not when I'd just told Silas that I knew I needed to stay put until he got back from France. And my substitute guardian should have also known that I didn't go places with

Brian. We visited each other's condos and chatted there, but the only people I ever went out with were either Candace or someone from my own family.

But no one swooped in to save me, or to intervene as Brian pressed the remote for the garage door opener, and signaled that I needed to enter and climb into his older but meticulously maintained Audi A4. Mouth dry, I fastened the seatbelt, then waited as he got in and turned the key in the ignition.

Maybe I should have tried to elbow him in the throat as he was backing out of the garage, but I didn't know if I'd be able to grab the wheel before we crashed into the bank of garages directly behind us. Instead, I sat mute and unmoving in the passenger seat, watching as he pulled out onto Cordova, then headed over to Arroyo Parkway.

To my surprise, however, he went south, where the parkway would eventually turn into the 110 Freeway. I'd assumed he would be taking me to Lucius Montfort's mansion in San Rafael, which meant we should have gone north and west.

If that mansion even was in San Rafael. The topography I'd seen in my vision had seemed to indicate that much, but I didn't know for sure.

There was so much I didn't know.

Still, I didn't want to telegraph my uncertainty to not-Brian. "Aren't we going the wrong way if you're taking me to Lucius' house in San Rafael?"

That question earned me a sharp sideways look before he returned his attention to the narrow, winding highway in front of us. "How did you know where it was?"

Ah. So the vision had been right. Well, that was something, although I didn't know for sure what I would be able to do with that information. "I have visions. Or didn't your master tell you about that?"

A faint scowl etched itself on the semivive's features. "He told me. We just didn't know that you'd had visions of his house."

"I see a lot of things," I said, my tone somewhat snotty. *Too bad I didn't see this one coming....*

Apparently the same thought had crossed not-Brian's mind, because the frown disappeared, replaced by a small, mocking smile. I hated seeing such unpleasant expressions on my neighbor's familiar features, because they only served to reinforce the realization that he wasn't himself anymore, that something else had taken control of him.

We cut through downtown, the lights in the highrises beginning to appear through the approaching dusk, and I experienced a pang as I thought of the night I'd spent with Silas, of how happy I'd been to wake up in his arms. And that had been only a few hours ago. I couldn't believe this was the same day. If only I could somehow hit rewind on the events of this afternoon, go back and tell him that he couldn't leave me alone.

Only he hadn't thought he was leaving me alone. He'd thought there would be someone in place to make sure this sort of thing didn't happen.

Except it was happening.

Since it was now early on a Sunday evening, the traffic wasn't as hideous as it normally might have been. Too bad, because if we'd been sitting in bumper-to-bumper traffic, I might have had the opportunity to open the door and escape that way. I would have gladly taken the risk of dodging traffic if it meant getting out of that car. Unfortunately, you didn't really have that option when cruising along at sixty-five miles per hour.

We headed west on the 10 Freeway. I wondered just where the hell not-Brian was taking me. Maybe Lucius Montfort had safe houses all over the greater L.A. area, and the mansion in San Rafael was only his main base of operations. I just didn't know.

However, when we got off the freeway at La Cienega and began heading north, that creeping sensation of cold returned. I couldn't say I knew these neighborhoods like the back of my hand, especially as darkness fell and day slipped into evening, but I knew enough to recognize this route as the one I would take to get to my sister's house and studio.

Sure enough, not-Brian jogged over onto Melrose, then turned down the side street where Vanessa's home was located. I saw her black BMW SUV in the long driveway, with a dark gray Mercedes S-class with tinted windows parked next to it. I didn't recognize the Mercedes, but I had a feeling that it belonged to Lucius. All the windows in the house were dark, and the fixture next to the front door was off as well. I could see the edge of the driveway because the solar lights that bordered it had just begun to flicker on, but overall the place had an empty, abandoned feel, despite the cars sitting in the driveway.

"What are we doing at my sister's house?" I asked.

"You'll find out soon enough," not-Brian replied. "Get out."

I did as he instructed, even though my limbs were stiff with dread. My mind couldn't begin to conjure Lucius Montfort's reason for meeting me here. However, I guessed it couldn't be anything good.

Because it was hard to see where I was walking, despite the solar lights, I stumbled slightly in the high-heeled boots I wore. Almost at once, not-Brian was at my side, his hand on my arm. However, I knew he wasn't being solicitous. He just wanted to make sure I wouldn't have a chance to bolt.

Down the driveway, and up the two steps that led to the concrete front porch. The semivive put his hand on the front door handle, turning it so we could enter. That right there told me something was terribly wrong. Vanessa would never leave her front door unlocked. Not in this neighborhood. Despite the best locks money could buy and a security system that put mine to shame, she'd still been broken into several times.

We entered the foyer, which was pitch dark. I couldn't say I was exactly glad to have not-Brian's hand on my arm, but clearly he was able to see better than I could, because he guided me through the entry and on into the living room.

In here, it wasn't completely dark. Three pillar candles flickered from atop the mantel, which was carved from a single piece of gray driftwood. Very spare, very beautiful, at least from my recollections of it. Now I couldn't make out much detail, except the subtle gleam of candlelight along the hand-rubbed wood.

Unfortunately, those candles gave off just enough light that I was able to see something of the scene before me. I froze in place, body cold and stiff with shock, even as I stared across the room at Lucius Montfort, who sat on a plain wooden chair in the middle of the room, his thin-lipped mouth smeared with blood. In his arms, limp like an abandoned lover, lay my sister Vanessa, her head tilted back at an impossible angle. More blood dripped from a pair of raw wounds in her neck.

Lucius' eyes, now almost silver-bright, met mine. "I'm sorry, my dear," he said, and gave me an almost rueful smile. "Sometimes I simply can't control myself."

I opened my mouth to scream, to cry my denial into the world, to say that this couldn't possibly be happening. But in that same moment came the sharp prick of the hypodermic in my arm, and still Lucius Montfort smiled at me, showing blood-streaked teeth.

Then I was falling, falling into the dark.

I didn't know if I would ever hit bottom.

www.ingramcontent.com/pod-product-compliance
Lightning Source LLC
Chambersburg PA
CBHW051332250626
47155CB00007B/2570